The Best of ETHEL ANDERSON

The Best of ETHEL ANDERSON

CHOSEN BY

JOHN DOUGLAS PRINGLE

ANGUS AND ROBERTSON • PUBLISHERS

This selection first published in 1973 by
ANGUS AND ROBERTSON (PUBLISHERS) PTY LTD
102 Glover Street, Cremorne, Sydney
2 Fisher Street, London
159 Boon Keng Road, Singapore
P.O. Box 1072, Makati MCC, Rizal, Philippines
107 Elizabeth Street, Melbourne
222 East Terrace, Adelaide
167 Queen Street, Brisbane

Published with the assistance
of the Commonwealth Literary Fund
National Library of Australia
card number and ISBN 0 207 12564 3

Registered in Australia for transmission by post as a book
PRINTED BY JOHN SANDS PTY. LTD. HALSTEAD PRESS DIVISION

Contents

Foreword

Ethel Anderson

ALTHOUGH ETHEL ANDERSON (née Ethel Louise Mason) was born in Leamington, England, in 1883, she was a fifth generation Australian. Both her parents were Australian and she was brought up and educated first at Picton, in New South Wales, and then in Sydney. When still a young girl, however, she married Austin Thomas Anderson, a British officer serving in the Indian Army, and left Australia to live with him, first in India and then (after the First World War) in England. She did not return to Australia until her husband retired from the Army in 1926. This was unwise because Australians are quick to disown any Australian writer who has the temerity to live overseas.

Ethel Anderson then compounded her error. It was bad enough to marry a British officer who rose to the rank of Brigadier-General. It was worse still when her husband, on coming to Australia, was appointed to the staff of three successive Governors of New South Wales (Sir Dudley de Chair, Sir Philip Game and Sir Alexander Hore-Ruthven) and finally Private Secretary and Comptroller to the Governor-General, Lord Gowrie. Australians could not believe that anyone who spent much of her social life in and around Government House could be a serious writer (she was), let alone that, when her husband died in 1949, she might have to write for a living (she did).

To some extent Ethel Anderson's own manner tended to confirm this misconception of her as an aristocratic grande dame. Those who visited her in her old age at Turramurra, as I did, found her a delightful, amusing, but somewhat formidable old lady. She sat in a drawing-room surrounded by bric-à-brac collected in India and flourishing an immense silver ear-trumpet —she was very deaf—like the trunk of an elephant. She used this instrument rather in the same way as Billy Hughes is alleged to have used his hearing aid. When she was tired of listening to you, and wanted to talk herself (which was most of the time), she simply removed the trumpet from her ear and switched you off. But her conversation was witty, erudite and very much to the point.

She was neither sweet nor gentle, the two adjectives usually reserved for old ladies. Though she adored her own friends and family, she did not waste time in any general but vague affection for the human race, and she was able to regard its sufferings with equanimity. I think this emerges from her writing. Her Indian tales reveal no sympathy for the toiling masses or her Australian tales for the convicts. Perhaps only Ethel Anderson could have permitted one of her characters, Dr Phantom, to remark, on observing the Rector entering Mrs Furbelow's lean-to: "the latest addition to the poor widow's family of twenty is about to pass, non-stop, through this vale of tears."

But her dedication to the art of writing was professional, thorough and absolute. She was a considerable scholar, knowing a little Greek and a lot of Latin. She was well read in French as well as English literature and especially admired Verlaine, Lamartine, Violette Leduc and—significantly—Colette. There is a good deal of Colette in her own sensuous descriptions of fruit and flowers and wine. She was also, though this is incidental, an accomplished pianist, a keen amateur painter and a discerning critic of contemporary art.

Ethel Anderson always considered herself a poet rather than a prose writer. Her poetry, like her prose, was professional, scholarly and marked by a highly individual manner. If it now seems rather less successful than her prose this may partly be due to an excess of self-consciousness. She was always experimenting with rhymes and metres, either imitating Horace's Alcaics or Sapphics in English verse or borrowing the speech rhythms and sound-effects of Dylan Thomas. As a result she never quite seemed to find a style which wholly suited her. She began, in her first edition of *Squatter's Luck*, by trying to adapt the classical tradition of Bucolic Eclogues to the Australian countryside which she loved so well. These poems are flawed, I think, by curious errors of taste: it was surely a mistake, for instance, to call her squatter's faithful companion and hired man Eustace! One also suspects that she did not really know very much about the practical side of farming. One or two of her poems read rather like pages from a seedsman's catalogue or a list of sheep for auction by Pitt Son and Badgery. One cannot help comparing these poems adversely with the surer touch and more lyrical feeling of David Campbell, who is himself a grazier.

Later, however, in the second edition of *Squatter's Luck* and in *Sunday at Yarralumla*, she turned to more intimately communicated personal experience, though she was still concerned to reveal the beauty of the Australian countryside to those who did not know it or did not appreciate it. I find these poems more satisfying though still not as successful as her prose.

One can see the same search for an individual style which suited her in her four published books of stories. The first, *Adventures in Appleshire*, appeared in Sydney in 1944 (six of the stories had already appeared in the *Sydney Morning Herald*). They are rather slight, charming sketches about her life in Warwickshire in England where she and her husband lived for a time after the First World War. Today they seem a little dated, a trifle Angela Thirkellish, with their cosy gossip about servants and the local hunt ball. But they already reveal her talent for lyrical description of flowers and fruit and trees, her amused observation of human foibles and, in one story, "Hold Gold", the first signs of that fantastic comedy which was to prove her true métier.

Indian Tales, published in 1948, is much stronger. The stories are all about north India, some based on her own experiences as the wife of an officer serving on the frontier, others based on incidents in the history of India. (After her death another collection of Indian tales was published under the title *Little Ghosts*. This contains five of the stories from *Indian Tales* but also nine new ones. Since, however, I suspect that most, if not all, of these were written about the time she wrote *Indian Tales*, I propose to discuss them together.)

It can be argued, perhaps, that these stories too are marred by a rather old-fashioned attitude towards India and Indians for which the young wife of a British officer before the First World War could be forgiven but which will hardly pass now. She had a great admiration for the Hindu Rajputs and their wives and for those peoples whom the British used to call "the warrior castes". For the rest of India's millions she seems to have had little sympathy, and her treatment of Eurasians is at times uncharitable and even offensive. In spite of this defect, however, several of the Indian tales are extremely well written, and three of them, "Chess with Akbar", "Mrs James Greene" and "Twenty-four Elephants", are something more. "Chess with Akbar" is an imaginative account, based on historical evidence, of the Emperor Akbar's last game of chess at Fatehpur Sikri in which the chess-men were living men and women. ("In changing their squares the slave girls stretched their arms above their heads, laced their finger-tips together, and rotated till their skirts were spinning waist-high; they sank down in the posture called 'lotus-bud asleep'.")

"Mrs James Greene" is something of an oddity. It is an extremely powerful story, again based on historical evidence, of the young wife of Cornet Greene of the Green Bays, who was murdered with his fellow officers by the sowars of his regiment on the first day of the Indian Mutiny. Mrs Greene with a few other women and an old man escaped the massacre of civilians which followed immediately, only to fall into the hands of a local rajah who decided to gamble his prisoners in a cock-fight. Mrs Greene's beauty and courage—she was only sixteen though she had a baby daughter—won the admiration of a young sowar in her husband's regiment who was present. Mrs Greene had been kind to his own wife when her first child was born. The sowar rescued Mrs Greene, hid her in his own house in Sitapur, and sheltered her there until the Mutiny was over. All her companions were killed.

Mrs Greene never left the sowar's house. Slowly, against her will, she fell in love with him. He had already been stirred by her youthful beauty.

> It was on the sixth spring of her sojourn under Mirza Khan's roof that Mrs Greene hung up on the bough of her peepul-tree the tinsel swing garlanded with champak flowers, and spread out on the smooth lawn of her garden the sweet-scented couch of love, the quilt of neem flowers and jasmines, the neatly arranged rows of frangipanni blossoms, and waited for Mirza Khan to visit her.

Nearly forty years later, a famous traveller, walking through a bazaar in a remote Punjab village, had his attention caught by the vivid blue eyes of an old beggar woman who was leading by the hand a blind old man, a very stately, white-bearded figure, soldierly and dignified. . . .

> The traveller stopped the woman and asked if she was not English. After a little she admitted it and, when asked her name, replied, "Mrs James Greene—spelt with an 'e'."

The oddity of this story which, as H. M. Green rightly says in his *History of Australian Literature*, "comes near being a masterpiece", is that it is quite different from any other of Ethel

Anderson's stories. It contains none of her wit and humour, very little of her poetry and lyrical description. It is a plain tale told with great power and restraint. It suggests that Ethel Anderson could have achieved success in quite a different style from the one she chose, but perhaps she herself knew that she could not sustain it. Even so, I do not know a better short story in Australian literature.

The third Indian tale which deserves mention is the delightful, bitter-sweet, "Twenty-four Elephants" in which, I believe, she first discovered and brought to perfection her true talent. (I am assuming, of course, that it was written before, not after, *At Parramatta.*) Once again this is based on a real historical character, Sir David Ochterlony, a Scotsman who served the East India Company in Oudh towards the beginning of the eighteenth century. Sir David lived like an Indian prince and, like an Indian prince, had his own harem or High Seraglio, though this was not a term Sir David himself cared to hear used. He merely said "ma hoose", or referred to its inmates as "ma wee lassies" or even "the leddies".

Every evening, as their sole recreation, "the leddies" were packed into the howdahs of twenty-four elephants for their evening excursion "to eat the air".

> The third elephant carried the Princess Arnawaz, a Persian, her two sons, her "confidential friend", the ladies Farida and Nahid, and two concubines. These ladies might be called the smart set or even the fast set of the household they adorned. Their dark and flashing eyes were rimmed with kohl. Their cheeks were painted with ceruse. Their bare waists were as supple as a flue of silk. Their nails were stained to a beautiful red with arkhanda. Their unveiled loveliness (for they were Persians) shamed the thirty-six stars called Wujah. So lovely were they that while their lackeys shouted "Band! Band! Make way for the Princess Arnawaz!" their ayahs squatted on the roadway and burnt rue to keep off demons, and all the bystanders exclaimed "Wah! Wah!" These resplendent beings moved off on the young elephant, So Sorry Cannot Wait, who was panoplied in blue and silver.

One evening one of the elephants does not return. Sir David, informed of this by an Indian boy who has the unusual ability to count to twenty-six, summons a meeting of his women in the Grand Seraglio and holds an inquiry. He quickly discovers that the Princess Arnawaz and her attendant ladies are missing—and also that they are all enceinte. Later he receives a pathetic message, together with a present of grapes from Khorasan. The letter ran as follows:

> "Beloved,
> "We, unworthy women, wounded to the marrow of the heart, left the felicity of Your Honour's protection, and wilfully deprived ourselves of the sunbeams radiating from the warmth of Your Magnificence, because we, unworthy vessels, wished our promised children, should they be daughters, to be allowed to live."
> Only then did Sir David realize that the dowager, the Begum Miriam (rigorously schooled in the harem of the Emperor Aurangzeb) and Usbeg the Persian (the Keeper of the High Seraglio), so highly recommended to him by Shah Shuja (who had written of him, "He is economical and orthodox extremely"), had been, as it is called, "old-fashioned" in their rule of his household. Following the ancient custom of the country, the Begum Miriam and Usbeg the Persian had allowed no girl-babies to survive the moment of birth.

But it was in *At Parramatta*, published in Sydney in 1956, that Ethel Anderson's gifts reached their maturity. This book is not quite a collection of short stories and not quite a novel. All the stories are set in or near Parramatta at the time of the Crimean War and the same characters appear in each. Though each story stands on its own, there is some development both of character and plot. Girls grow up, fall in love, marry and have babies. There is a certain vagueness about time, but we are told in the second chapter that the Reverend Phineas McCree is eighty-four and by the last chapter he is ninety-nine! That suggests an elapse of fifteen years, though his grandson, Donalblain, is four years old in the second chapter and "in his last term at the King's School" in the last, which suggests a shorter period. We are told repeatedly that "the Crimean War was not yet over"; since the Crimean War lasted only from 1853 to 1856, time seems to have moved more slowly in Parramatta than in Europe!

There are also some minor historical errors. The system of assigning convicts to private employers was brought to an end in 1841, so Dr Phantom could not have got his First and Second Murderers in 1854. But it would be quite wrong to take *At Parramatta* as an historical novel or a piece of social realism. *At Parramatta* can be most readily compared with the novels and short stories of Ronald Firbank (1886-1926), an English writer whom Ethel Anderson greatly admired and who plainly influenced her.* One does not read Firbank's *Cardinal Pirelli* to get an accurate picture of the Catholic Church in Spain in the nineteenth century or recommend his *Prancing Nigger* to students of the socio-historical development of Haiti. One reads them for their indescribable and idiosyncratic mixture of wit and poetry, satire and fantasy. So, too, *At Parramatta* is a fantastic comedy which Ethel Anderson used to express her own love of the Australian countryside as well as her highly developed sense of human absurdity. When Mrs McCree looks across the fields towards the Razorback and recalls her childhood in the Picton hills, she is voicing Ethel Anderson's own childhood memories. When Ethel Anderson describes, with her usual accurate detail, the uniform of the Bombay Horse Artillery and notes that the horsehair streamers, which had then replaced the old ostrich feathers on their brass helmets, "could stand up to the most brisk engagement", whereas the High Command had found that "during a long, hot battle, the feathers lost their curl", she is drawing on her own rich experience of military nonsense.

Real blood and real suffering do not appear in these stories. The only violence is a battle, fought with pumpkins and melons, at the Parramatta Royal Horticultural Show. Indeed evil is allowed to appear only once, in the remarkable story of Donalblain and the ducklings, though there is never the least doubt that Ethel Anderson recognized it when she saw it. *At Parramatta* belongs rather to the world of Shakespeare's *Midsummer Night's Dream* or Iris Murdoch's novels. Girls are mated and married off with ridiculous celerity when it suits their author's whim. A man has only to look at a girl to fall madly in love with her. It is a curious mixture of farce and fairyland.

Yet—and this is one of the qualities that makes Ethel Anderson unique—all the images and metaphors are precise, accurate and often earthy. If this is not a real world it is a world of real things. Ethel Anderson never wrote of pears; they were Jargonells or Bergamots or Golden Pears of Xaintonge or *Buerré du Roi*. ("Yes, I thought I could not be mistaken! The skin paler than the finest champagne! The shape, symmetrical, but slightly squat, if one could apply so bald a word to so desirable a form! Pipless! Indeed the faultless fruit.") Sometimes her passion for accuracy leads almost to pedantry. Lesser writers might describe a young woman's tantrums as being worthy of a great

* In a letter written to me on 15th November, 1957, Ethel Anderson said: "I think I would have *died* without Ronald Firbank when first we returned: I have studied him!"

actress. Ethel Anderson despises such vagueness: "Mrs Siddons as Lady Macbeth, Malabran as Desdemona, Wilhelmina Schroder-Devrient as Leonora, Pauline Viardot-Garcia as Orpheus, though (to heighten the pathos) they would have worn tights (except, perhaps, Lady Macbeth), even in their greatest hour could never have raised such a tempest of emotion as Babette did now, pouring out a torrent of words in an unknown tongue. She was superb."

Throughout the book one is continually surprised and delighted by the vivid, precise phrase. "The Vicarage buck-board, an unwired aviary of chirping girls, and drawn with cloppy animation by 'old' Ruby, who was rising two, then set off, to creak, to hesitate, to side-slip in the ruts of the sandy track that led from Mallow's Marsh to Lanterloo Bay." "The punt slapped and staggered its way across the surging river." What good writing that is! How fresh and admirable! And the wit is pervasive, delicate, ironic and slightly acidulous. It is difficult to choose examples from so much richness but here are two:

> Fragrance, his first-born, was Mr Thistledew's favourite. Mrs Thistledew, with infinite tact keeping the less pleasant facts of life from him, as much as possible, hid her other girls very carefully in the background; it is really doubtful whether her husband guessed that he had more than four daughters; he had never, that was certain, seen all seven at once. It was a shock his wife had spared him.

And this:

> Juliet had already seated herself in the driver's seat, her whip set at the correct angle, the reins smartly assembled. She looked quite enchanting.
>
> Indeed she caught the eye of the Governor himself. He was, at that moment, trotting past, helter-skelter, with a great clattering of hooves, as he was driving tandem in his London Curricle.
>
> His Excellency was a descendant of King Charles the Second—as indeed who is not?—and whenever he appeared in Parramatta all women between the ages of sixteen and sixty would inviolably withdraw into hiding until he had passed.
>
> With predatory smiles creasing his distinctly "Caroline", rubicund, yet swarthy face, he was about to pull up beside Juliet when the A.D.C.-in-Waiting leant across to say urgently, "That is Miss Juliet McCree, the granddaughter of the Vicar of Mallow's Marsh, and she is twelve years old" —and clucked twice (to the horses).

> "She is a personable girl for her age," commented Sir Charles, as he acknowledged salutes from Dr Phantom and the Vicar and the small crowd that had quickly gathered, and he moved off reluctantly with a spectacular display of horsemanship.

It would be even more ridiculous to try to summarize these stories. The two main characters are, I suppose, Dr Phantom and Dr Boisragon, who are partners in medical practice but in every other way opposed. Dr Phantom is kind, generous, romantic and, until the very end of the book, a bachelor. Dr Boisragon is selfish, complacent, arrogant and very much married (his first wife dies giving birth to her twentieth child; he then promptly marries again). Most of the other characters are related, closely or distantly, to Dr Boisragon. (As an experiment I constructed a family tree which actually worked!) After the two doctors, the principals are the family McCree, the Rector and his wife, their widowed daughter-in-law, the flighty Peronel, and their grand-children, Donalblain and the enchanting Juliet McCree.

A good many of these characters are introduced in the brilliant first chapter which seems to me the very summit of Ethel Anderson's achievement. (Unfortunately none of the others quite reaches this peak.) Dr Phantom returns from a visit to his patients laden with gifts of fruit to discover a children's party in progress in his partner's house. But something is wrong. He is baffled at the sight of "seven little boys and girls, of ages ranging from four to, perhaps, ten or eleven years, each holding in their trembling hands a black papier-maché basin; each standing on a separate step of the stone stair-way that led down to the slowly-meandering waters of the Lane Cove River."

Dr Boisragon, looking even more stern than usual, informs him that one of the children has stolen an apricot—a Red Roman—which he was keeping for his wife. Since none of them will admit to the theft, he has determined on a scientific experiment. He has given all the children an emetic. The two doctors stand on the step nibbling fruit from an ample basket until nature takes its course.

Juliet McCree is discovered to be the culprit. Dr Boisragon is outraged by her perfidy, though the child argues that it was not theft because she did not know that the Red Roman belonged to anyone.

> But, don't you see, Uncle Peter, it is only *you* who see anything wrong in it? When Papa used to go shooting

> duck—whose ducks did he shoot? And when you go catching fish—whose fish do you catch? And you know perfectly well that when God gave Adam the earth—as for all I can learn He did—He gave him every blessed thing! And I have never heard anyone say that what belonged to Adam does not belong to me. And whether I took a Red Roman, or whether any of my cousins, or my brother Donalblain (who is four) took a Red Roman, it is only a person like you, who thinks so much of owning a thing, who makes a sin of it. It is just the natural thing to do.

Juliet is packed off home in disgrace with the First Murderer. who drove Dr Phantom's Hyde Park carriage. The other children (slightly pale) continue their games. Dr Phantom and Dr Boisragon go down to the river.

> "At this time of the evening," Dr Boisragon took Dr Phantom's arm, "it is pleasant to sit on the steps facing the water, where one occasionally gets a puff of sea air, and since the children's party is in full swing in the house, let us linger here for an hour before going indoors."
>
> The partners took their places on the step where the basket of mixed fruits still adorned the parapet. Dr Phantom, having set down his own basket of pears by his side, made an incision in a Golden Pear of Xaintonge with thirty-two sharp white teeth.
>
> "I have been thinking over that depraved girl's case," Dr Boisragon murmured, having embarked on a second pear. "I see that her first sin—*theft*—was the cause of her second sin—*lying*—but, delving more deeply into the cause of her crimes, I am of the considered opinion that the child's inability to control her carnal appetite was the primal reason for her downfall. *That girl is a glutton!* Did you notice the way she kept eyeing those grapes?"
>
> "Yes, I did," Dr Phantom rejoined, averting his eyes.

I have deliberately made the extracts from *At Parramatta* the longest part of this collection of Ethel Anderson's work. I believe it is her best work and that it should be recognized as a minor Australian classic. I realize, however, that this must always be partly a matter of individual taste. There will always be some readers who will prefer her lyrical descriptions of India or even the powerful short story, "Mrs James Greene". But for me there can be no doubt. Horace Walpole once wrote that "Life is a comedy to those who think, a tragedy to those who feel." Ethel Anderson was one of those who think.

J.M.D.P.

England

Whether on Malvern's cloudy height
Or in the valleys of the west,
The western valleys, still alight
With all you once held dearest, best;

Whether by Severn's silent stream,
In meadows crisp and cold with snow,
Or lost in fields by dimpled Teme,
Where freshets spring, where cherries grow;

Where are you now? By deep-cut fold
And scented bough all things you loved,
Steep'd in the moon's part-shuttered gold,
Wait for you; yet unchanged, unmoved.

Hem'ly

When first we went to live at Low Hill I did not word an advertisement "Wanted, cook-murderess, three in family, five kept". There was no necessity for it.

On the very day we moved in the vicar's wife called and said, "I have arranged for Alice, the cow-keeper's daughter from Stoulton (we pronounce it Stowleton) to come to you as between-maid at nine pounds yearly. Luckily, Kathleen Hicks (the name was once spelt Hwaekks and pronounced " 'Icks") is able to undertake the work of parlour-maid. She will expect fifteen pounds yearly, all found. With Madam Smith's Tom for your boots-and-knives, at five shillings a week, sleeping in, and Mrs Matthew Corbet's Len as your gardener and odd-man (Len will bring his own cider) you should be well set up."

There was the slightest of pauses. An angel, flying fast, might have passed.

"Olive Bickerstithy from Bindles Wood will go to you on Mondays and Fridays. She will do your laundrywork (she pronounced it "larndrywork") and redd your stone floors at half-a-crown a day."

Another angel hurried by.

"And Emily Dipplechip, from Upton-Snodsbury, is free, and willing to come to you as cook-housekeeper. She is a good plain cook."

The vicar's wife, whose nephew, as she told me later, had written a poem called *The Golden Journey to Samarkand*, then rattled off the usual, long-familiar litany. "Emily Dibblechip is clean in her person and keeps her kitchen spotless. She is honest, sober, truthful and industrious. Though she does not look it—indeed, she has a lovely figure—she is as strong as a horse. She can do you a dinner for twelve if you do not want more than five courses. Her 'made' dishes are excellent, excellent! Her roast pheasants are never dry, and she can whip you up a palatable tart. She asks twenty-five pounds yearly, with her beer and laundry."

Preparing to mount her bicycle in the pouring rain, the Vicar's wife continued, "Emily has a light hand with pastry." Riding off in the rain, with a clanking chain, she added, vaguely, "Of course, dear, if there is a full moon or anything of that sort, send for me at once."

At noon that day Miss Emily Dibblechip—a cousin of "the" Mr Halfred Dibblechip, as she told me—arrived, a lad wheeling her Saratoga trunk in a wheelbarrow.

A most elegant and exquisite figure, Emily wore a bottle-green redingote, buttoned from neck to hem with brass buttons sporting the cipher of the Croome Hunt. Her head was cribbed in a crocheted sun-bonnet, made of fingerthick Berlin wool, multicoloured, and ornamented with hundreds of loops. Her curious nutty eyes were about as responsive as boot-buttons.

However, everyone liked her, and within ten minutes she was at work in the stone-flagged kitchen, dressed in a pink print, beautifully made, and so stiffly starched that it crackled like paper.

We had one small misunderstanding.

"I suppose, ma'am," she said to me darkly, on her second day, "you calls me 'Himilee' because you 'igh folks think 'Hem'ly' is too grand a name for the likes of me?"

The moon was then no bigger than a nail-paring.

In complete and efficient harmony the household which the vicar's wife had so kindly chosen for me watched the new moon increase from a crescent to a crooked sixpence, and finally swell to that big, self-assertive, orange balloon that is the English harvest moon.

Sunburnt reapers cut the corn, apples were gathered and stamped with bare feet into cider, ripe blackberries loaded the hedges, mushrooms sprang up in fields that still showed the wide-rolling furrows of the Saxon plough, and sloe-gin was brewed in every cottage, until there came a night when I woke up in my oak-beamed bedroom to see, through my lattice, a majestic moon riding a phosphorescent sky.

In every farmyard for miles around the dogs were barking.

Howls from Sneachill, Muckhiel, Egdon, Drakes-Broughton, White Ladies Aston and our own Low Hill, reverberated in eerie cadences. It even seemed to me as if someone was baying at the moon from one of our attic windows.

I woke my husband.

"Nonsense," he said.

Next night, he woke me.

"I really believe I can hear a woman sobbing," he admitted. "There is a lot of knocking going on, and, do you know," in the freshly lit candle's light he looked so astonished, "I think I can actually hear someone sharpening a carving knife!"

Together we peeped over the banisters.

Below us, Alice the cow-keeper's daughter, terrified and crying bitterly, was polishing the stairs. Standing over her was Emily, wearing a long, white, relentless-looking night-gown, frilled at the neck and wrists with goffered pleats. In each hand she held a carving knife, the thin one used for ham and chicken, the fat one used for beef and mutton. She would sharpen one against the other, and if Alice slackened work she would make threatening darts at her, hissing abuse.

We could hear her calling the shrinking Alice "My fine 'igh madam" and other less dignified names.

When we crept down and asked for the carving knives, Emily gave them to us at once. She went happily up to her attic with a length of rope, while my husband got the car and drove across to White Ladies Aston to fetch the vicar's wife.

Meanwhile, I pacified the cow-keeper's daughter, and put her to bed on a sofa in the drawing-room.

Between her gulping, hysterical sobs, Alice told me that at the first sign of trouble from Hem'ly, Tom and Kathleen had " 'ooked it horf 'ome".

It occurred to me that a glass of hot rum and milk might soothe Emily, so I went up to her attic with a jorum.

I found her, the rope round her neck and thrown over a beam, standing on a chair and just about to jump off it; but the brew I carried had a seductive aroma, and when the vicar's wife arrived a few minutes later, Emily was in bed, holding my hand and sipping hot rum and milk while I admired her night-gown. It was really most beautifully sewn.

"You see, dear," murmured the vicar's wife, "poor Emily is not really dangerous."

Downstairs, while we drank cocoa, and Emily slept like a child up in her attic, I heard her story.

In her first place, when she had been too young to know better, she had murdered the butler. The Judge said she was justified. The village admired her nerve. "If you will keep her for a bit, dear, till the moon has waned," the vicar's wife concluded, "she can then go off and stay with her grandchildren. She has six—children of that butler's son—and she is devoted to them, except when the moon is full."

Emily had such a light hand with pastry that I said "Yes."

I had not considered the effect these events would have on our house-party till Orlando, a Cambridge undergraduate, and the son of an old schoolfellow who had been at Eton with my husband, when leaving next morning, thanked me for "a really marvellous visit", adding as he stepped nimbly into a black and yellow Wasp (the car of the moment), "It seems such a pity that you could not ask Ibsen down. I am sure he would just revel in it here."

A Difference with the Croome

I HAD BEEN picking mushrooms one lovely autumn morning, and I was just getting into dry shoes when, looking out of my bedroom window, I saw the deputy-master of the Croome jump the hedge not twelve feet from me.

Since our house was laid flat on the clay and the rooms at Low Hill were eight feet high at one end and a mere seven feet at the other, I saw the leaping horse almost on a level with my eyes.

The hedge, only a week earlier had been a rasper, a bullfinch which no one could jump, but directly the hunting season began the hedger set to work, slashing the thorn boughs nearly through and plaiting them into a wicker fence, some five feet high, a piece of living basket-work that would soon sprout again.

I had just time to realize how smart a pink coat, a black topper, brown-topped black boots, and leather breeches could be, when the rest of the field swept through our orchard and hedge-hopped after the master. Hard breathing, grunts, a clink of steel, a clatter of hooves, and some language of a ripe vintage marked their passage.

Leaning out of the window, I could see the hounds, some seventeen couple, spread out among a network of fields that looked like green pocket-handkerchiefs bordered with leaves and berries. They nosed about beyond our garden, beyond our Saxon cider-press, our Norman dovecote, our tall pear-trees. Sterns like barbers' poles white, tan, black, and, more rarely, sterns of that badger-pie colour that is a very old foxhound colour, waved madly.

The hounds were feathering, trying to pick up a lost scent, and the huntsman was cherishing his hounds and nudging them on to a foil. I could see the whipper-in rattling about on a grey, meaning business. A smutty-faced hound was getting a whiff on a warm hedgerow.

Since there was a check, the tail of the field stayed gossiping under my window. Merthys on Rainbow and Geoffrey on Jazzband, still sitting in their saddles, were trying, with their whips, to wind the winch that brought the bucket up from the eighty-foot well. They were fresh from a kill at Broughton-Hackett, where Merthys had been blooded, and her rosy face was stained with a brown streak.

In our day the Dianas following the Croome did not squeeze their delightful bodies into male attire; they wore tailored habits, top hats, exquisitely folded stocks; they kept their hair tidy with veils. And they rode side-saddle.

I could hear a girl saying, "So absurd to dress up like this to ride over miles of grass! We meet only yokels, farmers, rustics!"

"But, my dear girl, we wear pink and dress decently out of compliment to the men who let us ride over their land! Do you think the farmers would tolerate us if we were shabby?"

They moved off, tittupping like rocking-horses over the hedge.

There came a call, "Hark forrard!" where a hound had spoken. A cracking whip and "Back!" from the huntsman, a "Tally-ho! Yoi! Yoi! Try!" from the whipper-in, a gay "huic, huic, huic, to him," and a few sharp twangs on the horn and they were off!

The fields one moment were vivid with hounds, men in pink coats, and galloping horses, and vocal with the music of the hunt; then the soft autumnal silences closed down on us, the ripe berries showed ruby-like, the sloes twinkled, the hips and haws blushed scarlet in a world in which every tree had put on its own compelling beauties of russet, gold, tawny-orange.

A movement caught my eye.

Peering through the green branches of the ancient yew, which had fallen, and, with its roots in the air had continued to grow through two centuries, leaning out over the pond in which St Oswald had kept carp, I saw the fox, the pest, lying along a giant bough, his head between his paws, (or should I say "his mask between his pads"?) a derisive smile on his ginger-whiskered snout.

He waited five minutes, then he jumped down and strolled up our drive, past the lauristinus and golden poplars, and through our gates on to the highway. There he sat and did a little hunting on his own account. The hounds were still in audible cry after nothing in particular—a hare, perhaps—when, casually glancing over his shoulder, the old fox loped off in the direction of Farmer Smithin's ricks.

How thrilling the swift movement of the hunt had been! I leant out of the window next the porch in front of the house, trying to recall the names I had heard the huntsman give the hounds. One had been Bonnybell, another Cobweb, another Corset. There had been a Lollypop, a Nicety, a Prowler, a Nipperkin.

Hearing a clatter of hooves trotting down the short drive, I came out of a brown study to see a man I knew mounted on a grey and superbly turned out in the customary kit. Our house being what it was, he had only to stand up in his stirrups to bring his face nearly on a level with mine.

"Our day's run was completely spoiled," he began.

"You lost the fox?"

"Yes."

I became knowledgeable.

"I saw those starlings," I said in a chatty way. "They could soil the field and spoil the scent, I know."

"It was not the starlings."

"No? Well, I noticed the hounds feathering our fields. I suppose it was the sheep, I noticed."

"It was not the sheep." He fixed me with a frosty blue eye. "The scent was foiled by someone wearing number four shoes and carrying a basket of mushrooms."

"Oh, surely someone wearing number four shoes and carrying a basket of freshly-picked mushrooms would never spoil the trail of that awful, rank-smelling old fox! Surely such—er—a person would never—er—carry a scent as strong as that old fox?"

"Oh, yes," said he, "such a person could. Such a person *did*! Walking smeuze for smeuze through the hedges, wandering here and there, such a person could carry a scent much, much stronger than that awful old fox as you are pleased to call him!"

He rammed his shining topper down over his yellow satin hair, wheeled the grey round a bay-tree in a tub, and rode off. He did not look back.

I leaned further out.

Tufts of Christmas-rose foliage, green as young lettuce, were showing in our nut-plat, where chessboard arcades of golden nuts, filberts as well as hazels, glowed against the scarlet-berried hawthorns. The sky was blue. The English earth was lying "all Danäe" to "her close bosom-friend the maturing sun". But life seemed very bleak to me. I had made a discovery about myself. I had disadvantages hitherto unguessed. I could foil the scent of a fox. Yes, a dreadful old fox!

Hold Gold

AMIABLY conversing about this and that, the vicar's wife and I were strolling along Shoe Lane, which is the fourth turning to the left on the highway between White Ladies Aston and Bindles Wood. She was wheeling her tricycle; I was keeping an eye on our Aberdeen terrier, Punch, who was engaged in various olfactory activities of his own.

The sun shone. The hedges along the lane were in full flower, but slightly less fragrant than they had been, so that the scent of hawthorns past their prime rather tainted the freshness of the honeysuckles. The pig-pen motif became *crescendo*, *fortissimo* and *diminuendo* by turns as we approached, hurried by, and left behind the cottages perched on the lane's high banks and half-hidden by poplars.

The vicar's wife was just about to impart to me her secret recipe for making proof-brandy out of cowslips, her most treasured possession ("it is one of the few things the dear vicar does not know I know," she was saying) when, quite suddenly, she ran her tricycle into the bank at the side of the lane, turned her back on the roadway, and gazing at the top of a poplar whispered urgently, "Don't look! On no account take any notice of the man!" She raised her voice and asked in a loud voice, "Is not that bird a thrush, dear?"

It was humanly impossible for me not to look over my shoulder. Jauntily approaching was the bizarre figure of "Old Gold", whose dilapidated cottage "marched with" Low Hill, though I had not yet spoken to him.

Old Gold had a weak chest. This he protected by wearing the back of his coat always (as a sailor might say) "in the wind's eye". Since the slight breeze then blowing, hardly more than a zephyr, came from the east, and Old Gold was walking eastward, he had his greenish swallowtails buttoned up his back. This gave him an episcopal appearance; the tails, flapping about his knees, looked for all the world like a bishop's apron, and his tartan trews, begged, one imagined, from some Highland soldier, were tight enough to be mistaken for gaiters. He wore large gold loops in his ears. On top of his floating white curls was balanced a Glengarry bonnet with a fluttering ribbon. His brilliant blue eyes radiating goodfellowship, he tittupped towards us, tripping along on his toes as coquettishly and buoyantly as a ballerina.

Obeying the vicar's wife's sibilant commands, I turned my back on the lane, and carried on with her a stilted and highfalutin' conversation about a non-existent bird.

Old Gold drew level with us. He stopped close behind us. He raised a piercing falsetto in ribald song.

It was a song (as far as I could gather) about some Duke and his three "dainties", but most of the words he used had no meaning for me.

"No decent man would sing that song unless he were very drunk," the vicar's wife murmured in my ear; again raising her voice she reiterated for the sixth time, "Yes, dear, I think it is a thrush." Lowering her voice she added, "That is a hideously profane medieval ballad, sung only by four-bottle atheists."

The song really sounded quite shocking, and Old Gold, launching out into the twentieth verse was pirouetting round us when, providentially, a haywagon, driven by Farmer Inkberrow, lumbered down upon us, and he, taking in the situation at a glance, said to Old Gold, "You come hup 'ere, my man," and emphasized his invitation with his long whip. Old Gold was borne out of our sight standing on a bale of hay, and still singing.

Seeing that the vicar's wife was really distressed by all this, I took her into the bakehouse, a few yards further down the lane, and in this cheerful atmosphere of new bread and red-hot cinders we found the baker plying an immense shovel, while rows of steaming loaves—crusty cottage-loaves with Victorian figures, deliciously plaited loaves, and saffron buns—were assembled in rows on trays or on the long trestle tables.

Coming into the bakehouse to greet us, Tabitha Bleek, the baker's wife, at once began to press restoratives upon us.

"A sup of sloe-gin, mum," she murmured, in her rich contralto, "just to stay you since you've been hupset, like."

"No, thank you, Tabitha, I never touch gin, as you know. Perhaps if you had a stick of liquorice, I might dissolve a little on my tongue; I always find it so sustaining."

"I'll fetch ye a stick. But do ye take a sup of cowslip wine, mum, since you've been so affronted, like."

"No, thank you, Tabitha. A peppermint drop, perhaps, if you have no liquorice handy?"

A tender look flitted over Tabitha's whitened face, in which only her kind brown eyes were not dusted with flour. Off she went, smiling to herself, to return with a tray, bottle, and glasses.

"Hit's cherry bounce, mum," she explained. "You'll taste a thimbleful—just to please me?"

I heard the vicar's wife say, "No, thank you." I said "No, thank you." Yet, somehow, looking back, I seem to remember very clearly what cherry bounce tastes like (yum-yum) and I seem to retain in my mind's eye a picture of the vicar's wife, seated on a wheelbarrow, near the one on which I was balanced, a stick of liquorice in one hand, a sherry-glass fully of cherry bounce in the other.

With Tabitha standing by, and William Bleek plying his long-handled shovel, I then heard the full tale of Old Gold's worst enormity.

Seraphically sipping, the vicar's wife remarked, "Old Gold can play the fiddle divinely when he chooses."

"He played in the Church Choir with me and Matthew Brims, ma'am," explained William Bleek, standing in front of a bank of still glowing red ash. " 'E were fiddle, I were trombone, Matthew were clarinet. Before we got the horgan, hit were. One Sunday, while vicar, 'e were in the pulpit, fumigating like, Old Gold began playing that wicked song, low at first, then so loud as the vicar heard 'im."

The vicar's wife took another sip and hummed the air through closed lips.

"Hit doesn't go quite like that, mum," William Bleek ventured to say, and reaching out a floury hand he took his trombone down from the shelf, and essayed the tune.

" 'E goes more thataway," he said, pausing.

"Yes, yes!" exclaimed the vicar's wife and hummed with more animation.

It was a delightful tune, roguish, rollicking.

I hummed, too, while William played the air on his trombone, and William's young wife warbled away in her deep contralto.

"Everyone recognized the tune, of course." The vicar's wife broke off singing to continue her story. "Then, to everyone's horror, that wicked old man began singing the words!"

"No!" I exclaimed, really shocked, but sipping . . . sipping.

"Yes! He leaped out of the choir-stalls, cutting absurd capers up and down the chancel, and sawing away at his fiddle at the same time. William behaved with great presence of mind."

"Surely, I did that," agreed William, complacently. "I tipped the choir horf to sing the National. Matthew and me played trombone and clarinet to top-notches, as you might say."

"With the whole congregation—there were quite twelve people in Church that day; it was the harvest festival—singing God Save the King, dear Lucius and the verger chased Old Gold round and round the church."

"Hit were fair terrible to see 'em dodging round the font," William commented solemnly.

"Finally they managed to eject him and lock the door."

"Hold Gold said as 'is hexcuse like, as 'e couldn't 'elp 'isself. 'E says as that tune come into 'is 'ead and 'is 'eels, both to once, like," William said. With a far-away look in his blue eyes he put his trombone to his lips and blew the air sweetly and clearly.

It was a marvellous tune. I could not resist humming it. The vicar's wife hummed it. Tabitha Bleek, the baker's wife, trolled it out in her rich contralto.

"What on earth is that tune you are all singing with such abandon?" asked an amazed voice, and I looked round to see Orlando, with Bethia, as usual, in tow, leaning against the posts of the wide-open double doorway. Orlando (who was staying a week with us) was looking very handsome and Shelleyish, with an orange bow as big as a child's sash tied under his chin. "I seem to know the thing, yet I can't quite place it."

Bashfully William, holding a shovel before his face, like a shield, whispered to Orlando.

"You don't say!" ejaculated Orlando, utterly staggered. "What! That tune!—and all the ladies singing it!"

"Well, sir, you know what ladies are," William muttered to Orlando, as man to man. "The vicar's wife began hit, and one thing led to another like."

"We were merely humming it," I said, hiding my glass. "None of us know the words. It is the song Old Gold is always singing."

"Do you mean to say that any one in this village knows the words of that old ballad?" Orlando asked. "Why, it's the old song about 'Duke Noah and his Dainties Three!' I have never before met anyone who knows the whole thing! Does Old Gold know it right through?"

"Surely 'e do, surely, surely!" William replied soothingly, astonished at Orlando's excitement.

"Jehoshaphat! What a stroke of luck!" Orlando fumbled in his corduroy pockets for his pad and pencil. "Tell me where I can find the feller, there's a good chap." Red with emotion he added, "I say, William, do you think he would come and give our Cambridge Archaeological Society a talk on it?"

As Orlando, being reassured on this point, rushed away to find Old Gold, I called after him, "Orlando! Orlando! How old is that song?"

"It first came out in the Poets' Corner of the *Ararat Gazette*," Orlando called back, making a bee line for "The Three Feathers", Old Gold's usual haunt.

The Dairy Maid

I FIRST saw Rose Bickerstithy one winter's noon. Except on the holly there was not a leaf on our trees. There was not a flower in our garden. One Robin Redbreast, a bachelor, hopping about on the holly berries, was playing at being a Christmas card. He gave the only note of colour to our orchard, where melting icicles dripped from every bough, and where even the grass had turned brown and drooped in drab tufts over the waterlogged, partly-thawed clay. A watery, reluctant sun was climbing among those dun, slate-toned, mountainous clouds which always herald a fall of snow.

Looking out on this frozen scene, where in the distance the Malvern Hills, usually so blue, were now black, I stopped at the stair window beside Kathleen, blue-eyed, golden-haired, very neat, even in this extreme cold, in green print, a plain white cap and apron. She had not yet donned the black dress and frilly cap and apron, in which, at lunch, she went through the ritual of offering me a grilled chop and a rice pudding.

She waved a duster. "It's Old Rose," she announced, her tone as frosty as the frost outside. She said nothing more but went on polishing the leaded panes. I could now see Old Rose, briskly wheeling down the drive a perambulator which contained, not, as one would expect from the look of her, a great-grandchild, but piled up pyramids of salt fish. I ran down to give her a cup of tea and enjoy a chat in the sheltered porch at the front door.

Sitting beside Old Rose, while she drank hot tea out of a saucer, it dawned on me that she was very lovely. Straying wisps of wet white hair, a felt hat which had obviously spent as much time blowing about the road as on her head, a shapeless, threadbare drugget coat, a man's boots much too large for her small feet—all these detracted nothing from her charm, from the childlike candour of her blue eyes, the exquisite sensibility of her elfin face, much lined yet still flushed with the wildrose complexion of her youth. I offered to paint her if she could spare time to sit for me. She was, to my surprise, delighted. But she made conditions.

"I must be wheeling me kerridge. And ye must wait till I git me a pair of gloves, like. Me hands ain't what they were."

Next Monday she came to sit for me.

She wore white cotton gloves. She posed behind the perambulator, very clean, very wistful, very proud, the salt fish decently covered with a piece of green plush embroidered with woollen flowers, really a charming piece of Victorian needlework, done, I was told, "by Her Leddyship to Croome" somewhere in the 'forties of the last century.

I could not fail to notice that my household disapproved of Old Rose. Kathleen had evidently refused to carry in our morning tea, for it was brought in by Annie, looking scared, and I had to send back the brown earthenware tea-pot and get my usual silver one—after a long wait.

Conversationally, I found Old Rose limited. Her chief topics were her kerridge and the poor profits made by hawking salt fish through six villages. "I favours Egdon, Sneachill, Low Hill (it ain't properly a village, 'tis only a hamlet), Stoulton, Drakes-Broughton and Bindles Wood," she told me, saying that this was all she could "manage, like" because there was a five-mile walk to and from Worcester. I calculated that this made a round of fourteen or fifteen miles.

"If I hawks in the snow I gets more kindness. 'Tis bad business hawking in a wind. When the missis opens the door a pictur' will blow off the wall, or some'at, then she gets snappy and won't buy."

Of course she told me about her sons.

"D'ye know Jarge, the pork-butch, to Drakes-Broughton?"

"Yes, I know the pork-butcher."

"Well, he's my son!"

A long pause.

"D'ye know Freddie the sweep, to White Ladies?"

"Yes. I know Freddie the sweep."

I knew him, indeed, only too well. The day he swept our kitchen chimney the whole house was so coated with soot that all the maids just sat round and cried. It was too awful. And there, in the midst of the weeping women stood Freddie, jet black, and saying, complacently, "Well, girls, I got the first prize to Evesham, for me roses!" Then he looked sly. "I waters them with me barf water."

I said again, dryly, "Yes, I know Freddie—the sweep!"

"Well, he's my son," Old Rose said.

Another pause.

"D'ye know Willie, the poacher, to Abbott's Wood?"

"No, I haven't met Willie."

"Well, he's my son. But he's about mostly at night."

Old Rose liked the finished picture. There she was, wheeling her glossy pram, her white gloves well accented on the shining handlebar, her hat made to look as much like it may once have looked when Lady Coventry had worn it to Ascot in 1845. I had been given the whole history of the hat.

The picture was framed in Worcester and duly handed over to Old Rose. A few days later she brought it back.

"I want ye to certify as it's the true portent of me, Rose Bickerstithy, to Bindles Wood. Me sons have signed it, and taken their Bibles as they're me sons."

So they had! There, on the reverse of the picture, was a statement: "This is to swear as this here be the true portent of our mother as bore us, and we takes our Bibles to it." The mazy signatures of "Gorg", "Freddie", "Willie", followed.

I wrote, at Old Rose's dictation, "This is to certify as this here be the portent of Rose Bickerstithy, to Bindles Wood, painted by me, and I takes my Bible to it." This I signed, and off she went, quite happily. I still had no notion who she was!

For some two years after this Old Rose would look in now and then and drink tea with me in the porch. I learned nothing more about her except that she had once been dairymaid "to the great house, to Croome". "And your next place?" I asked, tentatively. She was evasive.

There was, in Bindles Wood, a farm that dated from King Richard the Second's time. Like our own Low Hill, it had been patched, re-built, and added to. Still, there it was, as described in Domesday Book, with the same acreage, the same woods, the same brook, the same family farming it.

Farmer Yarl of Bindles Wood Farm was an immense man. He was quite six feet five, and must have weighed nineteen stone at least. As young men, he and his ten brothers had kept their own pack of foxhounds, but by the time I met him he was helpless, and sat in a wheelchair in the sun, drinking cider from a two-handled mug.

It is etiquette, when drinking cider from a two-handled mug, to hand the mug to any visitor, who takes the free handle and "drinks even" with the host. But for this custom I would have gone more often to see Farmer Yarl, for I liked his wife, a woman with a face like a bishop's.

To my intense surprise, on going one day to see Farmer Yarl

and his wife, I found Old Rose sitting in an arm-chair beside the farmer and "drinking even" with him out of his two-handled mug. It was a warm summer's day. Honeysuckle, in full flower, was overrunning the hedges. Wall-flowers made the old stone wall as fragrant as the hedges. There was a hum of bees, busy in the clover patches. Brooding over everything about the farm was a timeless sense of peace.

Small green apples had formed in the heart of each apple-blossom. In the fields calves were running, lambs gambolling. Hens clucked outside the great barn. At that moment that corner of England seemed to be drenched in the warmth of uncounted centuries of maturing life, and there, drinking together, sat Old Rose and Farmer Yarl. Presently Mrs Yarl brought them more cider. Old Rose had the cup and held it up for the farmer's wife to refill.

Looking at those three old faces I knew that Farmer Yarl's wife was waiting on his mistress; his childless wife was waiting on the mother of his sons.

India

Thrusts, from Calcutta to Kabul, the Grand Trunk Road;
Blows, from west to east, fiercely, the autumn tornado;
Who is this battling woman with the twig besom
From sunrise to sunset sweeping against the wind?

The Grand Trunk Road trails right across Asia;
The Banyan leaves litter the bitter sky;
The Indian dust presages—soon, soon, the Earth-moon;
Who is this creature of so much hope, so little wisdom?
It is Sucreete, the ryot's wife, earning five annas.

Nishat and Shalimar

THE WOMEN of Hind are gentle. Their beauty is of the moon, not the sun. Indeed, many of them are descended from the moon, as their pedigrees show. They are modest. In ten years among them I did not see, out of doors, a bared neck or bosom. Coolie women, even, are demure. In fording a stream they will tarnish their tinsel skirt-borders, dearly bought.

The women of Hind are little of stature, slenderly, delicately made. Their hands are so small that no marauder can rifle the crevices that, in palace walls, serve them as jewel-boxes.

India is rich in the hoarded beauty of raiding centuries. In the zenanas are rubies "big as pomegranates", which sparkle like iced wine, emeralds "like myrtle sprays", diamonds, pearls. The fabrics in which Moslem women dress are fashioned with an artistry perfected by a thousand years' slavery—so diaphanous the kincobs and muslins, so regal the stiff brocades larded with gold and silver, jewel-inset, dipped in dyes of fabulous worth.

The ladies of Hind are veiled in, mewed in, dependent.

Delicately nurtured, the cloistered ladies of Hind sip sherbet, or a grenadine of pomegranates, or, rarely, a maraschino of black cherries. They make a meal of the unpressed, round, delicious dates of Basra, perhaps, or finger-long grapes conserved in snow, from Kabul. Though chaste, they are from childhood versed in the nine ways of love.

Yet, unveiled, and stripped of their jewels and kincobs, such wives, mothers, and sisters of kings have been sold naked in the Persian market for two shillings apiece.

Yet the Princess Sangagota could say of women, "We are both thieves and sanctuaries." She could swear to her husband, then dethroned and facing death, "I am the lake, you are the swan. When you depart for the mansions of the sun, we part not", and die with him.

Yet the Princess Raziyz-ad-Din in the garments of the wronged could face, alone, a Delhi mob, swaying it to reign in men's clothes among Moslems, as King, not Queen.

Yet she who was called the Resplendent Lady, a silver veil flying from her helmet, could fight in the mined trenches of Ahmednagar, defending her city with balls of copper, balls of silver, balls of gold, using at last pearls, rubies, emeralds—and that for a cause not hers; and Nur Jehan, going to the rescue of her captive husband, could ride into battle in the forefront of her army, her baby granddaughter on her knee; could kill at her husband's bidding (or for her own convenience) tigers or men.

The men of Hind are ungentle, ardent in war.

A Rajput goes into battle crowned with flowers, wearing a bridegroom's robe of saffron. An Afghan or Punjabi charges downhill singing "*Zakhmi-dil* (The Wounded Heart)", a love-song. To Jats, Mahrattas, Sikhs, Dogras, Pathans, the joys of the sword are greater than the joys of bed or board, though Akbar kept five thousand women.

The eyes of these men, clouded over (as I have seen) with a film of softness, sad, like the eyes of cattle, may blaze with a cruelty past the limits of torture. They are strong. Babar's father, the King of Ferghana, even in old age "never hit a man he did not knock down". Akbar could ride two hundred and forty miles in a day and a night. He took pleasure in guiding, while it fought a rival, an elephant gone must. Jehangir could run the length of the battlements of Agra fort, carrying a man under each arm, leaping the void between bastion and bastion.

Murder, conquest, rapine, lust—these were the pastimes of the Emperors of Hind.

Yet Feroz Shah made a thousand and twenty gardens.

Yet Babar, in all his wanderings, noted the name of every flower he saw. In the mountains of Ghorband he collected thirty-three varieties of tulip. He built the gardens he called Flower-Scattering, Gold-Scattering, the Garden of Fidelity. He planted in Kabul the Garden of Felicity. He praised the gardens of Samarqand, naming them Perfect or Heart-delighting. He bought for his tomb in Istalif the Garden of the New Year, the loveliest garden then on earth, where grew oaks and the flowery arghwan-tree—the yellow bauhinia. And Shah Jehan, for love of a lady, built the Shalimar garden in Kashmir, planned earlier by Jehangir, also for a lady's love.

The plains of Kashmir are fertile. Between the Jhelum and the Western Himalayas they are abundant in beauty, thick-starred with cloud-like mulberry-trees, with cirrus poplars and chenars, with wilding apricots or cherries, or pink spiked almond-trees sharp-set against snowy ranges, far distant.

Growing green is the grass in the wide rolling valley of Kashmir! Strown wild, the yellow violet there; wild, there, the narcissus, wall-flower, daisy, bluebell, crocus. Wood-wild, there, the white, the blue, the purple miles of iris. Wild on temple steeple, palace dome, mosque, house-top, byre, the Kashmir tulip, striped with crimson. In bricked-in burying spaces, orange lilies promising eternal life; in rocky clefts, step-madonnas, pink, with leaves of grass—all wild!

The hills of Kashmir are favoured. Shaded, there, the tower-tall pine, shaded columbine, bright azalea, snow-loving rhododendron, outcast Persian rose. Shaded, there, delphiniums, primulas, Jacob's Ladders—blue as heaven. Shaded, monk's-hood, salvias, slipper-orchids, iris of chestnut-brown and gold.

Lovely, these, but lovelier the radiant gardens of Kashmir, built by lakeside, stream-bed, spring-head.

Making beautiful the dawn by the north-west pedestal of the hill Baba Wali, the Wah Bagh, where Chinese pilgrims came along ages back to worship the sacred lotus in the fountains of Elapata, the Serpent King, where Akbar cried, "Wah Bagh! Oh, what a garden!", where Jehangir built a pavilion of yellow breccia. Remote, on Lake Manasbal, the Daroga Bagh, set there by Jehangir for his Persian morsel. Sighing for lost summers, Akbar's Garden of Zephyrs on the Dal Lake, most mournful of pleasure grounds. Basking on a sunny promontory, the Nageen Bagh. Musical, the Hazrat Bagh, whose limpid fountains slip over carved ducks, fish, or cranes into the Jhelum.

The garden of the spring at Verinog has twenty-one water-jets carved like lotus-buds. I have not seen Verinog. But I have camped by Achibal. There, among terraced ricefields never still, a thousand rivulets quilt the air, a thousand freshets, runnels, springs, sing sweetly, giving the sacred Jhelum life.

There, from Baltistan, or Little Tibet, or Turkestan, or Yumba-Matzan, or Gartok, or from the fringing desert-snows of Asia, come pilgrims, or shepherds, or goatherds with long-haired Pashmina goats. They care not at all for the garden of Achibal, once so beautiful that God sent Gabriel hot-winged from heaven to forbid its completion—"for fear," He said, "it might coax my angels out of paradise."

Most beautiful of all these gardens are the Nishat and Shalimar gardens, in Srinagar. Copying the Eridu of the Assyrian paradise, with its saena bird and homa-tree, the cascades of the Nishat Bagh—the Garden of Gladness—tumble down twelve terraces named after the signs of the Zodiac. They topple down stone aqueducts, rimmed with pansies, with urns filled with double stock, scattering diamonds on the red-russet tassels pendant from the tall chenars and the bee-haunted thickets of lilac, swirling over water-chutes carved to guide them into patterns, ripples, sucked-in dimples, crystalline shawls, past thrones, baradaris, pavilions, and tanks where twenty singing fountains break up through their troubled waters. The chenars sway. The poplars ripple. Deep, deep, the lake-blue, where, so far below, these gay cascades entering not unannounced shake, quiveringly, a thousand lotus stems.

Beyond the lake-waters a hill-crowning fort shimmers in mid air. Niched higher, in shifting snow-driven mists—India's Cloud Messengers—the distant ice-ferns on the farthest horizon glitter thriftily. Flattering them, the lake repaints them.

It was Nur Jehan's brother, the Persian Asaf Khan, who built this garden.

In the long canal below the Shalimar the lilies are over the boatman's head. The lily-leaves, in a low shikara, blot out the sun. Below the Shalimar's malachite pavilion, the green willows weeping in languorous shade, zephyr-waved, brush the face. But the spirit of the Shalimar garden itself lives, not in flowers, though here roses mantle the earth like seas or snows; not in fountains, though here a thousand water-jets are as murmurous as bees or churring doves; not in trees, though here, stepping down three terraces, sylvan sierras agitate the lawns.

Love is a man's best monument! His gardens laid waste, his conquests fallen to other swords, his palaces and temples ruined, his kingdom, once the world's chief wonder, turned to dust, it is as a lover that Jehangir is remembered. And in this garden his love lies shrined.

In her pictures his fair high-breasted Persian is not shown veiled. She wears a turban decked with heron's plumes—a man's adornment. Her single silk-muslin upper garment does not hide, at all, her beauty; her interlacing jewels augment it. Her skirts, of grenadine the merest, are flowered, but not opaque.

Palace after palace was built for love of her, kingdoms were won for her, garden after garden recalls her lover's devotion. But it is in the uncounted roses of the Shalimar—the abode of love—that Jehangir and his Nur Jehan, his Light of the World, are nearest to us.

Falling here in winter the snows do not bury their love; in

summer the roses, scattering petals, cannot hide it. The fountain's spray cannot dim this immortal legend of true love. In dreams, in flower-song, in tree-murmur, still on this magic hill their love lives on.

The lovers of Hind are passion-swayed, abating not one of the nine delights of love.

Chess with Akbar

"You go past the house of the Turkish sultana," murmured Hamida Begum, "but do not forget to turn left—not right—when you pass the Palace of the Amber Princess, or you will find yourself buttonholed by that chit Rupmati, whom my son has discarded, and who has taken up her lodging over the gateway. She pokes a shameless nose through the unlatticed window, and lets no one pass, and the chance of getting a message through to my son would be too good to miss. Try one of these crystallized orange-flowers, dear?"

Little Sri, the newly purchased Burmese slave, called in Akbar's harem the Silver Chersonese—her skin was so fair—accepted the sweetmeat and sighed.

"Resplendent Lady," she answered in her indifferent Persian, "how shall I recognize Bibi Mariam's house? It is not a week since the Keeper of the High Seraglio bought me in Agra bazaar, and what with standing there in the broiling sun the whole day, and the passers-by staring and pinching me, and all that bargaining going on, first with one dreadful old man, then with another—why, I am dazed still!"

Bibi Hamida, Akbar's mother, was not impressed.

"For fifteen years I followed my husband, Humayun, in the desert or over the northern hills, often without a roof to my head; indeed, even on the very day my son Akbar was born, there was I, eating berberries in a sandy waste, not a drop of water to be had, and the juice as bitter as gall. As for the sun"—Hamida spat out a mouthful of the betel-nut she had been chewing—"and the thirst! A berberry's no bigger than a bullace. Hardly a taste of moisture! My husband's horse fell dead, his men were going mad, yes, dying like flies, and didn't care a rap for him, and no one would give him a mount—that churl Tardi Beg refused him the very horse Homayun had given him—till, in the end, that funny old woman gave up her pony and rode a camel. As for the sand! It was piled up in ridges, like waves, and in the middle of all this, up comes that wretched goldsmith with his fingers crossed, to show we'd not be welcome where we were going, for Marwar meant to murder us. And you, miss, talk to me of standing a few hours in the sun! Have another orange-flower, dear?"

Sri accepted one and swallowed it without enthusiasm.

"Resplendent Lady," she ventured, "it grows late. The Emperor's game begins within an hour. I should be in my place."

"Costing all you did, I should hope so." Hamida spoke acidly. "With the money you fetched, your captor will bind his wheels with silver and shoe his bullocks with gold. The price of girls goes up and up. My late husband's eunuchs never paid more than two shillings apiece for slaves or concubines, be they who they may." Hamida hitched her pyjamas higher round her bare wrinkled waist. "I've known queens to be two a penny in Kabul bazaar."

Sri, standing there in her finery, looked so much abashed that the old lady relented.

"Get you gone," she said, not unkindly. "You'll tell Bibi Mariam's house by the winged figures painted over the door. She got a Portuguese Christian up from Goa to paint them. She calls them angels." She added, as Sri made a humble obeisance, "You are to be the White King's pawn, and I daresay you'll do well enough. I didn't gather whom my son plays against tonight, but I hope that Akbar wins, dear, and then we shall have the pleasure of keeping you."

As Sri vanished through a curtained archway, Hamida looked after her with some complacence. "My son should be pleased with her, at any rate. It went against the grain a bit to give her all those emeralds, but Akbar expected me to make her smart, and you know what he is!"

Babar's sister, that very old princess who was Hamida's aunt by marriage, and Akbar's great-aunt, lifted her shoulders in exasperation. "Against the grain, Bibi! I should think it might! She will be worth a year's revenue to Rajah Birbal—if he wins her. Of course, dear, Akbar is the greatest conqueror, the most loving husband, the kindest father and the best son in the world, and the image of you." She leant across to push a wisp of white hair under Hamida's veil. "And I would be the last to criticize him after all his kindness to me; but, sometimes, Bibi"—Khamzada Begum threw up her eyes and helped herself to a sugared violet—"sometimes I ask myself. . . ." Her attention wandered, and she sniffed the air, saying vaguely, "Was he saturated with lime flowers—or was it verbena—when he visited you at least two hours back?"

Though she could not deny that the room was still heavy with the scent her son affected, Hamida was not pleased. " 'The dust of the rose-petal belongs to the perfume-seller,' " she quoted sententiously, looking offended.

"It's not Rajah Birbal who is to play chess with Akbar tonight." Khamzada's granddaughter, Akbar's bracelet-sister, a widow of thirteen, put down the wild-rhubarb stalks she had been dipping in sugar and crossed to Hamida's side. "It's not one of the usual players the Emperor meets tonight. No, it's some stranger."

"Some stranger!" Hamida exclaimed, piqued that she had not been first with the news. "Well, I'd rather Birbal did not win. He's at the back of all this interest my son takes in Yogis and Brahmins, and that priest, the Portuguese Ridolfo Aquavira. Did you notice, Khamzada, that when Akbar looked in to embrace me before going to the Hall of Audience his forehead was marked Hindu-fashion, and he had jewelled strings tied to his wrists—the Sacred Thread, if you please!"

Hamida Begum threw a defiant glance at the ten or twelve Hindu and Rajput wives who were her visitors. "A fine thing for a follower of the Prophet (on whom be peace!). A ruler of the Mogul! Well. Some stranger, you say?"

Khamzada took up a handful of rhubarb and began stringing the stalks.

"Oh, that complacent hussy!"

Every head turned in the speaker's direction.

The bundle of black tissues from which the voice proceeded rose slowly and, supported by two whisk-bearers, hobbled over to Hamida's divan.

It was Dildur Begum, in whose house, as a girl of sixteen, Hamida had first met Humayun. For forty days she, a poor sheikh's daughter, had resisted her royal lover, saying, "The man I marry must be one whose collar my hand can touch, not one whose skirts, even, it cannot reach."

It was this Dildur Begum who had finally brought off the match, and to show her gratitude Hamida kept her in honoured ease in her household, though many people found her trying.

"Who is a complacent hussy?" Khamzada asked.

"That chit Sri, the Silver Chersonese! Has she the look of a slave who expects to change masters—certainly for the worst—within the hour? No, not she! My whisk-bearers tell me that she kept the other slaves in fits of laughter last night. She described all the tricks she'd used to escape being bought by a man she didn't fancy. She said she'd crook her neck, or loll her tongue out like an idiot, or squint. Oh, she's a caution, that slave! If Akbar loses the match, the zenana is well rid of her."

The cracked tintinnabulation of a bell, sounding from the Hindu temple whose lotus-like dome showed among the flowering trees below the seraglio windows, called the Hindu and Rajput visitors to prayer. The Turkish sultana, a sulky beauty (with a figure salient), went off with them, her parrot on her finger and stars in her ears. Hamida Begum and her Moslem companions were left to themselves.

Two of the old ladies who remained with her were the old great-aunts whom Akbar visited daily. If it was a day of hot wind, which disagreed with him, Hamida would say, "The princesses would pardon you, dear Shadow of God, if you should miss today's visit."

Akbar would answer, "They have neither sons nor brothers—who will cheer them if I don't go?" And go he would, not unmindful of their highly spiced gossip.

"Did you hear"—Khamzada's granddaughter picked up a jade tamboura and sounded its strings with a careless thumb—"that the slave they call the Silver Chersonese told Rupmati—before the scandal, of course—that she came from just such another place of diamonds and yawns as this?"

"Well, indeed!" ejaculated Hamida, shocked. "Yawns!"

"She'll see something yawn, I daresay, before she's much older." Dildur Begum drew her black veil across her mouth. She preferred that only her eyes, still bright, and enlarged with kohl, should be visible. "Who is the stranger who is to play chess with Akbar this evening?"

Airily young Fatima touched the silver strings. "It's the Burmese admiral. Didn't you hear? Abul Fazl Allami had fixed new rates of pay for the marines, the nakhodas, in Akbar's fleet, and in the carracks for Mergui. The Siamers have protested that the Emperor's sailors are paid too highly, and spoil their market. There's been quite a breeze. Everyone thought the affair was settled when this Admiral Tani came, quite out of the blue, with further demands. And after the cabinet meeting he challenged Akbar to play chess tonight. The Emperor stakes the usual sixteen dancing-girls, and the Admiral—what do you think?"

Fatima paused and twisted a jade stop, just to tantalize her listeners.

"Tell me, tell me!"

"Nothing less than the lordships of Tired Hill and Pillow Mountain, those barbarous fiefs he has just conquered. They lie above Mergui, where there is a good harbour, and Birbal says Akbar is very keen to win them."

Cups of nipa wine (a wine made from a tree, and a luxury forbidden to Moslems) were circulating, and the jade cups were often replenished from the big Martaban jar that had been hidden behind an almirah. The royal ladies became very cheery as they gossiped and sipped, reflected a thousand times in the mirrors that lined walls and ceilings, their veils thrown aside for the heat, the choli—the tight bodice that covered the bust—unbuttoned or discarded.

Not a breath stirred the dark foliage of the mango-trees under the palace walls. Even so near sunset the heat was oppressive. The red sandstone arches and minarets of the vast building, set regally along a ridge above the burning plain beyond which Agra was hidden in a white haze, glowed crimson, their glare so dazzling that Sri, enveloped from head to foot in a muslin chuddah, felt stifled as she hurried along, her clogs tapping the marble pavement. She soon picked up her fellows, the slaves who had been dressed by other ladies in Akbar's harem. Each had attempted to outdo the others, and when the odalisques were finally set on the black-and-white marble squares of Akbar's famous chessboard, on the western terrace of Fatehpur Sikri, the sunlight streamed through diaphanous skirts and veils and glittered on a thousand gems. Sri, the Burmese girl, in white and silver, looked like a figure carved in rock-crystal; only her skin, tinted like a pale rose, glowed in the warm light. As she stood among the other white pieces on the board, her eyes sought, anxiously, the balcony on which Akbar and his three friends presently took their places.

The Emperor Akbar was beardless, and wore merely a scanty moustache above his pouting lips and cleft chin. A few coarse hairs stood out, stiff as a pig's bristles, in front of each ear. A wart on his left nostril was considered a beauty, and a sign of good luck. A short man, his fingers reached well below his knees, for his arms were abnormally strong. His muscular chest showed great thews and sinews that distended his muslin coat: he invariably wore white muslin.

Seated with Akbar were his three famous friends, Rajah Birbal, a fine man with drooping moustaches and strong features; Abul-i-Fazl, the historian, his beard rolled round his chin, and pearls in his ears; and Faizi, the Poet Laureate, a mystic. It was Faizi's aim, as he said (for the Indian poets talk always in hyperbole), "to expand the breasts of religion and make the womb of God fertile". Faizi's poem, "Admonishing the Rose", sung that evening for the first time by thirty of Rajah Birbal's concubines, is famous today:

Let not the intrusive wind,
Rose,
Rob your skirt of discretion;
Let not the rifling gale,
Rose,
Rob your pocket of chastity,

is an exact translation of it, and it was sung while final preparations for the game were being made.

Though the sun had all but set, the sandstone terraces were still stained red. Some flamingo-pink clouds floated like little boats across a sky the colour of pistachio nut.

The first torches had been lit and fastened in their iron baskets when the Burmese admiral arrived and took his seat in the pavilion from which the chess-players were to direct their moves.

Directly the White King's pawn saw the new arrival she looked anxiously at his wrist, round which he wore twisted a bracelet of jasmine stalks, the flowers gone, the leaves wilting. Seeing it, her whole face lighted up with joy. The Admiral, for his part, his gaze travelling indifferently across the slave-girls' jewelled ranks, soon picked her out, though he gave no hint of recognition.

This Burmese admiral, or Siamer as he was called, was a person of great importance. He was styled, in his own tongue, Perpetual Viceroy of Trang and Tavoy, Lord of Many Peoples, and Conqueror of Tired Hill and Pillow Mountain. Tani was his name. As his office of Admiral was hereditary, he was young. He was, too, extremely handsome, "a man of courage, of commanding presence and like a captain", as reports of him relate. They note that he was "whiter than the men of Bengaloon, and somewhat browner than the men of the kingdom of Chimay"—that is, of China.

The game of chess that Akbar played that summer evening over four hundred years ago was different, slightly, from the game of today. The Queen was then called a "Minister", the

Bishop a "Counsellor". The manoeuvre called "castling" was unknown. In some circles pawns had just achieved the privilege of a double march in the first move. It was, in effect, a simpler game, and Akbar was a master of it. Tani was a beginner.

As the Lord of Many Peoples looked round him he compared Akbar's splendours with his own more barbaric glories. He marvelled at the flaring torches, the rose-red terraces, the malachite pavilions, the groups of living chess-pieces in their ordered array. There were the black-and-white kings in their chain armour and heron's plumes, the knights on their skirted hobby-horses, the odalisques in their radiant clothes. In changing their squares the slave girls stretched their arms above their heads, laced their finger-tips together, and rotated till their skirts were spinning waist-high; they sank down in the posture called "lotus-bud asleep".

Watching all this, Tani remembered his much-valued conquests, Tired Hill and Pillow Mountain, which he was at the risk of losing—"for the sake of freeing a slave to whom I have never spoken," he mused, ruefully.

The game proceeded, and within an hour Tani was left with seven pieces; Akbar, eleven.

At this stage a servant approached and, knocking his forehead on the pavement, told Akbar (on being given permission to speak) that the Turkish sultana had just been delivered of a fine boy.

Akbar (who kept five thousand women) had, born to him every year, some five or seven sons, heirs male of his body; and at that times as (sometimes) now, an Indian prince might leave behind him seventy or eighty sons. (Daughters? It was not etiquette to bear daughters.) Since it was customary to distribute gifts on the birth of a son, Akbar, as ceremony demanded, was forced to break off the game and go to the Turkish sultana's palace. At his own birth Akbar's father, Homayun, penniless and a fugitive, had divided a musk-bag, his sole possession, among his followers. Tonight Akbar took to his High Seraglio a dancing-girl from Delhi, a tray of diamonds, and nine rolls of kincobs and silks; details of which are meticulously recorded in Abul-i-Fazl's court accounts.

During Akbar's absence the chess-pieces dispersed and moved about the terrace, where the glare of the torches left dark corners, and among the rose oleanders in the shadow of a minaret Tani, having signalled to her, found the Silver Chersonese waiting for him.

She stooped to make a slave's obeisance and touched the twisted jasmine stalks bound round his wrist.

"Salaam, Bracelet-brother," she murmured softly, smiling into his dark, slanting eyes.

"Salaam, Bracelet-sister," Tani made answer, unsmiling. "I came in answer to your appeal, but I shall most likely lose a kingdom for it. When your messenger gave me your bracelet-token I attempted to buy you, but the Emperor's eunuch would not sell. There was nothing for it but to challenge Akbar to this game of chess, in which I was told you were to be among the sixteen slaves, the prize."

"Have you no hope of winning?" Sri asked, trembling.

"Hardly." Tani stood upright, his arms hanging by his sides, his double-handled dagger thrust through the tightly twisted folds of his sarong. He was bare to the waist, but so covered with jewelled chains and ropes of pearls that his pale flesh scarcely appeared. "When I caught sight of you, standing for sale in Agra bazaar, I wondered 'Who are you?' "

"I am the Queen of Acheen," Sri replied, "but no one will believe it. I was going by ship to Junk Selon when one of Akbar's carracks appeared. Our vessel was taken, and the raiders would not ransom us, but thought it less bother to sell us all as slaves, though this is a thing forbidden by the Emperor."

"If I fail to win?" Tani asked.

She touched the hilt of his dagger. "If you fail, I shall not live."

A gong sounded, recalling the chess-pieces to their places.

The shadowy figures under the angle of the red tower faced one another, hesitant. Looking Tani straight in the face, Sri laid her young body against his, then drew back, to say, "When I gave my jasmine bracelet to a fellow slave to deliver to you, I had little hope that he would do this; when I saw you had it, I had small hope you would accept it, and rescue me. You are here. I dare, at last, to hope."

It is an ancient and chivalrous custom in India that a woman in need may appeal to a man to save her by sending him a bracelet. This makes her his bracelet-sister, and him her bracelet-brother. The young widow Fatima, Khamzada's granddaughter, had sent Akbar a bracelet when she was about to be burnt alive with thirty other women on her husband's funeral pyre. He had accepted it. He had ridden two hundred and forty miles in a day and a night to save her.

Tani had responded to Sri's appeal, as custom demanded, yet

caring nothing for the girl who made it; but now her touch, her beauty, had fired his blood. His indifference gone, he followed her back to the terrace, determined to win.

His return was unnoticed by Fazl and Faizi, who were discussing the game; and, standing behind them, he listened to their talk.

"Tani is a poor player," Faizi remarked, studying the re-assembled players. "Akbar has for once left a fine opening to his opponent. By an initial move of the knight, and the White King's pawn, Tani could get checkmate in two moves."

"Akbar could see through the knight's manoeuvre," Abul-i-Fazl said, laughing. "He would counter-play it."

But when Akbar returned from his High Seraglio he was dazed with opium. Tani made the move for which he had Fazl to thank, and Akbar, bemused, failed to perceive the obvious and effective answer to it. Tani then signalled to the Chamberlain, who with a white wand touched the human chess-pieces into action, and the Silver Chersonese, the White King's pawn, left standing in her place throughout the game, made a double march uncovering check.

Tani had won. It was checkmate to Akbar.

Abul-i-Fazl's chronicle vouches for the truth of every detail of this contest debated nearly four hundred years ago on the red terraces of Fatehpur Sikri, and it is from him that we know that Tani, Perpetual Viceroy of Trang and Tavoy, Lord of Many Peoples, went off with the sixteen dancing-girls, the prize. From another source we learn that in 1603 a queen of Acheen, who refused to pay a bill for "some Amorous Representacions in Wax", purchased from the East India Company, numbered among her other titles that of Lady of Tired Hill and Pillow Mountain.

Akbar played no more chess. Suspecting the friend he had loved above all others of disloyalty, he sent Birbal on a campaign that meant virtual banishment, and from which he never returned.

In the days of their unclouded friendship these two had agreed that whoever died first should appear to the other. When Akbar abandoned Fatehpur Sikri he gave out, as the reason, that there was no water there. But this was not the truth. The ghost of Rajah Birbal appeared nightly to him; it was from this apparition, with its bloodstained clothes and reproachful eyes, that Akbar fled.

Even today, in the deserted garden below the red towers and

terraces, in the sad haunts of the spider and the water-weed, where the lotus lilies have been choked in the tanks, and the roots of the great banyan-trees have grown up through the marble pavements, the ancient gardener speaks of the shaitan, the ghost.

Not many years ago the writer of this history and her husband were leaving this garden, and as the old man was about to shut the gate stopped him, saying, "There is still someone in the garden, who passed us by the fountain."

But the Mali shut the gate.

"That is the shaitan," he asserted carelessly.

So this story remains, the one living link with that radiant assembly, when Akbar played his last game of chess, long ago.

Twenty-four Elephants

ONCE UPON A TIME, on the twenty-fifth day of the month Aban, which is the eighth month of the Persian year, when the sun still continues in Scorpio, it happened by some divine mischance that the Angel Usrosh presided over the destinies of that day out of turn—a fact that the soothsayers all advanced as the reason for the calamities about to be related.

Unaware of the fatal influence on their lucky stars, the ladies of Sir David Ochterlony's household went out at six o'clock to "eat the air" as they habitually did at that hour. They were dealt by over-excited household officers—like so many packs of cards—into the howdahs of twenty-four elephants.

Sir David's country house, near Muriamin, in the Kingdom of Oudh, rose out of the waving fields that surrounded it as white and lonely as a full-rigged sailing-ship in an uncharted ocean. Its lime-washed outer walls were tall enough to hide the windows of its single upper storey. The roof, on which its fair occupants spent most of their time, was screened by a parapet. Day in, day out, they could see nothing but blue sky, or rain-clouds, sun, moon, or stars. The pool, creamed over with green scum, in which they were meant to bathe, was mysteriously unacceptable to these ladies, for the reason that bubbles of air sometimes came to the surface. Their evening outing, therefore, was their one recreation.

As they lurched and swayed along the highway, arched from one horizon to the other by an arcade of banyans, peeping out of their howdahs they could see, between the cathedral-like splendours of the great trees, mud villages heaped like brown-paper parcels above the corn. They would pass a marriage procession, the bride hidden in a gay palki, the groom all agog on a white pony with a turquoise necklace. They would see a child driving a buffalo, ryots crossing a ford, a flight of peacocks, a badmash—an outlaw—on a country-bred stallion, a woman leading a camel: all were a cause of excitement and speculation.

It was a brilliant affair, this evening in the month Aban, when, to the certain knowledge of every astrologer in the kingdom of Oudh, the Angel Usrosh presided in place of the Angel Ird, who should have been on duty.

The air was so pellucid that the domes, cupolas, and minarets of Lucknow city, viewed across many parasangs of corn, sugar-cane, or gram, and even the square tower of Dilkusha Bagh, the Dearheart Palace, quite twenty miles to the east, were clearly etched against the farthest horizon.

Vivid as looking-glass, the shining ribbon that was the Gumti river turned and twisted through the reaches of the unending plain, chequered with every shade of green in its nearer acres, and dyed with every tint of blue and lavender in its remoter edges; ridges, these, which did not seem to end, but appeared to roll upwards and return to the beholder disguised as turquoise mists flecked with apricot.

The air, after heavy rain, was cool. It was fragrant with the scent of many flowering trees.

Even as early as five o'clock the elephant lines had buzzed with activity. Grey forms, lighter than the shadows of the mango-topes in which they had been picketed during the heat of the day, emerged to stand knee-deep in flowering mustard while their keepers laced and buckled them into their elaborate trappings.

In addition to the mahout who governed it, each elephant had four or five personal attendants, an innumerable retinue of lesser fry—water-carriers, sweepers, grass-cutters, leaf-gatherers—and many skilled tailors and embroiderers, who made and cared for the harness and the rich furniture of the howdah. To look across the yellowing fields while these men took the padded saddles and saddlecloths, the fringed headpieces, the gilded and cushioned howdahs from the boxes in which they were stored, and, swarming over the enormous beasts like ants, equipped them, was to watch an army at work.

The names of the elephants were duly tabled and their expenses paid monthly by Sir David.

Murad, the head mahout, had come to Sir David from the Jam of Ramnagar with excellent references. He was the accountant for the elephants' bills. They far exceeded the cost of housekeeping.

The nicknames given to these valuable and necessary animals usually hinted at some quality in their characters or some detail in their pedigrees. Grass Growing Under Feet and Tardy Arrival were slow, even for elephants, though they could move quickly on occasion. Peeping Lotus Bud and So Sorry Cannot Wait were young females. The immense tusker Impossible Splendours, an adult male called Prince Pleasant Greenshoot, and a brute of uncertain temper cajoled under the flattering appellation of August Official Thinker were Cambodian elephants. They had been imported from Siam. Their mahouts were Siamese.

There were two Persians in the elephant lines, servants of the young elephant called Flap Ears, a name which in the Bactrian vernacular means Poet (he was a dreamy beast), but for the most part the keepers of the elephants were Mohammedans. Many of Sir David's upper servants were Hindus. Since these rival religions bred quarrels, Sir David, who cared nothing for the cause of such disputes, found it simplest in the long run to award a favourable judgment to Hindus or Mohammedans alternately. The bickering that smouldered endemically in the stables would always flare up into a final outburst in his office.

On this ill-omened day in the month Aban (the Angel Usrosh presiding out of turn), there was more than the customary bustle when—as listed by Murad—the twenty-four elephants shuffled round to the women's apartments and waited patiently by the discreet side-door that gave access to them. Each howdah was then packed with its full complement of women and children.

The tally of departures, afterwards scrutinized so anxiously by Sir David, and verified on oath by scores of witnesses, was meticulously kept by the Keeper of the High Seraglio—Usbeg, a Persian who had been highly recommended by Shah Shuja. High Seraglio was not a term Sir David himself cared to hear used. He merely said "ma hoose", or referred to its inmates as "ma wee lassies" or even "the leddies".

Many of his ladies were not of his own choosing but gifts from friends or even business acquaintances. The Rajah of Bundelkhand, for instance, had sent him, on his birthday, an elephant carrying six hill-gypsies; girls of sixteen who wore only grass skirts and black stoles, and who were so unapproachable that they would have no truck with other members of the harem; and when Sir David had looked in on them one afternoon on a friendly visit they had received him standing back to back, each one armed with an ugly steel weapon resembling a bill-hook. They were pretty creatures, all the same.

Another old friend, the Akhund of Swat, had given Sir David, one Christmas, thirty dancing-girls from Delhi—a handsome present this, for such nautch-girls were then regarded (as they still are) as the most nimble of ballerinas. Several fellow nawabs, dying, had dispatched to him with pathetic letters begging their acceptance their whole collection of wives, children, and concubines—not knowing what else to do with them. Victorious princes, passing his way, would sometimes leave Sir David as many as forty unwanted captives. Frequently some rajah of his acquaintance, on going through a process that might almost be described as stocktaking, would sent the Scottish nawab the oldest and ugliest of his discards; for Sir David was known to be the kindest and most generous of men, and he would invariably grant a safe and luxurious asylum to all such poor castaways.

Of course he had his favourites.

It was the unwritten law of his harem that when the High Seraglio went out "to eat the air" the reigning favourite should travel on the leading elephant. This was always the most splendidly caparisoned: who would stand in the road to watch the passage of more than the first few of a string of twenty-four elephants?

On this inauspicious day Murad himself drove the leading beast, Impossible Splendours. Its tusks were sawn off short and capped with gilt filigree work. Gold bands set with rubies were placed in them at intervals—like rings. Its ears were pierced on their upper edges, and long brush-like aigrettes were suspended from them. It had a collar of precious stones. Across its vast forehead was looped a diadem fringed with pearls. Gold discs, linked with ivory medallions, much carved, were spaced along the red Morocco-leather bands of its harness. Its saddle was of scarlet leather, its saddlecloth of pink brocade. As for its howdah—who shall describe its glories! Its curtains were sewn with peacock's feathers and slabs of looking-glass. Its poles were of beaten gold banded with agate. Its cushions came from Tunisia. Every vast hoof of this elephant was plaited with golden thongs. Lustrous tassels threaded with uncut emeralds waved from every joint of his harness.

Into this howdah went the reigning favourite, the Begum Iquilima, who was named after Adam's daughter, her four sons, her "confidante", the begums Sucreeti and Roshanara, with their infant sons and four concubines. The next elephant bore the six hill-gypsies and no concubines, for these little firebrands bit or otherwise mishandled any other passengers.

The third elephant carried the Princess Arnawaz, a Persian, her two sons, her "confidential friend", the ladies Farida and

Nahid, and two concubines. These ladies might be called the smart set or even the fast set of the household they adorned. Their dark and flashing eyes were rimmed with kohl. Their cheeks were painted with ceruse. Their bare waists were as supple as a flue of silk. Their nails were stained to a beautiful red with arkhanda. Their unveiled loveliness (for they were Persians) shamed the thirty-six stars called Wujah. So lovely were they that while their lackeys shouted "Band! Band! Make way for the Princess Arnawaz!" their ayahs squatted on the roadway and burnt rue to keep off demons, and all the bystanders exclaimed "Wah! Wah!"

These resplendent beings moved off on the young elephant, So Sorry Cannot Wait, who was panoplied in blue and silver.

All this time the baby elephant, Zoozoo, who was entirely painted over with a pattern resembling Nottingham lace, and who was further adorned with a necklace of blue beads as big as oranges, rollicked and lolloped about, mewing piteously. He nuzzled first one elephant and then another, endeavouring to find his mother, Pearl of Heaven, the sixth elephant on the string, who, being on duty, disowned him and refused to acknowledge him. He was ultimately hauled back to his stable.

The fourth elephant was without splendour. An uncurtained knife-board effect seated ten of Sir David's younger sons, gay little boys, who had begged to be allowed to take their toys with them, and did so.

The fifth elephant, the bad-tempered August Official Thinker, harboured the dowager, the Begum Miriam, the "chaperone" of the harem, who had been recommended by no less a person than the Emperor Aurangzeb, the Great Mogul (the White Snake, as his brothers called him), several more mature matrons, and a plethora of concubines—"occupants of lower seats", as they said, who were always petted and made much of by the older begums.

It was well over an hour before the bustle and chatter, the squeals and whispers, the vituperations and even the slaps that heralded the departure of the ladies had died down in the hall, and the last elephant, Prince Pleasant Greenshoot, burdened by six coal-black widows, a bequest from the estate of the late Ensign Shipp of Bangalore, had turned out of the laurelled and ilexed drive into the highway.

Peeping through a chick—a curtain of threaded beads and reeds—Sir David had watched his household's departure with many chuckles of pure joy. He was one of those men for whom life held no dull moments.

This particular Sir David Ochterlony (there were others of that name) was governor of a large and important province in northern India, and his official duties brought in their trail many difficult problems. It greatly helped his simple mind, so sheltered in early youth by the rigours of a "manse" training in the neighbourhood of Peebles, in a Scotland then less bonny than the ballads led one to infer, to study the plots and counter-plots, the workings of the thousand and one disputes, that agitated without intermission the peace of his unofficial life. From them he drew a rich experience that strengthened his judgment when he was dealing with the cabals of his civilian officials and the turbulent and treacherous people over whom he ruled. In such racial and family intrigues he was able to trace a pattern that would have baffled Freud and amazed Rousseau and Adam Smith.

As he turned from the window when Prince Pleasant Greenshoot's perfect posterior had whisked through the gate in an elephantine trot, Sir David, not for the first time, was puzzled by the recollection of a scene which (as he recalled) had taken place in that very room on the twenty-fifth day of the preceding month—the Angel Ird presiding.

The house was quiet, for the household officers—all being eunuchs—had retreated to the taikhana, the underground rooms, to practise the coloratura roulades, the piercing trills, the thrilling cadenzas, with which, at concerts, they delighted to assuage His Honour's leisure hours. Having for the nonce nothing else to do, Sir David put away the file of papers marked SONS, CAREERS FOR, grouped under the headings Navy, Trade, Madras Army, Civil Service, Political and Missions (Sir David was always careful to make due provision for all his dependants), and, unlocking a drawer in his desk, he took out the notebook endorsed QUARRELS, HOUSEHOLD; MURRIAM, OUDH, Vol. 290.

With the help of the jottings he had made at the time, Sir David was able to reconstruct, perfectly, this mysterious intrigue which had so teased and puzzled his memory.

His Hindu bearer, Punchum, with his master's permission (though he had no knowledge of its import), had taken a message to Toz, in Persia, for the Princess Arnawaz.

Punchum had left behind him his son, a chokra aged eleven years, whose duties were to polish His Honour's boots, to care for His Honour's clothes—distributed on a network of strings and ropes across the corners of his dressing-room—and to remove and polish His Honour's spectacles. The boy had done his work well. His ministrations had been found particularly soothing in this last-named small attention. Sir David had good long sight, but he had to use glasses for reading, and in the summer these soon became clouded over. It was troublesome to remove and polish them himself; he would therefore push a dimmed pair on his forehead, and put on a fresh pair taken from his tray. When left long alone, Sir David would have as many as four pairs of spectacles perched on top of his head, while another set of the horn-rimmed owlish circlets balanced across his nose would emphasize the limpid blue of his childlike and inquiring eyes. His hair, unfortunately, was the wrong shade of red, but he was otherwise a handsome, hawk-featured man—without a superfluous ounce of flesh on his body, for he kept himself fit by violent exercise.

His notes made the reconstruction of last month's quarrel easy. The keeper of the elephants, Murad, his two assistants, Farid and Ibraham, and the mahout of the elephant So Sorry Cannot Wait had invaded his office—the room in which he now sat—and (such a formidable row of bearded men) had accused the chokra of theft. They had forced the boy to bring in the roll of bedding on which he slept outside Sir David's dressing-room door, and, opening this diminutive bundle of rags, had displayed the stolen articles.

One infant's shoe, much worn.

One torn envelope.

One medicine bottle.

One piece of broken china patterned in blue.

On this betrayal of his guilt the chokra had drawn the end of his turban over his mouth and murmured, "I am one whose barque is overfreighted."

When Sir David had asked him, "Have you no explanation to offer?" the chokra had turned his face to the wall and answered, "I have drawn out the molar tooth of hope."

Since it was the turn of the Mohammedan faction to have judgment given in its favour, and since the boy was a Hindu, he was dismissed. The triumphant Mohammedans had taken from him his white turban with its red-and-gold device, his white coat with its scarlet cummerbund. They had replaced the stolen treasures ostentatiously on His Honour's desk, and the chokra had withdrawn from the Presence, to be seen no more.

But Sir David had continued to wonder why. Why this conspiracy to destroy so small and helpless an unbeliever? Only one hint had occurred to him, and this seemed preposterous in its implications. Was it because the chokra could count?

As Sir David well knew, the simple people of the countryside could seldom count beyond ten. They ticked off the numerals on their fingers like women. But the chokra was known to possess the gift of counting up to twenty-six. How he did it was his secret.

Sir David, while absorbed in this conundrum, had been conscious that the elephants had returned, and that the ladies had yet once again been decanted from their howdahs. However, he had been much too preoccupied to watch the unloading as he had intended to; he was still in distressed meditation over another incident which had also baffled his conjecture. His mind dwelt on the grief of the Begum Roshanka. She had been weeping for days. She had refused to be comforted and, to his amazement, shrank from him if he drew near her. She could not be induced to disclose the reason for her sorrow.

As he meditated, a sound made him look up, to see the chokra whom he had dismissed stand salaaming in the doorway. He bade him enter.

After many obeisances the boy took off his shoes and, entering the room, stood by Sir David's desk shaking with fright yet with a scarcely hidden air of triumph.

However indigent he may be, it is the custom for a poor man visiting a rich man to bring a gift. A tray of spices? Heaps of ginger, curry-powder, or cloves? Almonds and raisins? A Pashmina kid bleating at the end of a rope? A roll of Dacca muslin? Such offerings were beyond the chokra's power to parade, even though it was usual merely to touch and return them. He had brought the beggar's gift, one green leaf. Like the child he was, he had chosen a pretty one, a colocynth leaf, striped white and green. This he laid on the desk, and he folded his trembling hands and bowed his humble head and looked very like a supplicant.

"After wounds—retaliations!" he remarked in a quavering voice.

The chokra was quoting from the Koran, the Mohammedan's holy book, and for a Hindu to do such a thing was positively eerie. Sir David realized that the matter was serious, and prepared for a long session. "Speak, boy," he commanded, and pushed up his glasses, for they had suddenly clouded over.

"I am water and clay."

"Truly."

The chokra had rehearsed the next bit, and he continued glibly: "This threshold-kissing dunderhead was feeding a she-ass on water-moss by the corner of the potter's field at the spot where the water stagnates below the bank of rushes."

"Yes?"

"The sahib knows the place?"

"I know it well."

"This miserable one's next brother was beating a drum to drive the birds away from the corn the potter is growing to feed his father-in-law's sister's cousin's doddered ox."

"I am in no hurry."

"This foolish one's next brother was making scales out of the halves of an orange—thrown away," the chokra meditated, "by Yacob, the tax-gatherer. It had neither pith nor pulp."

"Proceed, O enlightened teller of miraculous happenings," Sir David interjected by way of encouragement.

"Near the door of his hut His Honour's butcher, who lives at the far end of the potter's field, was eating a dish of sheep's guts, stuffed, and it smelt very good, so this abject one ran away from the pain of it to the highway, and lo! His Honour's house came out of his gate hidden in the howdahs of twenty-four elephants. This vile one counted them. Twenty-four elephants! Nothing fell from them to distend the stomachs of the poor, so this clod of earth waited for their return, because, Huzoor, sometimes the Princess Arnawaz will throw down a few coins—some sequins or pice—for the needy."

"And does she now?" Sir David was interested.

"Sir, this despicable cumberer of the ground waited by the gate, and in two hours' time twenty-three elephants returned. This camel-hearted son of little worth counted them. Assuredly there were twenty-three."

"Did you take notice which elephant was missing?" Sir David asked, hiding his emotion.

"Which is heaven? Which is the rope?" asked the chokra cryptically. By this he meant to imply that he did not know the answer to that question.

Seeing that Sir David was about to rise, the chokra deftly removed the accumulated four pairs of spectacles which had been pushed up onto his red brush of hair (it was the *wrong* shade of red) and, polishing them, laid them on the tray. His heart sang for joy because His Honour allowed him to perform this service without comment. Furthermore, the chokra, anticipating his needs—for Sir David never went with uncovered head into his harem—dived into the dressing-room and returned with his headgear, a kind of beret, a wide-brimmed pleated affair of blue cloth which, like a sailor's hat, had ribbons falling from it.

Sir David did not reprove him for this intrusion. He thanked him and, looking down into his eager eyes, said, "You may return to my service, and your pay will be ten rupees a month."

Having raised the child to the seventh heaven, Sir David cocked his beret very much over one ear, squared his shoulders, and marched out to do battle with his household. The chokra, being a prudent lad, remained behind. He ran to beg an advance of pay from a friend, and, having obtained the money, flew, rejoicing, to the bazaar to buy food.

In a picture of Sir David painted about this time, he is shown wearing just such a beret. His pantaloons are very full and gathered—it might almost be called smocked—round his ankles. His shoes are picot-edged at the top. His silk shirt has deep lace frills falling on his collar and cascading over his knuckles. It is fastened by a dozen gold buckles. He is shown wearing a red loose-fitting coat, its revers being turned back from neck to waist and frogged with braid, the same braid holding the gathers of his voluminous sleeves in place. In his portrait he carries both sword and dagger. He may very likely have been so attired when he went, inwardly fuming with rage, outwardly perfectly calm, to inquire into the mystery of the missing elephant and to learn (how his heart misgave him!) which of his ladies had run away from him—the ungrateful minx!

On leaving his office Sir David walked through the hall, which occupied a square space of perhaps half an acre and was paved with fragments of blue and white china set in cement, even the wide steps of the staircase being so decorated. Among a medley of palms and crotons a great many tigers paraded, for Sir David liked to see them about, and though they were stuffed, and though their red flannel tongues plainly showed the ravages of moths and silver-fish, they looked sufficiently impressive.

The gallery above this entrance hall was supported by white and blue pillars and railed, like the banisters, with arabesques of wrought-iron painted blue and white. As the balcony was the thoroughfare for all intercourse between the ladies of the harem, it was usually as busy as Fleet Street. Today all was silent.

To wear a red garment is a sign of anger. His Honour guessed that the eyes peeping through the apertures of every door in sight must have read the warning portent of his coat. He decided to hold the inquiry in the Hall of Obeisance. Sending for Usbeg, Sir David ordered his whole household to assemble in this state apartment.

At the top of this large room there was an armchair resembling a throne. It had a gold background and was set on a red carpet. On this Sir David sat, while his whole household and all his eunuchs and officials assembled round him. This hall, or Place of Obeisance, was decorated in black filigree-work edged with silver on a dazzling white ground. Mirrors, not more than five or six inches wide, joined floor to ceiling at intervals of about a foot. The effect of this decoration was mysteriously brilliant. While no forms were wholly reflected in the looking-glass, colour vibrated there. A row of crystal candelabra, swinging on chains from the roof, was lit by a thousand candles. The floor was made of wooden bricks thinly patined in gold and silver. It reflected every spark of light.

The ladies were veiled. Only the six hill-gypsies in their short grass skirts and narrow black stoles, their bill-hooks—their steel kukris—clutched in their hands, and standing, as their custom was, back to back, lent a somewhat barbaric touch to the oriental splendours of this gathering.

There was a good deal of movement.

Each begum had two whisk-bearers. Each slave, even, had a fan-bearer. Each concubine had a slave to undulate her fan. The room was overpoweringly scented with attar of roses, pan, sandalwood, jasmine, and a thousand perfumes.

When all were present, Sir David called on Usbeg to produce his list of departures for that evening. On this exact record being checked with the return lists, it was found that the elephant So Sorry Cannot Wait was missing, and it further transpired that the Princess Arnawaz, her two sons, the ladies Farida and Nahid, the two concubines, and the mahout Murad were not among those present.

The evasive answers made to all Sir David's questions greatly protracted the inquiry.

"How did it happen," he demanded, "that the mahout Murad, who set out on the elephant Impossible Splendours, which beast is now in its stable, is missing, while the mahout of the missing elephant So Sorry Cannot Wait is present in this room?"

"*Allah a'lam* (God knows)," Usbeg replied.

"*Allah harim* (God is good)," his assistant asserted.

The ancient matron, the Begum Miriam, who was the chaperone of his seraglio, coming forward had murmured through her veil, "Allah has stitched the earth to the sky with arrows." By this she meant that the matter had completely baffled her intelligence. "This is indeed a house of sighs," was the contribution to the discussion put forward by the reigning favourite, Iquilima, who was bathed in tears.

"The magic wind that wafted Solomon's hosts to victory has deflected the paths of those unworthy ones," was Usbeg's final flight of fancy. He would say no more.

The ladies all swore that the Princess Arnawaz was "as pure as the enchanted waters under Mahomet's throne". And that she had no lover. The whole household swore the ladies Farida and Nahid were equally pure, and that they, too, had no lovers. And they swore that neither of the two concubines was less pure than those same enchanted waters, and every lady in the zenana swore this by the oath most sacred to her—that is, "By the ten fresh and shining crystals of the Beloved", by which she meant Sir David's own ten fingers.

And when all the other ladies had contributed to the discussion such exclamations as, "Out, alas!" "Fie!" "Indeed!" "Ah!" "This is the place of surprises!" "How Allah has darkened the felicity of His Honour's house!" Sir David had learnt nothing more than that the two mahouts had changed elephants at the place where the Lucknow road joined the Grand Trunk Road and that the elephant So Sorry Cannot Wait had then headed in a brisk trot in the direction of Persia, Toz, and beyond.

He also learnt that all five ladies were *enceinte* and near their time.

From the evasive manner of everyone present Sir David suspected that there were dark undercurrents of which he had no cognizance, but he could learn no more.

He dismissed the assembly.

He found nothing in any of his notebooks to clarify his judgment in this difficult matter, so he took a chance. He addressed a letter to the Princess Arnawaz to the care of her father's house in the town (or village) of Toz, and he began the letter with the equivalent of, "Ma puir wee lassie." This missive, together with all her clothes and jewels, and all the treasures of the other missing ladies, he dispatched by the hands of his bearer Punchum in the panniers of a string of trotting camels. He added the sum of eight thousand aspers. It may be remembered that Punchum had already taken some mysterious message to Toz, but he would not divulge it. He remained dumb, saying merely to any question put to him, "Allah returns to Allah."

It is recorded in Sir David's biography, written by his son, Sir Ottoman Ochterlony, of the Indian Civil Service, that after the departure of the Princess Arnawaz his father took no further pleasure in his High Seraglio. He never again visited his ladies, whom he kept, liberally pensioned off, in his villa outside Lucknow. This revulsion followed the receipt of the letter sent by the Princess Arnawaz in answer to his. It came on the thirteenth day of the solar month Tir, the sun being in Cancer, the Angel Tistry, the Guardian of Cattle presiding.

A present of grapes from Khorasan, each one the length of a finger and each grape separately wrapped in cotton wool, accompanied the letter, which ran as follows:

> Beloved,
>
> We, unworthy women, wounded to the marrow of the heart, left the felicity of Your Honour's protection, and wilfully deprived ourselves of the sunbeams radiating from the warmth of Your Magnificence, because we, unworthy vessels, wished our promised children, should they be daughters, to be allowed to live.

Only then did Sir David realize that the dowager, the Begum Miriam (rigorously schooled in the harem of the Emperor Aurangzeb) and Usbeg the Persian (the Keeper of the High Seraglio), so highly recommended to him by Shah Shuja (who had written of him, "He is economical and orthodox extremely") had been, as it is called, "old-fashioned" in their rule of his household. Following the ancient custom of the country, the Begum Miriam and Usbeg the Persian had allowed no girl-babies to survive the moment of birth.

Mrs James Greene

MRS JAMES GREENE at sixteen was not exactly a bride. She had a daughter three months old. However, she was still so new to the duties of a housekeeper that the cookery-book which her Great-aunt Hannah had given her as a wedding present could, on occasion, absorb her whole attention.

Her husband, Cornet Greene of the Green Bays (as his regiment of irregular cavalry was nicknamed), stooping to kiss his wife good-bye when he was leaving for the usual morning parade in Sitapur barracks, found her less responsive than was her custom to his deft caress. A subaltern's wife who for the first time was to entertain a general, who was to give that very night (3rd June 1857) her first really important dinner party, might be forgiven if a little thing like an after-breakfast kiss—which is mere marital small-change, in any case—had but her half-hearted notice. She was weighing the rival merits of fish soup with croutons—"Jimmy, what are croutons?" she had asked without raising her eyes from the page, and he had told her, "Snippets of toast"—or of the Prince Consort's Favourite Sweet—"Just fancy, Jimmy," she had murmured as he tweaked her ear, amused at her earnest air, "milk and rice only!"—and so enthralled was she that for the first time in their fifteen months of married life she had almost allowed her Jimmy to mount and ride away without her customary blandishments—the butterfly kiss and the waving handkerchief.

How glad, how very glad, she was afterwards to remember that, as he put his foot in the stirrup, she had tossed aside her book, rushed to the mounting-block, and flung both arms round his neck—passionately, for she was a passionate young creature—and that, in doing so, she had murmured in his ear, "You know that I love you better than all the rice puddings and all the generals in the world, don't you, darling?"

Laughing, Jimmy Greene had ridden down the drive, his scarlet jacket, black stock, steel gorget, and braided dolman gleaming brightly in the tropical sunshine. He had waved to her as he was about to turn from the drive into the high-road, where the neem-trees hid him from her sight.

So they parted, never to meet again.

For as Cornet Greene rode onto the parade ground where his regiment—unmounted this morning—was already drawn up in the neat unbroken lines that had been his pride, a *feu de joie* that sounded like paper tearing had ripped along the front line and he and all his officers there assembled fell from their chargers, shot dead by their own men.

The sowars then dispersed to kill every European man, woman, and child that they encountered. Simultaneously in every British cantonment in Oudh the prearranged revolt broke out. On that fatal day the mutineers began to loot, to burn, to torture, to pile into dreadful heaps, living and dead alike.

In the well at Cawnpore where screaming children were tossed alive among the hideously mutilated dead and dying; in the white-washed shambles of Dinapore where (until Lord Curzon obliterated them) stained fingerprints could be seen patterning the skirting-boards (the men's high up, the women's just above the ground); throughout all the provinces of Oudh and Behar black terror stalked the white race suspected, quite unjustly, of forcing Hindus and Moslems alike to bite cartridges greased with pig-fat, to break a rule vital to their religion. Their priests had told them that all ammunition was so greased. The resulting mutiny was, to all Indians who took part in it, a crusade, a holy war; no cruelty, therefore, was considered too revolting to be practised.

Meanwhile, on that first morning of the rising in Sitapur, Mrs James Greene, seated in the cool central room of her house with one foot on the rocker of her child's cradle, turned the pages of her recaptured cookery-book.

"Khuda-Baksh," she was saying to her cook, "last night you made an omelette and charged me for eight eggs. This book says that four eggs are the utmost—" So far had she got when shots rang out on the parade ground.

Khuda-Baksh heard them. He had been waiting for them. He leant quickly across the cradle and snatched the book from his young mistress's hand.

Aghast at such unheard-of impertinence, Mrs Greene looked at her swarthy bearded servant, terror growing in her eyes. The man's evil intention was clearly shown in his dark, treacherous looks.

Taking her child in her arms, Mrs Greene backed against the wall.

"Khuda-Baksh," she cried, trying to keep her voice firm, "put that book back on the table and leave the room at once! When the sahib comes home—"

"He will never come back!" Khuda-Baksh laughed. "He and all the sahib-log in India have been killed."

Shadows blocked the doorway.

Some near neighbours, Sir Harry Johnson and Miss Binnie, with two soldiers' wives, rushed into the room.

The baronet was an old man. The exertion of running had deprived him of breath. He stood panting and speechless while Mary Binnie gasped out, "The sepoys are murdering all the English in cantonments. They are even killing the children. Oh, what shall we do? Where shall we hide ourselves?"

"In the taikhana!" Mrs Greene exclaimed immediately.

In every house built in the early days of India, either by French, Dutch, or English, there was what was called a taikhana, a set of underground rooms meant to be a refuge from the intense heat of summer. Many were kept secret, and provided with a secret outlet, to be used in time of danger. The Greenes' taikhana had a concealed door opening onto the river-bank nearly a quarter of a mile from the house.

Looking to see what had happened to Khuda-Baksh, Mrs Greene found that he had vanished, intimidated by the sight of Sir Harry, whose feeble, shaking hand held a revolver—a pistol, as it was then called. She guessed that the man would not have gone far, but she hoped that they would be able to gain entrance to the underground rooms before he returned, bringing others with him, as he was certain to do.

"Come through this archway," she urged her companions. "Quickly! Quickly! Thank God that Jimmy always makes me carry the key of the taikhana in my pocket. Hold Baby, Mary, while I get it."

Stooping, Mrs Greene lifted the voluminous shirred flounces of her crinolined skirts and found the pocket sewn into the lining. She fished out the key, unlocked the strong door of solid teak that appeared to be merely the panelled back of a cupboard, and led her trembling friends through it.

The main rooms of this taikhana were lit by fanlights of thick glass let into the ceiling. They were not hollowed out directly under the house, but were situated under the plot of ground between the bungalow and the river, the Surayan, that ran at the foot of the grounds.

"We have no food, so we shall not be able to stay here long, but after dark we might slip through the river door at the end of the tunnel that leads to the ford," Mrs Greene was explaining, when sounds of running feet and a crackle of musketry sounded faintly far above them.

"The mutineers!" Mary Binnie exclaimed. "Oh, if they find us we shall be brutally murdered!"

Sobs choked her utterance. Ten minutes earlier she had seen her sister with her infant child and little son hideously massacred. Sir Harry, too, had tears streaming down his furrowed cheeks. His grandson, Ensign Johnson, whom he had come to India to visit, had been shot down and then hacked to pieces in his presence. The two soldiers' wives had seen their husbands decapitated, and all their fellow women killed. They had seen the mutineers march off in triumph with the heads impaled on their bayonets.

Three months later the Viceroy's wife, as she drove along by the waterside at Allahabad, was to see the miserable band of women who were to be the sole survivors of experiences which had entailed unspeakable suffering. She was to write in her diary that night, complacently: "It shocked me to observe that these wretched females were so insensible to the delicacy of their position." Lady Canning had not learnt, with Elizabeth Barrett Browning, that "Hopeless grief is passionless."

In the initial hours of this ordeal which was to end for all but one of them in a terrible death, Sir Harry, Mary Binnie, and the two soldiers' wives—widows, that is—though they were dissolved in tears, though their irrational gestures of dismay told how deeply their feelings were moved, had still to follow the primal instinct for self-preservation which is inherent in the very nature of man. These poor fugitives wept for those they had so tragically lost; still, they also feared for their own safety, and they clearly showed the terror that overwhelmed them.

Mrs Greene alone was calm. She had her child to care for, and nursing it, her neat bodice unbuttoned, her white, blue-veined bosom partly covered by a lace handkerchief, she sat on the floor of the tunnel apparently unmoved, her child at her breast and a gentle and maternal tenderness lighting up her lovely face.

"We must wait till darkness comes, then we must make a dash for the ford, cross the river, and try to make our way to Lucknow, which is, I think, our nearest British post," she said to Mary Binnie, who though distracted was slightly more composed than the other three. "News may reach our people that a mutiny has broken out in Sitapur. They may already be sending men to rescue us."

She did not guess that in Lucknow, too, regiment after regiment had rebelled and murdered their officers; that a remnant of the surviving English was to stand one of the noblest sieges in history in that unfortified house now known as the Residency.

It was cool in the taikhana.

Even when the mutineers above them burnt the house down (thinking they were hidden in it), the shuddering group far below ground came to no harm, though like all old Dutch bungalows it had a thatched roof which burnt fiercely.

After an hour or two there was silence above the fugitives. It became apparent that the servants had known nothing of the taikhana's existence, and the entrance to it was now concealed in the ruins of the house. Evidently, too, the secret of the passage to the river had been well kept.

"Those glass panes," Sir Harry said, looking up, "surely those must have been noticed by your gardeners?"

"No, I think not," Mrs Greene answered. "They are deeply set between two pairs of iron gratings. From above they look like the deep drains they are intended to imitate. We are safe for the present."

The long hours of daylight dragged.

The house above the little company was a heap of ashes and tumbled piles of masonry. It was useless to venture back to such ruins. For all they knew, there was no one left in the cantonment, or in the civil lines adjoining it.

Mrs Greene was a vigorous young woman, robust in faith as well as in body. As she leant back against the wall of the tunnel and hushed her child to sleep, she said to Sir Harry, "Let us pool our knowledge. I know the surrounding country so little. To get to Lucknow we must cross the river—I know that much! Fortunately the ford is passable; only last evening I watched the coolie women wading across it, and the water barely reached their knees. Yes, it was knee-high, no more."

"I know the track that leads to Mitauli," Mary Binnie said. "Rajah Lone Singh of Mitauli is friendly to Europeans. He was dining in mess with my brother only a week ago."

"Yes." Sir Harry spoke thickly; he seemed to have had (as indeed, he had) some sort of stroke that impeded his speech.

"Yes, I met the Rajah of Mitauli the night I dined in mess. He is quite friendly, I think."

Throughout the day Sir Harry had seemed to be in a sort of coma, his old white head nodding on his chest. He had been inert, not asleep.

"Yes," Mary Binnie eagerly agreed, "Rajah Lone Singh is a friend. He will help us. He is a splendid man. My brother admired him immensely. I have often ridden on the other side of the river and passed his house at Mitauli. It is not more than five or six miles away. Oh, do let us try and reach it before daylight tomorrow!"

"Yes," one of the soldiers' wives put in, "it is better to try and get help from the Rajah than to attempt to make our own way to Lucknow, which is fifty miles away at the least. How can we hope to go safely through a country where our enemies are as thick as flies?"

The other woman agreed with her.

"There is a full moon," she reminded them. "We must bolt out of here directly it gets dusk. We'll have to get away before the moon rises."

"True! Let us go as soon as we can. We might find something to eat, at any rate, though the idea of drinking river water makes me shudder," the woman who had been a sergeant's wife added in agreement.

Directly daylight faded they crept out of the taikhana by the river door.

They made their way through the long unkempt and half-burnt grass, every few minutes waiting motionless to look about them for some signs of their enemy. There seemed to be no one near, but the darkness made it hard to distinguish objects a few yards away.

The water when they reached the ford ran swiftly, yet it was scarcely knee-high, and by clasping hands they crossed the river safely, though Mrs Greene and Mary Binnie found their floating crinolines a great handicap. It was fortunate for them that the two sturdy soldiers' widows could twist their skirts round their hips and help the two ladies to keep their feet.

Feeling (quite irrationally) more secure when they had once reached the opposite bank of the Surayan, the fugitives rested and drank thirstily, well hidden by the tall sugar-cane which grew there. They picked some stalks of the ripe cane and sucked the sweet juice, which greatly revived them.

The women had been both alarmed and distressed to find that

Sir Harry moved with difficulty. They realized that he would be a great drag on their progress, for he stumbled over stones or clumps of cane or scrub as if he could not see the obstacles that lay in his path. It was not so dark but that the black outlines of more solid objects showed still darker in the dusk. Sir Harry, too, fell several times.

They had scarcely got safely into the shadows of the sugar-cane when the moon rose and flooded the whole panorama with light.

The country was flat and, as flat country does, it seemed to magnify the size of everything. Under the brilliant moon the river shone like a sheet of glass, every dark piece of flotsam on it perfectly visible.

They were lucky to have crossed in time.

They were just thinking of moving on their way when pandemonium broke out on the farther side of the bank about sixty yards above their hiding-place. There the Surayan was deeper and could only be crossed by swimming, or in a boat.

Pouring headlong out of the shadows of a bungalow that stood some twenty yards back from the river came a frenzied mob of English people—men, women, and children. The men, it appeared, were trying to shepherd the women and children to some place of safety; they had waited too late. The moonlight had taken them by surprise and made their movements apparent to their foes.

As they ran, many of these poor people were mercilessly shot down by the pursuing sepoys. Others were cut down by the curved swords of the cavalry soldiers, the men of Jimmy Greene's regiment.

Some fugitives reached the river only to sink, wounded, below the turgid waters, churned up now by all the struggling swimmers. Very few reached the opposite bank. Even among these, several were hurt by long shots from the sepoys' muskets. In the end only thirteen or so dodging through the cane seemed to the onlookers to escape, for the time being, the dangers which threatened them.

Mrs Greene and her companions, their faces pale with horror, watching this dreadful massacre of their friends, hurriedly debated whether it would be wiser to turn upstream and join the larger party, or keep to their original plan of throwing themselves on the mercy of Rajah Lone Singh. They decided in the end to make their way to Mitauli. They realized that Sir Harry could make little effort for himself; his feet dragged, and the two soldiers' widows had constantly to support him on either side.

Mrs Greene doubted, too, whether with her child to carry and hampered by her long skirts she could make much headway through the close-knit cane; besides, how could they make certain of finding the other party?

It was after very little discussion that they made up their minds to make their way to the house of that nawab whom they believed to be friendly.

So simply did Sir Harry, Mary Binnie, and the two soldiers' widows—Mrs Simmons and Mrs Pike—make the resolution that was to lead to their deaths. For the party of thirteen which they had seen cross the river, protected by some native police, did, finally, though after many hardships, reach their friends in Lucknow.

Mrs Greene, like Mary Binnie, had often ridden past the village of Mitauli where Rajah Lone Singh had his house. She guided the forlorn little company through the tall sugar-cane which had been their salvation, for it both fed them and hid their movements, and by two o'clock in the morning they had reached their goal, a flat-roofed white two-storeyed building enclosed in a red brick wall which had trees waving over the top of it, like feathers in a casque.

They beat with stones and sticks on the fast-closed gates.

After twenty minutes someone heard them and they were admitted.

Daylight was even now creeping through the rose-flushed sky, palely beautiful in the thick opalescent mists of dawn.

Looking back, as she was in after years so often to look back on these first dreadful days, Mrs Greene, who was to suffer and endure so much, felt always that the moment when she and her four companions stood before Rajah Lone Singh and saw no kindness in him was the worst of many ordeals. She looked at his gloating, oily countenance; she read there no pity, only a treacherous satisfaction; the complacency of the bully who has found fresh victims.

Yes, as she looked at the Rajah when after two hours of waiting he had strolled out of his house to stand with two attendants on either side of him and hear their petition—that he would give them palki-bearers and escort them safely to their own people in Lucknow—she knew immediately that there was no hope for them. She realized that they had delivered themselves into the power of a brutal and implacable enemy.

The light was still faint, for a mist as white as milk hung over everything. The fugitives were grouped under an immense banyan-tree bearded with long roots that sagged down from every branch and made colonnades and pillars as stately as those in any great cathedral. The tree with its far-roving boughs covered quite half an acre of ground, each limb being as thick as the trunk of a well-grown oak, while the earth under the tree was quite bare and ribbed with the main-roots that sometimes rose five or six feet out of the black fertile soil. The leaves of this tree were bigger than a man's palm and of a rich incandescent green; its aerial roots were as thick as thatch.

Standing under it, the Rajah wore a white muslin coat folded across his strong and muscular chest. His wide striped drawers were not drawn round the ankles like jodhpurs but were very full, baggy, and patterned in stripes of green, red and black. His turban was of Dacca muslin, very fine and clean. He wore gauntlet gloves that reached his elbow, because he was a leper and sought in this way to hide his deformity.

Now, Rajah Lone Singh was a great gambler. He had won the estates he at present enjoyed at dicing with his brother, and when he had contemptuously given his guests leave to lie under his banyan-tree and had sent them out a chapati or two and a chatty of drinking water, he dispatched a messenger post-haste to a fellow nawab, a neighbour whose fields he coveted. Mrs Greene and her exhausted companions lying under the banyan-tree heard the beat of departing hooves and trembled; they now felt certain that Rajah Lone Singh intended to betray them.

Cock-fighting is a sport popular with Indian gentlemen. Rajah Lone Singh had a famous cockerel imported by caravan from China, and he had many times longed to pit this bird against an equally famous cockerel belonging to his friend Nawab Allah-ud-din of Surayan, for whom it had won a number of wagers. This nawab played only for high stakes. Rajah Lone Singh, being a miser and the most avaricious of men, had for some months been casting about in his mind to find some tempting stake which he could use in a match between his bird and the Nawab's, and yet risk neither land nor money of his own. In the poor English now claiming his protection he thought he had found what he sought. He would challenge Allah-ud-din to wager his corn fields against the baronet and four Englishwomen.

Sitting under the banyan-tree as morning changed to noon and noon to fiery evening and dark night, Mrs Greene and Mary Binnie, still outwardly more composed than the soldiers' widows, who wept unceasingly—the baronet, apparently, slept all day—judged from the preparations that were being made that the

Rajah meant to entertain a large party of friends that evening. There was a general bustle of activity that made it plain to any housewife that a big dinner was in preparation.

Mrs Greene, in spite of her fears, was so much a child that she was interested in all that went on. She watched some twenty chickens being chased, caught, and killed, and fat quail being taken from the quail-pit. A peacock was brought in. Several baskets of fish came up from the river which ran near. Trays of sweetmeats dried in the sun.

Regarding all this, it crossed Mrs Greene's mind that twenty-four hours earlier she herself had been making preparations for a dinner party.

When Rajah Lone Singh early that morning had listened to what the fugitives had got to say he had confined his attention wholly to Sir Harry. He had neither looked at nor spoken to the four women.

Indian men do not admire Englishwomen—white women, that is to say. Their pasty faces, they assert, look anaemic and unwholesome; beside the honey-coloured and flawless skins of Indian beauties they lack brilliance. Their hair, too, seems dull and lustreless in contrast with the satin-sheened oiled and raven tresses of zenana belles. Their figures (they consider) are bad; their heads, hands, and feet are too large. They have, in short, no grace of movement, no subtlety of rhythm in dancing, no charm of expression in their colourless washed-out eyes.

The dust-stained dejected women sitting under the banyan had nothing to fear from Rajah Lone Singh's attentions: had they but known it, he intended to pay them none.

When the red sun had dropped below the sugar-cane, and lavender mist lay like a table-cloth floating a few feet above it, a clatter of galloping hooves and much shouting from his running torchbearers and servants heralded the arrival of Nawab Allah-ud-din.

Stories of the destruction of every Englishman in Sitapur, of the terrible massacres of Cawnpore, Lucknow, Fyzabad, Dinapore; or Delhi, Agra, and Bareilly; tales of the risings in the Central Provinces, in Meerut, Patna, and Lahore, had been eagerly passed from mouth to mouth throughout the length and breadth of Oudh. They had lost nothing in the telling.

It was current gossip that the race of Englishmen was doomed to an ignoble extinction; the glory enjoyed by every rebel who had murdered one or two was the envy of every Indian.

Nawab Allah-ud-din had been unlucky. Directly the sun rose

he had ridden post-haste to Sitapur, hoping to take part in the general massacre, but in every case the victims he had selected had fallen to another sword or bayonet. In the five fugitives offered to him as a bait by Rajah Lone Singh he saw a chance to redeem his reputation. He would win them. He would gain much praise by openly insulting them. He would finally murder them with as much cruelty and publicity as possible.

Mrs Greene, her baby in her lap, was seated among the roots of the banyan-tree, which made a comfortable resting-place. Mary Binnie, in an effort to keep the mosquitoes from the child's face, was waving a flowering branch she had broken off from a nearby neem-tree; Mrs Simmons and Mrs Pike were lying asleep on a patch of grass beyond the limits of the tree, when two man-servants carrying lanthorns came out of the house and preceded Rajah Lone Singh and Nawab Allah-ud-din, who were coming out to inspect the prisoners.

Rajah Lone Singh coveted his friend's canefields, yet he was beginning to feel that he would prefer to keep his captives for his own amusement; he thought, "Perhaps I had better see that my cockerel wins the match; I can win the fields any time."

There is a certain disarming innocence about youth. Mrs Greene, at sixteen, was young even for that age. She knew nothing of sin or of the tempestuous passions of the human heart.

When Mary Binnie rose, trembling, to her feet as the two men approached her, Mrs Greene rose with her, more to keep the waving neem-branch within reach of her child's face than for any other reason. She stood up quite without any sign of fear and said "*Salaam*", the only Hindustani word she knew, by way of greeting.

Mrs Greene had been very proud of being a married woman. Since she had married early, a doting mother and five spinster aunts had constantly impressed upon her the need for dignity in a married woman. She showed dignity now.

Picot-edged frills, ribbons and furbelows—indeed every device known to the Victorian dressmaker's robust imagination—tricked out the many yards of her scarlet tartan dress, and made her voluminous skirts stand out like cumulus clouds. Her plainly fitting tight bodice buttoning up the front with a score of tiny tartan buttons had a white lace collar of the type called "puritan". It was fastened with a cameo brooch carved with the elegantly classical theme of Diana teaching Cupid to shoot.

Mrs Greene's pale-gold hair, parted in the centre, was bunched in feathery ringlets on each side of her very Dolly Varden face.

She had a firm well-rounded chin, a short retroussé nose, blue eyes set wide apart and made brighter by the dark lashes and arching eyebrows that were a deep fawn colour and very thickly spread. Even in this moment of trial there was a dewy freshness about her that would have charmed the most critical eye, but to the two Indian men she made no appeal.

Both Rajah Lone Singh and Allah-ud-din were brutal men, delighting in cruelty in the way that has hitherto stamped the Eastern mind as uncivilized to Western ideas.

As this helpless girl stood before the two men who held her fate in the hollow of their evil hands, no one knowing of the orgies of butchery that during the past twenty-four hours had gone to stain the pages of Indian history would have guessed that Mrs Greene had one chance in a thousand of surviving the next few hours, or at least the next few days.

A great many lights were now flitting about the courtyard. Servants carrying the exotic delights that were to furnish the forthcoming banquet hurried to and fro between the kitchen and the house—a two-storeyed stucco structure, more like a Cheltenham villa than the dwelling of an Indian landowner.

It happened that the chuprassy who carried the much-prized white cockerel which Allah-ud-din had brought with him, confined in a wicker cage, had set his burden down beside a brazier, an iron basket filled with burning charcoal which another servant had dumped carelessly down on the ground while he ran to answer a summons from the cook's godown. (The whole courtyard teemed with humanity, and the general excitement was causing a great deal of confusion.)

The two Indians were standing with their backs to the coop, laughing while they discussed their captives—now quite obviously their prisoners, not their guests.

The wicker coop was carpeted with straw, dry after the day's intense heat. Mrs Greene, who had been attracted by the beautiful fighting-cock's plumage, had been watching it idly when suddenly she saw that the straw, ignited by the brazier, was smoking. Without a moment's hesitation she put her child into Mary Binnie's arms and swooped in her brilliant tartan draperies straight across the courtyard.

She had unlatched the burning hatch and taken the cockerel in her strong young arms before anyone realized what was happening. There she stood, the coop flaming beside her, the cockerel safe. Behind her the great banyan-tree, garlanded with marigolds —for it was a shrine of some sort—caught the dancing light from the fire and became an unreal stage-like green, while the red flounces on her tartan dress glowed yet more brightly in the blaze that was now shooting showers of sparks upwards towards a starlit sky.

The servants who had left the coop darted up and would have taken the cockerel; but, still gently and firmly clasping the snow-white bird, whose curved tail-feathers flowed out from it, graceful as a playing fountain, Mrs Greene walked towards the spellbound Allah-ud-din.

"This bird is yours, isn't it?" she asked, smiling. "If I had been an instant slower it would have been burnt to death, poor creature."

She put the cockerel into its owner's hands.

"It was touch and go, wasn't it?" she added casually, halting a moment before him.

Nawab Allah-ud-din was a small man, active and muscular. He was not ill-looking. He had the hooked nose, the slanting eyes, the high cheekbones of his race, which had in it a Mongolian strain. His white linen coat and jodhpurs were spotless; his turban was a miracle of art, being wound with all its pleats festooned in a direct line with his left eyebrow, which was higher than his right; this gave him a dashing air.

The Nawab's ears were long and weighed down with heavy ear-rings. It may be that the women behind the purdah made a speciality of embroidering shoes for their menfolk. Certainly the Nawab's shoes and those of Rajah Lone Singh were equally resplendent in natty stitchings of silver wire and sequins.

There should have been nothing to alarm Mrs Greene in the quiet figure of the Nawab; but meeting his black, very shallow eyes, she had a moment of real terror. There had been no pity in Allah-ud-din's face. In its relentless cruelty, as in Rajah Lone Singh's, she read the same implacable menace.

She took her child from Mary Binnie and stood erect. She would show no fear.

"It's a fighting-cock, that bird, isn't it?" she inquired, carelessly strolling over to Rajah Lone Singh, whose laughter had been quieted by the incident.

"Yes." He smiled. "I mean to match my bird against the Nawab's tonight—for a wager." He and his friend exchanged amused glances. "You shall watch the fight. Yes. We will let the birds fight out here where you and your companions shall watch them."

Laughing again, the two Indians went in to the banquet.

During the past half-hour many men had been arriving in doolies and palanquins or riding trotting ponies. An elephant having a magnificent howdah on its back, its tusks encased in gold, had brought an old man and a graceful boy who wore a coat of pale-blue brocade.

Looking from the banyan-tree through the open french windows beyond the veranda arches, it was possible to see into a room with long tables and lines of turbaned guests. With the exception of the white-bearded Talakdar, who had arrived sitting with his grandson in the howdah of the elephant, the men were of little importance, being merely the Indian equivalent of the Irish squireen. They were mostly swashbucklers and landowners of small holdings in the neighbouring villages. Several of them were sowars, soldiers who had been serving with the irregular cavalry which, twenty-four hours earlier, had mutinied and shot down their officers. They could be seen still in their uniforms recounting their triumphs with rowdy abandon.

Looking through the windows at these carousing men, Mary Binnie and the soldiers' widows felt fear knocking afresh at their despairing hearts. They thought that these men, after drinking the arrack and other potent intoxicants in which, against the teaching of their religion, they were indulging, would be capable of any crime; a fear that was to prove only too well founded.

Even Sir Harry, awakened as the women had been by the noise, seemed to realize more poignantly the dangers which surrounded them. He struggled to his feet and with the aid of Mrs Simmons and Mrs Pike, who were strong, buxom women, he moved across to where Mrs Greene was sitting in her old place among the roots of the banyan-tree.

"My dear," he murmured, feeling difficulty in articulating, "I fear for you and your poor little child. I still have the pistol which I have hidden in the lining of my coat. I am old. If I were tortured I should not live long, but you and Mary Binnie and these women are young. There may be terrible indignities and suffering before you, and you might not die easily. This is perhaps the one moment left to you to decide whether you will take your own lives, and so evade the terrible future."

"Oh, sir," cried Mrs Simmons impulsively, "these Indian gentlemen might not be so unkind! I'd rather have my own life to live, whatever may come to me, than take a coward's way out."

Mrs Pike was of the same mind.

Mary Binnie, crying as if her heart was breaking, as indeed it was, sobbed out, "I know enough Urdu to understand what those men are saying. They mean to make us the stake in the cock-fight they are going to have. If the Nawab wins us from Rajah Lone Singh our fate is sealed. He is a villain. I have heard many tales of his cruelty."

Before Sir Harry could speak again, the banquet drew to a close. The revellers with shouts of laughter prepared to leave the house. Servants came out and traced a chalk circle on the hard, smooth earth behind the banyan-tree. The two fighting-cocks were brought out and given pills of some drug that was meant to make them more pugnacious. Golden spurs were affixed to their claws.

Chairs were arranged along the fringes of the chalk circle.

Flaming torches were affixed into the poles and baskets intended to hold them. They gave, within the circle, a light as bright as sunlight but less stable. Beyond the circle, however, all was dusk among the heavy foliage of the neighbouring trees.

The two fighting-cocks, perfectly groomed, were being held by the men who tended them when the riotous drunken men crowded out of the house and arranged themselves round the earthen arena. The birds were magnificent creatures. Allah-ud-din's entrant was the white cockerel Mrs Greene had rescued from the burning coop; Rajah Lone Singh's was a leggy orange-coloured bird, imported from China.

The fight began.

There is a monument on the China Bazaar Road, outside Lucknow. It has on the north face the names of ten or twelve soldiers killed within the Residency; on the south face are inscribed the names of Sir Harry Johnson, Mary Binnie, Mrs Simmons and Mrs Pike. Mrs Greene's name companions theirs.

The motto gracing the tomb reads: STRANGER! RESPECT THEIR LONELY RESTING PLACE.

It is true that Sir Harry, Mary Binnie, Mrs Simmons and Mrs Pike lie in that grave. The Nawab Allah-ud-din's bird won the match. The Chinese game-cock was left lying dead within the chalk circle. The exulting Nawab took possession of the prize—the English fugitives.

He forced them, lashed by long whips, to run before his trotting horse. After unspeakable indignities he murdered them in a mango-tope, not far from the place where their grave now stands.

Mrs Greene was not among the Nawab Allah-ud-din's victims.

In spite of the inscription on the tomb, she, in reality, escaped their dreadful fate.

It happened that among the soldiers who had been invited to Rajah Lone Singh's banquet there was a young sowar—a cavalry-man—called Mirza Khan. He had been in Jimmy Greene's regiment. When Mrs Greene's child was born this sowar's wife had also given birth to an infant—a son. Mrs Greene had a great many more clothes in her infant daughter's layette than she could possibly need, for she had a number of relatives who took pleasure in making the loveliest garments imaginable for her expected baby, among them being many boy-baby garments with the conventional blue bows. She sent a generous bundle of these to the sowar's wife.

Mirza Khan's wife had been delighted with the gift. They made her child look, she thought, most distinguished; so during the past three months she had constantly asked her husband to tell her any news he could about her benefactress.

It chanced that Mirza Khan on his mettlesome country-bred stallion had ridden into the Rajah's courtyard just at the moment when Mrs Greene had made her dramatic rescue of the white fighting-cock.

Indian men admire above all things bravery in a woman. Many legends of brave women are told in Indian history. Mirza Khan, therefore, being a brave man himself, admired the spirit Mrs Greene had shown. Dismounting, he gave his piebald mount to a groom to hold, and walked closer to where Mrs Greene in her brilliant red tartan dress was standing under the leaves of the banyan-tree. The flames still lighted up her face, so exalted now in its brave endurance of her ordeal. He watched her accept without flinching her captor's insulting words (which she did not understand) and insolent looks (which she perfectly comprehended).

Mirza Khan realized that nothing could save Mrs Greene from the most agonizing tortures if she were left in the power of the Nawab Allah-ud-din, and that the leprous Lone Singh would be an equally cruel tyrant. He slipped away, therefore, and sought out old Mosin-ud-Dowlah, the Talakdar who had arrived on the elephant. He was a kind and enlightened man, a well-tried friend of the English, who is now known to have assisted many of them to escape from the mutineers, and whose touching tribute to his friend Wellwood George Mowbray may still be read on the tomb he erected to his memory, in Lucknow.

This Talakdar's well-armed band of fighting retainers, his

wealth, and his recognized standing in Oudh prevented the disloyal faction from showing him any hostility. He was too powerful.

Mosin-ud-Dowlah immediately agreed to Mirza Khan's suggestion that he should smuggle Mrs Greene to a place of safety hidden in the howdah of his elephant. He caused his young grandson to divest himself of his blue coat and turban and baggy muslin pyjamas, and leaving the boy to borrow clothes from one of his grooms, the Talakdar gave these others to Mrs Greene.

So great was the excitement over the cock-fight now in progress that Mrs Greene, directed by Mirza Khan, easily slipped away into some tall growths of sunflowers that bordered the Rajah's mango-tope, where, taking off her crinoline and bunching up her curls under the turban, she, like Rosalind, put on a boy's attire. Mirza Khan brought her some coffee with which she stained her face and hands.

When she was ready, Mosin-ud-Dowlah established himself in front of her on the howdah, and together with his grandson and the mahout, they escaped on the swaying elephant through the open and unguarded gateway of Rajah Lone Singh's serai.

Once they were outside, Mirza Khan handed the child up to Mrs Greene, for he had carried it out with him, riding with his usual gallant bearing on his piebald horse, which had blue beads for a necklace, and a saddle chased in silver. Then, his drawn sword in his hand, he rode off in their company.

Mosin-ud-Dowlah at this time kept no harem. So the sowar, Mirza Khan, took Mrs Greene and her child into his house.

Mirza Khan, who was the son of a small landholder, a zemindar, had a house that was a little better than that of most sepoys, or sowars. It stood on the left bank of the Surayan, about three miles south of Sitapur, and it was enclosed in a high mud wall, the top of which was thatched, somewhat after the Wiltshire fashion, in order to keep the rain from dissolving it.

The bungalow itself was small and had a flat roof, and its doors opened out onto several trellised verandas. It contained, in all, seven rooms which opened into a central chamber, in the middle of which lay a large marble catafalque.

The presence of this tomb, a saint's, made it necessary for the sowar to open his house once a year to pilgrims of a sect which paid honour to the buried saint, whose sacred bones were said to lie in this queer sarcophagus.

As is well known, General Martin caused himself to be entombed in the dining-room of his vast mansion, La Martinière, in Lucknow, because he knew that the King of Oudh coveted it and meant to take possession of it after his death; his buried body prevented this robbery. The shrine was probably placed in the sowar's house for the same reason—that is, to protect the rights of the owner of the house.

Mrs Greene found that her kind rescuer's family consisted of his wife, whose child was born the same day as her own; a second inferior woman, whom the wife forced to attend on her husband when he was drunk, which was seldom, for he was a strict Mohammedan and rarely touched wine; and two old aunts of Mirza Khan's, to whom, since they were penniless, he had given asylum.

The sowar's wife received Mrs Greene kindly. For the first three months of her sojourn in this quiet household she was treated as an honoured guest.

In return for all the kindness she received, Mrs Greene taught the sowar's womenfolk the simple arts she had learnt in her English country home: tatting, knitting, the making of peculiarly good cheeses, and of various preserves, comfits, jams, pickles, and sauces, all very rich and unusual, which they sold with profit in the bazaar in Sitapur. She also taught the women to make elaborate patchwork quilts, to paste fish-scales and wind wool on wire into the semblance of the most beautiful flowers, and even birds. A canary holding in its beak a sprig of may-blossom, and having above it an arch of roses and wallflowers, was a favourite design of hers, and always sold very well.

This last pursuit greatly delighted the sowar's two old aunts.

Mrs Greene's child flourished. She was so wrapped up in her daughter's welfare that during those first three months she was not unhappy. News came through of the stand that the English shut up in the Residency were making. She heard from an ayah, who often crept into her room at night, that Sir Colin Campbell was coming to relieve the garrison there. She felt certain that once the revolt was quelled she would be free to return to her own country and her father's house.

The sowar had told her of her husband's death. She mourned him as an inexperienced girl does, with a deep and sincere sorrow, and with only an instinctive understanding of her own wretchedness.

Then, for a reason which she at first did not understand, she felt less free.

At the foot of the sowar's garden there was a summer-house—a chabootra, as it is called—which was set well out from the angle of the enclosing wall which ran alongside the river, here flowing smoothly right against this old red brick wall. The water was deep here, and the river fairly wide, so that it was a cool and sequestered spot, very pleasant to Mrs Greene, since the other women rarely went there. When she wanted to be alone she often sat in this chabootra, watching the paddy-birds in their lovely nuptial plumage, or the fish jumping out of the water after flies.

There were no buildings on the opposite bank of the river; behind the chabootra a grove of mangoes hid it from the house.

During the months she had been under his roof Mrs Greene had seldom seen Mirza Khan. He had taken service with the old Talakdar, Mosin-ud-Dowlah, and she heard him clatter off every morning on his piebald country-bred pony. Sometimes through her lattice she got a glimpse of the resplendent red-and-gold uniform he wore as one of the Talakdar's retainers. It was long after dark each night when he returned.

There was a small enclosed courtyard outside Mrs Greene's window in which she often sat at work. Happening one holy day, when the sowar was at home, to glance out as she sat at her window sewing, she saw him. He was stripped to the waist and wore wrapped round him the dhoti, the muslin garment which all Indian men wear. His turban was discarded and was looped over the bough of a neem-tree near by. He had a small brass jar from which he was pouring water over his head and over his light-brown glistening torso. He was a magnificent man. He had the strong, thick, youthful neck, the wide chest and narrow hips, the muscular arms of a fine fighting man, and he stood well over six feet in height. Since he was a soldier he took great pride in his appearance. He was meticulously clean. His beard was well oiled and brushed and curled round a string so that it curved in a shining roll from ear to ear, and did not hide the fine lines of his noble masculine throat and shoulders. His hair at this moment was coiled into a topknot on the crown of his shapely head. It was curled like a woman's, and more brown than black. As Mrs Greene instinctively paused to admire him and, fascinated, watch him, a puff of wind blew her curtain to one side, and Mirza Khan, turning at that moment, looked her full in the face with his dark and brilliant eyes.

She was immensely discomposed. She drew back behind her curtains with a scarlet face. How she hated herself! In her looking-glass she saw that her young face was brilliantly alive and that her eyes, usually so blue, were gleaming with a bright orange colour that startled her with its feline sheen. "I look like a tigress," she thought, shocked.

It was the memory of this incident—encounter, it might almost be called—that surged up to fill Mrs Greene with shame when, on a still, cool evening late in the summer, Mirza Khan entered the summer-house where she was sitting pasting fish-scales into the semblance of a rose, her child asleep in one of those baskets commonly called a Moses basket.

The lotus in the tank had shrivelled and drooped long ago into the water, the neem-flowers had come and gone, the fruit on the pomegranate was ripe and ready for picking, the corn was already cut.

The evening was very calm. Sunset clouds were drifting incredibly slowly across an infinitely pale sky more green than blue.

"Salaam, Gharib-Purwar," Mirza Khan began, touching his forehead with his hand in the recognized gesture of salutation, "I would like permission to speak to the Huzoor."

"Salaam," Mrs Greene answered, reddening. As she sat there in her tartan dress she, who had formerly been so self-possessed, was now pitifully self-conscious in her host's presence.

Since that fatal night at Mitauli she had spoken to Mirza Khan on two occasions only: once, when with tears in her eyes she had thanked him for rescuing her from Rajah Lone Singh; a second time, next morning, when she had again to thank him for the return of her clothes, and for some jewellery which, recognizing it to be hers, he had taken from a fellow sowar who had stolen it from her house.

The trinkets he had returned to her Mrs Greene, in the happy assurance that she could still do a favour, had given piece by piece to the sowar's wife, who was invariably kind to her.

"Mirza Khan," Mrs Greene now said, speaking quickly to hide her embarrassment, "surely the mutiny is over? Surely it would be safe for me to try and reach my friends in Lucknow?"

"Huzoor, not yet," Mirza Khan said earnestly. "There are still many bad characters on the roads. As soon as it is safe I will send a letter to Cawnpore—all the mem-sahibs have been taken there; none have been left in Lucknow. When it is safe I will make arrangements to take Gharib-Purwar back to her own people."

There are still many families in India which can claim descent from the Grecian generals who accompanied Alexander the Great across the Hydaspes—the Jhelum. Mirza Khan claimed to be descended from one of Alexander's generals, and, indeed, as he stood before Mrs Greene he had a very noble Grecian air about him, in spite of his deeply tanned skin.

"But, mem-sahib," he continued, "I came to say that tomorrow is the day that the tomb in my house is shown to the pilgrims who come to pay homage to the saint buried in it. The mem-sahib must hide. She must on no account be seen. Rajah Lone Singh and Nawab Allah-ud-din have never given up their search for her. Though the mutiny is put down there are no sahib-log near enough to protect her should these men find her."

"Oh, Mirza Khan," Mrs Greene entreated him, trembling and gazing into his face most pitifully, all her embarrassment forgotten, "you would not give me up to those wicked men?"

"Huzoor," Mirza Khan replied grimly, "all that one man can do, I will do."

He paused an instant, looking at her without speaking and meeting her eyes with a deep, unsmiling regard. The sky behind his blue-and-gold turban shimmered with an astonishing brilliance as he saluted her gravely and, turning, left the chabootra.

Before it was light next morning the sowar's wife brought Mrs Greene some Indian clothes. She gave her a sari—a full, much-pleated skirt of red cotton, striped round the hem with purple, green, and orange and much braided with tinsel. She brought her a rose-coloured chuddah—the wide sheet which Indian women twist into the waistband of their skirts and fling over their heads. She added a shirt of bright amber muslin, very finely woven and sewn with a gold thread neckband, and a voluminous pair of purple drawers, very full round the waist and fitting tightly round the ankles. A pair of red leather slippers, some glass anklets, and many ropes of turquoise beads carved to resemble flowers completed this outfit. There was also a headband gay with glass rubies and emeralds.

The sowar's wife on lending this dress, said it must be given back—it had been her husband's wedding present to her.

Mrs Greene then stained her face and body with coffee, for her waist above her skirt was bare. She hid her crinoline and her English clothes, and put on the Indian garments.

She covered her fair curls with black horsehair—fly-whisks, in reality—and the headband kept this in place. Mrs Greene thought this disguise complete, for the chuddah veiled her face when she chose to draw it close, and she did not, in any case, intend to leave her room when the house was full of strangers.

From the moment the sun rose, an unbroken line of pilgrims

filed through the room in which the tomb stood. Many were very poor, humble people, and they would leave the smallest of copper coins, or a handful of rice, or a few fading marigolds on the grave. Prostrating themselves, they would patter off some unintelligible prayers and petitions (for a petition is to prayer what night is to day—the inevitable sequence) and then they would go on their way, happy.

Coolies, naked but for a loincloth, some shopkeepers, some devotees from other shrines, a few soldiers very ragged but still in their uniforms, though every sepoy now had a price on his head, and some of Mosin-ud-Dowlah's retainers wearing the flamboyant scarlet-and-gold uniforms in which, peeping through her lattice, Mrs Greene was accustomed to see Mirza Khan ride daily away—such were the people who visited the shrine. Late in the day, to Mrs Greene's horror, she saw a contingent of servants from Mitauli enter—she recognized the man who had carried the coop; he was easily identified, for the man had a black patch over one eye.

Though Mrs Greene felt she need have nothing to fear, for no rule in India is so strictly kept as that which preserves the sanctity of the purdah—the entrance to the women's apartments—she shook with alarm as Allah-ud-din himself swaggered in and, making an ostentatious obeisance, laid an offering of many gold pieces beside the relics adorning the sarcophagus: the saint's begging-bowl and his worn flagellant's thong.

Though Mrs Greene for her own safety's sake should have withdrawn immediately from the peep-hole in her curtain (it was a trellis of holes cut out and sewn with thread, which made a lace-like aperture), a dreadful fascination kept her eyes glued to it; she could not tear herself away.

Indian men are perfectly well aware of the lattice, the door with its perforation of peep-holes through which the women in every Indian household peer out at the forbidden world. There is even a certain coquetry about the business. Nawab Allah-ud-din, casting his eyes idly on each aperture in turn, saw, suddenly, Mrs Greene's blue eyes sparkling through the gauze.

Triumph surged through him. He realized that at last he had located the woman who had eluded him for so long.

Aware that he had recognized her—his face plainly showed it—Mrs Greene realized with a rush of terror that her blue eyes must have betrayed her. She did not reason. Her daughter she knew was safe, playing in the zenana with the sowar's children. She ran through the outer door of her room into the trellised courtyard where Mirza Khan stood leaning on his long curved sword as if on guard—as indeed he was.

"Mirza Khan," she cried, distraught, "Allah-ud-din is in there! He recognized me as I was peeping through the chink in the curtain. Oh, Mirza Khan, you have been so good—do not let him take me away!"

So great was her fear that Mrs Greene forgot she was not wearing her English dress. She was not used to the management of the chuddah, the veil that should have shielded her. It slipped from her shoulders so that her beautiful body was clearly displayed in bright sunlight through the diaphanous shirt she wore as her only upper garment.

Mirza Khan's sect taught him to practise chastity, temperance, and obedience to a warrior's code; he was as strict an anchorite as any other man who had sworn to conform to an exacting religious ideal.

If Mrs Greene had been attired in her "foreign" clothes it is doubtful whether Mirza Khan would ever have swerved from his loyal intention of restoring his guest to her friends as soon as it was safe to travel through the still unsettled countryside.

But the sowar's wife, poor woman, in her wish to do her best for Mrs Greene to whom she was deeply attached, had lent her the dress she had worn on her wedding-night—it was as a bride that the lovely English girl now made her frantic appeal to Mirza Khan. Her stained body had no distasteful pallor, her blue eyes were (to him) like those of a goddess, as they besought him, bright with an irresistible and overwhelming brilliance, to save her.

Mirza Khan looked at his suppliant guest. His eyes, soft with that deceptive softness that denotes a tendency to the berserk rages which on occasion can possess men of the Mogul race, dwelt strangely, she thought, on hers. She saw, without understanding, their awakening fires. They were quickly veiled.

"Go back to your room, mem-sahib," Mirza Khan directed her, quietly. "I will wait there with you. I know Allah-ud-din. He will act quickly."

Comforted by Mirza Khan's gentleness and strength, Mrs Greene, returning, had scarcely entered her room where Mirza Khan took his stand directly to one side of the curtained archway into the larger, central room, when a hand drew the hangings aside, and Allah-ud-din slipped noiselessly through them.

His movements were as swift and menacing as a panther's. He was famous as a huntsman. In each hand he carried one of those squat two-edged knives which Indian men formerly carried stuck through their wide swathed belts. One of these knives he pressed against Mrs Greene's breast as she stood boldly facing him—boldly, but with a fast-beating heart. He kept his right hand free as he darted a snake-like gaze about him. He did not turn when Mirza Khan, stepping in front of him, cut him down with one movement of his long curved sword.

Mirza Khan left Allah-ud-din's body lying where it fell, and, having sent Mrs Greene across to his wife's apartments, he himself rode off across the river to see Mosin-ud-Dowlah, his master, and to acquaint him with all that had happened. Two hours later he returned with some of Mosin-ud-Dowlah's servants and some armed retainers, who carried off the body to their master's serai—a display of friendship and strength which prevented any further trouble.

During the next five months Mrs Greene saw Mirza Khan not at all. On those rare occasions when he was at home she could hear him through her curtains talking to his two old aunts, who adored him, or holding long murmurous conversations with his wife. Mrs Greene he had always treated as he did his two old aunts, with a most exquisite kindness and courtesy; they were his dependants; but now she never saw him to speak to.

In the spring when the mango-trees were in flower and the bees crawled laden with pollen into the orange rosettes of the pomegranates, Mirza Khan's wife, as was her custom, decorated the tiny pleasure-ground that abutted onto her outer door. She hung up on the bough of the big peepul-tree that shaded her lawn a swing with tinsel-bound chains. She decked this with garlands of the fragant champak-flower that has so overmastering a perfume. On a grassy knoll beside the lotus tank (the lilies were not yet in flower) she spread the couch of love, the ceremonial quilt of neem-flowers and frangipanni, and creamy-flowered scented jasmine boughs.

A parrot in a gilt cage swung from the boughs of a flowering cork-tree near by; a rich red-and-blue counterpane lay beside it.

Mrs Greene, who spent the best part of her days in the zenana, where she was on friendly and affectionate terms with Mirza Khan's family, particularly with his two old aunts, saw these preparations for the entertainment of Mirza Khan with an aching heart. She had learnt that her letters would always be returned to her, that she could hope for no communication with the outside world, or with her own people. Great kindness had been shown to her, but she lived apart from the warm and vital springs of life that made Mirza Khan's household so happy a community; whenever the god and lawgiver of this little world appeared she was excluded from the circle.

On the rare occasions when by accident they passed one another, he saluted her but did not speak to her; his eyes, she felt without understanding at first their message, seemed to her to be sad, hungry, and reproachful.

In the Indian spring there is a musically humming moth that flutters about in the zephyrous night air. The newly opened champak-buds have a sweetness that makes the senses swoon with a languid and overpowering delight. The jasmines, more potent, even, by night than by day, send out an intoxicating fragrance that makes each puff of air as glamorous as Arabia's fabled incense-tree.

It was on the sixth spring of her sojourn under Mirza Khan's roof that Mrs Greene hung up on the bough of her peepul-tree the tinsel swing garlanded with champak-flowers, and spread out on the smooth lawn of her garden the sweet-scented couch of love, the quilt of neem-flowers and jasmines, the neatly arranged rows of frangipanni blossoms, and waited for Mirza Khan to visit her.

Nearly forty years later, a famous traveller, walking through a bazaar in a remote Punjab village, had his attention caught by the vivid blue eyes of an old beggar woman who was leading by the hand a blind old man, a very stately white-bearded figure, soldierly and dignified. This traveller stopped the woman and said to her in English (for he was convinced that she was English), "Can I help you? Are you not an Englishwoman?"

This traveller said afterwards that the blue-eyed woman was clad in incredibly tattered rags, bespeaking the direst poverty, but that the old man was wearing garments of a much better quality, clean and neatly darned, and that the woman showed a most affecting and touching solicitude for his comfort, brushing the flies away with a whisk when they settled on his closed eyes, telling him in advance of every inequality in the ground, and, when the sound of the Englishman's voice alarmed him, clasping his hand in her own with a warm, reassuring pressure.

Since this woman looked at him in amazement and made no reply to his questions, the traveller repeated them. "Surely," he persisted, "you are an Englishwoman? Tell me—what is your name?"

So strange are the vagaries of the human mind that, hearing for the first time in so many years her mother tongue, this poor woman's mind flashed back to a moment when, standing proudly erect beside her young husband at a hunt ball in the Worcester Assembly Rooms, she had heard, for the first time, the same question addressed to her.

Surprisingly she answered now, as she had answered then, "Mrs James Greene—spelt with an 'e'!"

The traveller could not induce her to leave the old sowar, whose name, he found, was Mirza Khan, and to whom she appeared to be devoted. He was obviously entirely dependent on her.

A Seraglio Has Its Uses

BEFORE Sir Sri-Sri-Sri Bahadur spoke those fatal words, destined to carry so much anguish in their train, all was peace in his harem.

Through the wide seraglio windows, not-so-distant mountains, culminating in Kangchenjunga, shone, snow-white, in sunlight as cold as ice. Intruding through glass arches that extended from floor to ceiling, the sky was tinted every imaginable shade of azure. Even the mighty ice-ferns glittered with a cerulean radiance. There was, in all that vast wintry landscape, not one cloud in sight, and the palace, built in the Tibetan manner, was perched on so high a rocky bastion that, though Katmandu lay below it, nothing was to be seen but this sharp-set panorama of sky, snow, and ice.

In one corner of the Hall of Obeisance, an immense room, a group of ladies, their voices "uttering harmonic cadences", were playing cherry-pit. In another, hilarious odalisques were engaged in exhilarating games of chicken-hazard and tip-cat. Six sultanas gossiped apart with great amity. Clustered round the heap of Tunisian cushions on which Sir Sri-Sri-Sri reclined at ease, several more-favoured houris refilled the chillum of his hookah with balls of charcoal and tobacco, themselves, meanwhile, smoking the short pipes called chibouks which harem inmates affect.

All indeed was peace when, looking about him with that sarcastic, scheming expression which, of late, his ladies had grown to dread, Sir Sri-Sri-Sri Bahadur, Prime Minister of Nepal, Grand Master of the Most Puissant Order of the Gurkha Right Hand, Knight of the Most Refulgent Order of the Star of Nepal, Companion of the Illustrious Orders of the Tri-Shakti-Patti and the Sacred Tripod, taking his gurgling hookah from his mouth, said simply, "I am tired of the sight of so many blue legs."

He spoke in English.

In that seraglio English was usually spoken because the ladies, almost to a woman, had been educated in a Patna school where the nobility of Nepal acquired that Oxford accent their maharaja loved to hear. In moments of crisis, however, each would revert to her mother tongue, and now murmurs (*pianissimo*, it is true) in dialects resembling Sanskrit, Persian, Tibetan, Chinese, Arabic, Urdu, and Nepalese sounded from every group: ears were always stretched to catch the least word that fell from their tyrant's lips.

"I hate the sight of so much mottled flesh," Sir Sri-Sri-Sri Bahadur continued, holding the hookah at arm's length while the water gurgled up and down the tube. "It revolts my aesthetic! Your red, red noses, dear ladies, affront my finer feelings."

He put the stem of his pipe back in his mouth and waited complacently for the storm to break.

His wives were all of the first rank. Each wife had her own guru or priest, her own baid or doctor, and her astrologer or soothsayer; each had her own ladies-in-waiting, her slaves, and her cook. An individual cook was necessary, because these noble ladies came from the Baizai, that is, the Region of the Twenty-two Rajahs; or the Chaubisi, that is, the Abode of the Twenty-four Elect. Those who were Newaris could eat buffaloes, goats, geese, fowls, or sheep; they could drink beer and spirits. Those who were Magars could eat pork but not buffalo. Gurungs were allowed by their religion to consume buffalo-flesh but not hogs.

(It may be remarked in passing that there were no cradles in Sir Sri-Sri-Sri's harem.)

It was the Princess Padma who sprang up—furious—to voice the anger of the insulted wives. "Be exalted!" she rapped out briefly, reducing the terms of courtesy to their fewest words. "Has the Ineffable One then drunk dog's bane? When, on the Day of Judgment, the Mirror of God reflects the faces of all mankind, and each one will see himself in his true likeness, shall the face that looks back at Sir Sri-Sri-Sri be that of a toad?"

The Princess Padma was exceedingly beautiful. Her jet-black hair was rolled in a chignon on the crown of her imperious head. Her brows formed a crescent. The Court Poet said that her anklets, because they hid her ankles, were like the clouds that obscure the sun. He also said that her voice was like that of a she-camel calling in her coaxing way.

This young beauty's eyelashes were rimmed with collyrium, the tips of her toes and fingers were stained with privet. She kept her delicious body meticulously clean by the orthodox friction set up by her bone flesh-brush and a swallow-stone.

With her aquiline features, her dark flashing eyes, her vivacious manner, there was not a princess in Nepal who could touch her for looks, aplomb, or garrulity.

Hearing her, the wicked Prime Minister (he was a notorious rogue) merely laughed unpleasantly, and all the trembling ladies again began "dropping stars".

"An apple before reaching the ground turns a thousand somersaults." Undaunted, the Princess Padma quoted a Persian proverb and, hitching up the short black drawers she wore under her voluminous but quite diaphanous trousers, continued tauntingly, "Let the rustic enjoy his bath—indeed!"

By the first proverb the Princess meant her husband to understand that, though he might now lord it above them, his fall was imminent; by quoting the second she advised him, in the vernacular, to stick to his own occupation, or, in plainer words, to mind his own business.

Though they applauded her daring, how her hearers trembled!

However, the begums Lakshmi and Devi, both of the blood royal, feeling they must support her went to her side and, standing with their trembling fingers linked in hers, told Sir Sri-Sri-Sri (in elaborate hyperbole) that they would write and tell their mothers what a brute he was; and all the other harem ladies, continuing to "drop stars", murmured that they, too, would write and tell their mothers.

Laughing, their husband clapped his hands.

A fresh outrage made the whole seraglio dumb with horror. For, at this signal, in walked the eunuch Nasil Ullah! In a Buddhist-Hindu zenana! Incredible! But there he was!

This giant, this infamous one, had just been dismissed from His Highness the Maharaja's service for cruelty, theft, and the presentation of exorbitant bills. As the ladies knew, the scent account sent in by Nasil Ullah had been of such staggering proportions that His Highness had immediately dismissed him and had himself ordered twelve hogsheads of Alderman's Bouquet from Birmingham.

There were other more grisly tales told of this gigantic man, who, with four equally powerful assistants, brought in and set down before his new master a roll of red flannel, a bundle as large as a beer-barrel! Red flannel. Red, red flannel. Flannel of a hue so disastrous, of a quality so cheap, that all the ladies viewing it decided it must be flannelette—as indeed it was!

"There you are, my girls," said Sir Sri-Sri-Sri brutally. "In future my wives shall be warmly dressed, and my eyes shall no longer be estranged from enjoyment by the sight of so much goose-flesh."

He signed to the gigantic Nasil Ullah to leave the roll of flannel and go, commanding him, as he and his assistants left the room, to order some fifty durzees—tailors—to come next day and fit the harem out with red flannel trousers. "Leave the bale," he added. "The Illustrious Ones may like to admire its colour and quality."

So saying, Sir Sri-Sri-Sri withdrew.

The Princess Padma was a Newari. In babyhood she had been married to a bel-fruit. The fruit, after this mystic ceremony, had been thrown in the river Rapti, a sacred stream. The object of this ritual was to ensure that she could never become a widow, a state of disesteem in Nepal. The bel-fruit, swept away by a foaming torrent, might float or swim, decay or flourish—who could say? Who, therefore, could specifically assert the wife of a bel-fruit to be a widow or not? There was a further benefit conferred by this ceremony: a woman so blessed could put a betel-nut under her second husband's pillow should he cease to please her. This simple act constituted a divorce that was binding in law.

The ladies in Sir Sri-Sri-Sri's zenana were perfectly well aware of this ritual. Many were Newaris. Those who were not were that evening easily persuaded by the Princess Padma to undergo the bel-fruit marriage, and (after the roll of flannel had been heaved into the *oubliette*) they celebrated these mystic *noces* that very night.

The Princess Padma's own (hereditary) guru performed the rites. By midnight the bridegroom bel-fruits had been dispatched, poste-haste, to the Lesser Rapti, and the bel-fruit brides, with their sisters-errant—a bevy of thirty—each with a betel-nut concealed in her palm, were ready to enter into the second phase of the Princess's design.

On leaving his harem, Sir Sri-Sri-Sri had gone off to a gay drinking-bout in his own apartments. It was probable that by this time he slept, yet to make certain of it, the Princess Devi had sent by a slave a draught that was to be secretly poured into his "chirping-cup"—the last cup of liquor he took before going to bed. This concoction of bhang, hemp-leaves, and opium had been entrusted to her by her mother. It was sealed up in a bottle labelled:

DOSE

For use in emergency give him half.
As a last resort give him the whole phial.

There was, conceivably, a certain amount of risk attached to the administration of this nostrum, but the ladies were desperate. Wear thirty yards of flannelette round each leg? Never! Their minds were quite made up on that point.

According to the pundits there are two ways of ascertaining the arrival of daylight. One, by counting the tiles on a roof. The other, by holding a man's arm against the sky—should it be possible to see the hairs on the back of his hand, it is daybreak.

Both these tests having proved that day had dawned, and the Princess Padma's baid (her doctor), who had crept into Sir Sri-Sri-Sri's bedroom, having reported that he slept soundly, the ladies going, veiled, in single file, each attended by her own (hereditary) guru and her own baid, went on tiptoe to slip the betel-nut of divorcement under his pillow.

The Begum Devi, since hers had been the responsibility of providing the sleeping potion, went first. Her slender hand was seen to disappear under the pillow. Her guru, who witnessed the rite, was prepared to swear to its validity.

The Princess Padma of the Pangolin (for such was the name of her father's dominion), stooping over her husband, saw him—as did all his other wives—for the first time asleep. She noted the thick pursed-up lips, the down-drawn corners of the cruel mouth, the short and menacing hooked nose with its cut-back nostrils; she noted his Mongolian eyelids, slanting upwards towards thick eyebrows nicked in the middle like a bird's wing. She saw his coarse thick hair, as black as night. His muscular chest was broad for a man of his height. As she looked down on him some strange emotion welled up in her heart. She realized how dreadful it would be to have no man to shield her from the terrors of a world hitherto unknown, to be cast adrift, companionless. Determined, however, to be faithful to her fellow conspirators, and steeling herself to the deed, she advanced her hand to the pillow's edge, but irresistibly impelled, as she did so she bent lower to kiss with her salt lips the brow of her tyrant, her oppressor.

To her terror she found her hand caught in a vice-like grip. Her startled gaze encountered her husband's eyes—wide open.

She half turned, but the guru, the old priest, had vanished, and the door was shut.

It was quite three by the clock on the following day—an auspicious day, for it was the day called Roz-i-alast, the day of the original covenant made between God and man—when the petulant ladies who had divorced themselves (with the exception of the Princess Padma, who still slept), having spent the morning packing their few possessions into minute boxes of yellow wood, arched, and bound with elaborate brass hinges, and having written to their families letters which they had not yet posted—being without courage—made their way to the Hall of Obeisance.

There is a tale that when Joseph first entered Potiphar's house his wife—Queen Zuleika—and her ladies were cutting up orange peel to make marmalade, and that the beauty of Joseph so unnerved these fair Egyptians that they sliced their fingers instead of the fruit. They could not take their eyes off Joseph. It is as well that Sir Sri-Sri-Sri's divorced wives carried no knives. On entering this room they were as completely amazed as Queen Zuleika and her waiting women had been; but they were astonished by a different beauty.

Round the walls were ranged bales, bolts, and flues of—silk? They scratched off the wrappers in one or two places. Yes, silk! Of great strength, yes; of a very close weave, yes; and quite opaque—yes! But how fabulously lovely! The true Turkish blue! Thirty trays, each with a name on it—*their* names—contained, merely, Burmese rubies.

Before their amazement could vent in words, Sir Sri-Sri-Sri entered, and he seemed just as usual. He made no reference to betel-nuts. Behind him followed fifty durzees, and, since Nepalese women are not, as they say, purdah, or veiled to the sight of man, the durzees immediately took their measurements and settled down to cut and sew the new silks.

The members of the harem, anxious in the midst of their pleasure, whispered, each to her confidante, "*Did* every wife put her betel-nut under the Ineffable Pillow? Or did none?"

No answers came.

In the excitement of creating such dresses as had never before been seen in any Nepalese zenana, this subject fell into disuse. It was never clarified.

When the apparently reinstated wives had been habited, each in a whole bale of silk—thirty full yards (as was customary) going into the making of each trouser-leg—there still remained twenty bolts of aurora brocade. Not a word of protest was uttered when Sir Sri-Sri-Sri, remarking that it was a pity to waste so much good material, introduced into his household twenty new members—low-born creatures as strong as hill-ponies. They were all similarly attired in very baggy pyjamas.

"What Amazons!"

"What coal-heavers!"

"What coolies!"

Such comments were uttered in secret, and the new-comers were, to all outward appearance, amiably welcomed.

The kingdom of Nepal was thinly populated. Its rulers, laughing—Nepalese are great laughers—if doubtful about the reception of some new bill were accustomed to ask, "What will the Barwan Lakh"—the Fifty-two—"think of this?" Still, it was a rich country. The yearly revenue amounted to some nine million pounds English. As far as the Barwan Lakh were concerned, civil expenditure (with no roads, no hospitals, no dole to be considered) would have made only a temple-mouse feel rich. Taxes on mines, forests (there were most valuable trees in that region), land; a tax on rent amounting to half the value of the property; and the accumulated gains of many government monopolies—all swelled the revenue.

Taxes were collected by subahs, then transferred from outlying districts under escort and placed at the end of each financial year in the Mul Dhukati, the heavily guarded government cellars in the capital, Katmandu, where a surplus had been accumulating for many years.

The Prime Minister ruled the country, though theoretically the Maharaja was paramount. The Prime Minister, Sir Sri-Sri-Sri, had risen to office over the bodies of many other candidates. He was a ruthless man. He had a genius for intrigue. His mind was of so tortuous, so subtle, so shrewd a nature that his crafty machinations had so far defeated all plots to overthrow him. He had been six years in sole control of the Nepalese treasury. He had almost perfected the plan that was to astonish all India, when, reading the signs, he realized, in his clear-sighted way, that the faction against him, under the Maharaja's aegis, had grown so powerful that only immediate flight could save him. He prepared to quit Nepal secretly and in haste.

The Customs Office was, perhaps, the most efficiently run of all the Nepalese government departments. It was under control of Sir Sri-Sri-Sri's worst enemy. He was aware that he would have difficulty in getting past the numerous posts dotted along the ninety-mile road between Katmandu and Segowli, on the Indian frontier. The track ran for the most part along the margins of pebbly half-dry river beds, so deeply set below towering cliffs or vast mountain peaks, each crowned with a watch-tower or temple, that divergence from it was impossible.

Before his departure, therefore, the Prime Minister made every preparation to ensure a safe and successful journey. He saw to it that there were no "black-footed" bringers of ill luck among the carriers of his doolies, palkis, and palanquins. On the last Wednesday of the month preceding his projected flight, he broke fifty earthen ewers, exclaiming as he did so, "Evil is gone, and good is come!" He engaged a virgin to spin a left-hand thread, and, twisting this over a goblet, he drank three measures of wine. In addition to these helpful ceremonies he consulted several famous astrologers, wizards skilled in the art of reading the future in sand. This science was imparted to the Prophet Daniel by the Jinn Dibril and by him handed down to the soothsayers of Nepal, who were (and are) highly skilled in that black art.

The date of the day most auspicious for departure was learnt from the carefully cast horoscopes of the Prime Minister himself, his wives, his concubines, his eunuchs, coolies, and cooks, together with all the servants of his so numerous retinue. In these not one single portent of ill luck was to be detected.

Nothing that could ensure the success of the journey was left undone. His wives had all carried feather images of the Bird of the Heavenly Lote Tree. No one had encountered a crop-sick camel. No one had enjoyed eating the hunch of a camel during the stay of the sun in Pisces. No one had touched cheese, olives, onions, garlic, or meat while the moon was in her third mansion. Every demon having been propitiated, every jinn having been placated, every lucky dream having been tabulated, every omen having been propitious, Sir Sri-Sri-Sri Bahadur, Grand Master of the Most Puissant Order of the Gurkha Right Hand, Knight of the Most Refulgent Order of the Star of Nepal, Companion of the Illustrious Orders of the Tri-Shakti-Patti and the Sacred Tripod, left Katmandu in complete darkness, on a winter's night so cold that even the bears had retreated to their caves and not a soul was stirring abroad.

The only delay had occurred when the long cortège was halted for two hours at the back door of the treasury, the Mul Dhukati.

Twelve years later this chronicler met twenty-five of the ladies whose history is here related. During the interval the Prime

Minister had died (a natural death) in his superb palace in Allahabad. No fewer than twenty of his wives had availed themselves of the much-coveted privilege of burning on his funeral pyre. Ten had remarried.

It is seldom that a soldier's wife can penetrate the sanctity of zenanas, seraglios, or harems, but this historian had a friend, a judge's daughter, who had by good luck been governess to the heir-apparent of the King of Sikkim, and who had thus gained a right of entrée into all such royal retreats. This privileged lady was kind enough to carry her to a party given by the twenty-five widows of the late Prime Minister of Nepal. It celebrated the birthday of the only son and heir—an enchanting child.

An acceptance of Einstein's theory of time and space had gone to make this party memorable.

The violets used in decorating the impressive Hall of Obeisance had come from Peshawar, the primroses from Srinagar in Kashmir. The biscuits had come from Trincomalee, the dates from Basra, the prawns from Karachi. The cakes had been flown from London, the sweets from the Bosphorus. That all should have been assembled in one place at the moment of their utmost perfection had argued a certain amount of efficient staff work, and also the wherewithal to pay for such prodigality.

The local delicacies, cakes made of almonds and honey and served with a Dutch liqueur of peculiar delicacy, had their own virtues.

At this party the guests were received at the top of the marble stairs and just inside the ivory doors of the Hall of Obeisance, the twenty-five widows, *en règle*, standing in line. The boy in whose honour the festivity was given introduced everyone to them. There was a great variety in the names of the guests, but an all-prevailing unity in those of the hostesses. All were introduced simply as "my mother". The child's actual parentage was evidently a court secret. But it was plain that his "mothers" all doted on him with an equal affection. On the child's part a punctilious courtesy, an affectionate regard bestowed on all alike, a reverence without variation, extended to each one of these magnificently clad women, made any guess as to his own preference impossible.

The Englishwoman responsible for the inclusion of the least of the revellers in so distinguished a gathering (there were present reigning princesses from Nepal, Sikkim, Burma, and the Punjab) had imparted to her, on the drive there, the story of the Prime Minister's flight from Katmandu. It transpired that he had brought with him from that distant capital the whole golden treasury of the kingdom of Nepal. It was an almost incredible *coup*, considering that the most valuable gold-piece, an ashrafi, was worth merely twenty-five shillings.

How was this astounding feat accomplished? History is silent.

The stream of new-comers thinned: the son of the twenty-five widows of Sir Sri-Sri-Sri, having performed his duties of host with aplomb and vivacity, was prepared, it appeared, to air his English. He was a garrulous little boy. He presently engaged the two Englishwomen in conversation. He told them with pride that he was to go to Eton the following term, and that his imminent departure was the true reason for his birthday celebration.

"Would you say," he asked, hiding a wistful doubt about it, "that this school is a friendly sort of place? Do you think it is a place where a boy would feel at home, supposing he came from so distant and so different an environment as I do?"

To this question his guests could but answer that they hoped it might be so, and that it certainly was a beautiful place and full of interest.

"I can shoot—I have bagged my first tiger. At tip-cat I am unbeatable. Do you think my English is colloquial enough?"

A positive affirmation reassured him on this point. He grew proud, holding up his magnificently garnished head to say, "I am also very rich. I have millions of gold ashrafi."

Suitably impressed, his companions asked him, "Where do you keep them?"

The child began laughing in the ready Nepalese way, creasing up his slanting eyelids, and leaning forward, buoyantly confidential, almost in the laps of his interlocutors. "In the cellar!" The boy was convulsed with merriment. "In the very cellars under our feet! Oh, my father was a clever man! He gave me lots of hints, I can tell you."

"Is your gold in sacks?"

"Oh, no, no, no!" The boy rocked with mirth. "How could sacks have got past the Customs? The gold pieces, when my father escaped from Katmandu, were all sewn up into the legs of fifty pairs of blue silk trousers, and my fifty mothers—they wore them, and got past the Customs! Such a joke! Fifty pairs of trousers!"

Australia

Remote your home! Remote, and all but dumb
Its creeks, its paddocks where the opossums come,
Or spotted wild-cats climb; voiceless, until
False sarsaparilla purples all the hill,
And spring with warm mimosa warms the sense.
Then cow-boys, balanced on the stock-yard fence,
(Time beating heartily with tapping feet)
Precariously, with reedy flute, but sweet,
The moonlit airs at mopoke time assault
With trickling notes, judged music by default.

Juliet McCree Is Accused of Gluttony

Dr Phantom did not really care for children. It is doubtful whether any child had ever been invited to ride beside him in the dashing Hyde Park in which he made his daily rounds. This was a canopied and curtained vehicle, its four wheels rimmed with iron, and it was drawn by a piebald Waler, and driven by a white-gloved, personable murderer.

It was usual in those days for citizens of Sydney who applied for convict servants to ask for a murderer if any should happen to be available. They were in great demand, for, though apt to be impulsive on occasions of emotion, killers had generally been found to have warmer-hearted and more likeable dispositions than criminals of other persuasions. Dr Phantom, caring little for thieves, sheepstealers, pickpockets, lags, or the abductors of heiresses, employed, when he could do so, only murderers. Though he drew the line at poisoners (his dispensary being, he felt, a temptation) he was at this period particularly lucky; he was rich in the possession of "First and Second Murderers"—as he designated them—and his servants' hall, in the neat red-brick Georgian house, some twenty miles from the capital, had never been more cheery.

On this energetic afternoon in early autumn, when a mellowing sun shone obliquely down on a humming and triumphing world, "First Murderer" was on the box, a check-string with its wide band attached to his right arm, that had, on some earlier occasion, presumably wielded a lethal weapon (an axe was at that time the most popular tool), and Dr Phantom, sitting directly behind him, would jerk the cord to ensure attention before issuing directions as to which track should be followed, or at which house, shack, shanty, hovel or mansion he should stop.

In this beneficent district the fruit had never been finer.

The grapes growing in the direction of Dural had recalled to Dr Phantom a Tuscan summer.

The peach harvest, he noted, had never been more luscious. Lying at his feet two large baskets testified to an almost Olympian abundance; one was an Ossa of jargonelles, orange Bergamots, and

"Williams"; from a second willow-ark rose a perfect Pelion of grapes, apricots and plums (blue pedrigons), the first fruits of several orchards.

As Dr Phantom bowled along in his nicely shaded carriage his eyes lingered on the signs of an earlier optimism, on many a phalanx of raspberries, on plantations of gooseberries, and ordered battalions of strawberries. A particularly fine crop of these delectable berries punctuated the Undertaker's neatly kept plot with bright red nodules nestling on straw. It was an age when straw laid down on a roadway paid its sympathetic tribute to the difficulty of producing the coming generation, and discreetly muffled the departure of age; and straw was plentiful.

On this garlanded highway, where even the hedges were bright with rose-haws, the good doctor experienced the pleasure afforded to a reasoning man by the contemplation of a Universe based on reason.

He passed the chain-gang knocking sparks out of flint.

"They are dressing stone for the repair of the bridge," he (rightly) concluded.

He skirted the milkman's trotting cart which pleasantly recalled to him the hip-waddles of a Zulu belle. The cart was painted yellow and a scarlet scroll was ciphered with the words "Families supplied twice daily".

"He is delivering the late afternoon milk," Dr Phantom instinctively realized.

That, too, was a reasonable conjecture, though the statement on the cart was, perhaps, cryptic to the uninitiated.

Just outside Parramatta he observed the Rector entering Mrs Furbelow's lean-to. "The latest addition to that poor widow's family of twenty is about to pass, non-stop, through this vale of tears," was his natural inference; he was right.

But a sight that baffled his intelligence as his Hyde Park clattered to a standstill by the kerb outside his partner's brass-plated, two-storied yellowstone house beside the bridge in Parramatta, was the apparition of seven little boys and girls, of ages ranging from four to, perhaps, ten or eleven years, each holding in their trembling hands a black papier-maché basin; each standing on a separate step of the stone stairway that led down to the slowly-meandering waters of the Lane Cove River.

His first thought had been "Whooping-cough", but "No," he reminded himself, "I should have been the first to be informed of any such epidemic."

He found his partner Dr Boisragon (pronounced Borrygan) standing on the top step of the flight.

He looked grave.

He looked even more stern than usual, and his handsome face wore an expression that might almost have been called "pained". Though he was dressed with his customary ceremony in a full-skirted marine blue frogged coat, with yellow Nankin breeches, nicely moulded over Wellington boots and his own (almost famous) legs, with a thick, gold bemedalled watchchain caressing a buff waistcoat, a black satin stock meticulously folded under white linen points, and with a stovepipe hat, cocked sideways, as he always wore it, he might have been going to a funeral; to the obsequies of the victim of someone else's rapacity and incompetence.

"The grapes," Dr Phantom explained, handing him the larger of the two baskets which he had carried from the Hyde Park, "are from Widow Plunkett. The pears are selected from a basket given to me by Mr Jarvey, in recognition of the pretty compliments I paid him on his wall-fruit. The greenish apples are from Granny Smith, whose cottage near Castle Hill I passed in pursuit of a ruined stomach and a case of mumps out at Hornsby Junction."

Accepting the basket Dr Boisragon touched the grapes reverently with his sensitive hands—he had a surgeon's hands—"The bloom!" he marvelled, "How does Nature do it? Is it an efflorescence? Is it a quintessential patina?"

He set the heavy basket down on the parapet beside him and broke off a sizeable bunch of Muscatels.

"I must confess my ignorance." Meditatively Dr Phantom peeled with his equally sensitive fingers a Yellow Monday peach of august proportions. "No one, to my knowledge, has conducted research into the mysteries of the bloom on fruit. It may be a sort of attar of perfection, like the fragrant scum one skims off a tank of rose-water. It may be a fructuous halo, or nimbus, like that bright manifestation of Holiness which (we are informed) accumulates round the heads of saints."

He savoured his golden-fleshed peach.

"These," Dr Boisragon murmured, converting another grape to a corporate Christianity, "are gifts from the Gods of Plenty! What a country is ours! Begging the question of the scientific nature of bloom, I can rejoice in the luxuriance that showers on us such a prodigality of gifts."

He took a bunch of white muscadines from the diminishing heap.

"But I am a sad man! I have a heavy heart! I am too conscious of the serpent that lurks in our Eden, of the wickedness of the almost irreclaimable YOUNG!"

He sighed heavily and with an absent mind voiced the opinion that "The muscadine is, perhaps, the best white grape. Its juice is so pleasantly insinuating in texture—its flavour is so ethereal—a mixture of sharp and sweet—its bouquet (if one might call it so) is of so subtle an aroma."

Dr Phantom chose an apricot. (It was an *abricot persique.*)

"Yes. In this glorious Eden of ours, I am confronted by sin in its most loathsome aspect, by error in its most leprous form."

"Dear me," Dr Phantom agreed, easily, and without much due attention. "You are having, I gather, a party, a jollification, a romp-a-way for these children? Who are all these visitors?"

Dr Boisragon was eating a plum—a White Nutmeg.

Dr Phantom took a bunch of Black Frontignacs, and put them back.

"The three immature females in tartans and plaits are the indigent McMurthies, my poor sister Téméraire's brood. Her husband, as you know, is Captain of the brig *Rose*. The boy and girl standing on the step below them, whom I have heard referred to as 'the Coppertops', are my unfortunate eldest sister Jessica's grandchildren, Juliet and Donalblain McCree. With my own hopefuls, James and Grizel, you have been acquainted from their birth—surely you recognize them all?"

The glances Dr Boisragon cast on the children were dour in the extreme. Dr Phantom excused himself, saying, "Their colour is unusual. Are they not unnaturally pale?"

A douce sea-breeze, a zephyr faintly tinged and tinctured with ozone, and spiced with salt, which daily about this hour found its way up the estuary from Sydney harbour and the Heads and the Pacific beyond, stirred the hitherto placid waters of the river into infinitesimal wavelets, and blew the little girls' skirts about, flapping them like wings against their ankle-length *culottes*.

A number of seagulls, their presence so far inland perhaps presaging storm, were dipping and wheeling about the surface of a patch of ruffled water which, in the deeper reaches, hinted at a shoal of fish.

A group of saplings that dotted the sloping lawn right down to the water's edge also swayed and rustled, and their lively branches reminded Dr Phantom to inquire after—"The nectarine? Is it ripe? Did you poor wife enjoy it as much as you hoped? I see it has gone."

An expression of deeper suffering clouded Dr Boisragon's already gloomy face.

"My wife did not have the pleasure of putting one toothmark on it. It was stolen." He looked desolate. "It was a Red Roman."

It occurred to Dr Phantom that the group of children hugging their black basins looked, if possible, even greener about the gills, and, though he did not care for children, he averted his gaze from the rows of suffering upturned faces.

"Stolen? A bat? A parrot? Mr Jarvey told me of the depredations of many flocks of rosellas, or parakeets—or was it lorikeets?"

Half-sated, Dr Phantom ventured on a jargonelle.

"It was stolen," Dr Boisragon reiterated simply, dropping a handful of pips into a garden urn. "I inspected it at three o'clock, when we first assembled on the lawn for our festivity. I decided to allow it one more hour of sunshine before giving it to my wife. Noticing how warm the sun had become, I went, an hour later, to pluck it—it had gone. It had vanished. Under the tree—not a sign of it. Down the slope? Not a vestige of it!"

He sternly regarded the flinching rows of upturned faces.

"I questioned the children closely. They all denied having stolen it."

Dr Phantom ran a physician's discerning eye over the greening faces.

"Are the children sickening for something, do you think?"

"They are." Dr Boisragon's tone was succinct. "I gave them all an emetic. Nature never lies. I shall soon find out who stole and ate my nectarine."

"Surely, by observation, you might have detected the culprit? Children are transparent enough. I once met a fraudulent financier. What struck me at the time was the complete absence of all experience in his blue eyes. Knowing nothing about his defalcations, I said at the time, 'That young gentleman has got something to hide. He has obliterated his past from his expression.' And he had, too! Look at those faces! The girls in plaits and tartans have eyes as black as sloes, without even a highlight in the pupils. I know that type. To learn how they feel—look at their mouths."

The two doctors looked at the three tremulous mouths.

"I should say those girls were innocent."

"Deduction is well enough in its way. I prefer the certainty of the scientific method."

"Your boy James is like you. Is he six?"

"Yes."

"Rule him out. By this time he should have learnt not to risk displeasing you."

Though glad of this opinion on his son's probable innocence, Dr Boisragon was not certain he liked the inference.

"As for the coppertops, they are both suffering so acutely that their queasiness must soon take an active turn."

It did.

Their breakdown was the signal, it seemed, for which everyone had been waiting. Seven black basins bore witness to the efficacy of Dr Boisragon's emetic.

Dr Phantom was just remarking, "It strikes me that there is a guilty knowledge, a hint of hidden appeal to one's sympathy, in the squirrel-like eyes of the girl coppertop," when her basin demonstrated her guilt.

The regurgitation of the skin of a Red Roman was proof of it.

"Juliet McCree! You are both a thief and a liar."

Dr Boisragon had never been more impressive.

"You wicked child! What have you to say to explain away your downright lie?"

He was forced to wait till she was capable of answering.

"What excuse do you offer for your felony?"

"Felony, Uncle Peter?"

"How do you excuse your theft of my nectarine?"

"I didn't steal it."

Even Dr Phantom was shocked by such depravity.

"What—do you deny it? In the face of such evidence as that basin holds?"

"I just took it. I didn't steal it."

"To take what is not your own is stealing."

"But I didn't think it was not—" she retched—"was not—" she was violently ill—"was not—" she had scarcely got her breath when another paroxysm overtook her—"was not—" Dr Phantom turned away his eyes—"was not mine."

That innocence was no shield from suffering was being aptly demonstrated by the six other children who were noisily and liberally contributing to their basins.

"Wicked sinner! Look about you! Through your obstinate denial of your guilt you have caused great suffering to your young relatives—poor innocent children! Does that not shame you? Does that not soften you?"

Dr Boisragon grew more angry.

"Do you persist in saying that you did *not* lie to me?"

He took his pocket-book out of his buff waistcoat pocket.

"I will run through the notes I made when questioning you. Here they are." He flicked a page. "Juliet McCree—my question—'Did you steal that nectarine? My Red Roman?' *'No, Uncle Peter'*—That was your answer!"

He snapped the elastic band back and put the book away.

"I said, 'Remember, child, your hope of Heaven hangs on your answer. Speak the truth! *Did you speak the truth?*' You again answered, 'Yes, Uncle Peter!' What perfidy! To rob your dear Aunt of my gift! The fruit I had watched from the bud up! What do you mean, wretched liar, in saying you did not know it was not my nectarine? It grew on my tree."

"There are so many things everywhere, and I don't quite know who owns everything. It's all so puzzling, Uncle Peter, because when I filled my bucket with sand no one said I had stolen it, and when I dipped my mug in the river, no one said I was not to steal the Lane Cove River, Uncle Peter, and when we pick blackberries, and mushrooms along the roads or in the paddocks, no one calls us thieves, and I'm only a little girl, Uncle Peter, and I don't rightly know the way to get things that don't belong to me for nothing, Uncle Peter, the way you and Dr Phantom do, and I don't know whose sea-gulls those are, neither."

She again had recourse to her basin.

"What! Dreadful child! Do you accuse *us* of theft!"

"Oh, no, Uncle Peter, it's not quite like that. But you can get the things you want without stealing them, and you know what things belong to other people, and I don't yet! But I will try to learn, indeed I will."

"What a depraved mind."

"But you see, you know what is free and I don't! And you know what you must *pay* for, and I don't! I did hear the sound you were making with your words, Uncle Peter, but I did not understand what the noise you made really meant; and if you could please explain to me how you got the fruit in the baskets and didn't pay for it, and didn't really steal it, I mean, if it was someone else's, and you did not have to pay for it? Will you teach me how to get things that are someone else's and not pay?"

She suffered an attack of dry retching that was quite spectacular.

The six other children had filled their black basins and waited, white of face and wet of eye.

"Empty your basins in the river, my bairns, and then wash your hands and faces and go into the dining-room for tea. Since you have been proved to be innocent you may each have two pieces of the birthday cake Cook Jane has made for James. But, before you go, take leave of your cousin, Juliet McCree, for this is the last time that—with my approval or permission—you will ever speak to her. If God spares me, she shall never darken my doors again. Wicked, wicked child!"

"Goodbye, Juliet," the children murmured, awe-struck, walking uncertainly past her, their black papier-maché basins carefully carried in their weak hands; they had all been very sick—the emetic had been a powerful one, though perhaps slow in starting.

Juliet went dutifully down to the water's edge and emptied her basin into the Lane Cove River, and, in going up to the house to wash, she lagged well behind her cousins, not that she suffered any sense of guilt, but because she appreciated the drama of the occasion.

While awaiting Juliet's return, Dr Boisragon remarked genially to his companion: "It is an extraordinary thing that the expulsion of food—with us—should require so much effort. I believe that the Romans, before they had a banquet, tickled the backs of their throats and emptied their stomachs. They must certainly have practised regurgitation as an art, for they were a civilized people and I imagine that the hall of Augustus, the house of Maecenas, the villas of Horace and Cicero, could hardly have presented such unbridled scenes as those we have just witnessed! They must have had some nicer system of their own in the method of vomiting!"

Dr Phantom ran an eye over the row of lace curtains that draped the windows of the square, yellowstone house behind them.

"The ladies of your household?" he enquired, "How is it they were not present?"

As a matter of fact he had several times noticed the agonized faces of Dr Boisragon's younger step-sisters, Miss Loveday, Miss Tabitha, and Miss Matilda, peeping through the lace of upstairs windows.

"I can't understand," he mused, "why his womenkind left

those unhappy children to my friend's untender mercies! They must, by this time, know what he is like!"

He said this to himself, but as if replying to him Dr Boisragon broke off from his classical conjectures to say, "My dear wife was prostrate! She was inclined to be hysterical, so I ordered her off to her room to lie down for an hour or two. My sisters, too, attempted to gloss over an incident they regarded as trivial. Poor, silly women! I ordered them indoors, and I will thresh out the question with them tonight after dinner."

Juliet here came back, her face shining with tears and soap, her red hair, so wet that it looked dark, drawn off her forehead with two combs; she had tried to hide the stains on her apron by rolling it up round her elbows, with the result that the unfaded patch on her green cotton checked dress showed how old and worn it was.

The child looked peaked and hungry.

She had left her brother, Donalblain (who was four), happily eating bread and butter masked with "hundreds and thousands", and she could see the glow of the candles, round the birthday cake, and the six other children laughing and talking round the table, with its sweets and bon-bons, crackers and toys, and sugar animals, while the three aunts, having, as it were, come into their own, were busy "making it up" to the infant martyrs.

Juliet's straw hat (from China) was swinging from her arm by a green ribbon, and her reddening curls, which, as they dried resumed their gloss, were seen against a background of pale river-water and the brackish hillside of the further bank; the salt seemed to have cured the hanging leaves of the grey-boled trees; and it encrusted, too, the pool-brightened rocks. The sky was purely Tuscan as Dr Phantom had already noted.

Dr Boisragon, as Juliet joined them, at once returned to the pursuit of Truth.

"Do you not realize, Juliet, that if I had not hit on the expedient of interrogating Nature herself, six innocent children might, all their lives, have lived under the stigma of theft—of being *thieves*! And *this* for your crime. Do you not realize the enormity of your crime against society?"

"But, don't you see, Uncle Peter, it is only *you* who see anything wrong in it? When Papa used to go shooting duck—whose ducks did he shoot? And when you go catching fish—whose fish do you catch? And you know perfectly well that when God gave Adam the earth—as for all I can learn He did—He gave him every blessed thing! And I have never heard anyone say that what belonged to Adam does not belong to me. And whether I took a Red Roman, or whether any of my cousins, or my brother Donalblain (who is four) took a Red Roman, it is only a person like you, who thinks so much of owning a thing, who makes a sin of it. It is just the natural thing to do."

"Then, being naturally a thief, you are, naturally, a liar?"

"Oh no, Uncle Peter, I did not think I was a thief. So, of course, I was not a liar. Don't you see, there is no such thing as sin, it is only that some men, who don't understand God or what God said, begin to make their own rules to suit themselves, and they invent sin, Uncle Peter. I expect, if you thought a little about it, you would soon grow to see that this is the truth. It is just grown-ups who invent wickedness, and then accuse innocent children of it."

"Hopelessly casuist. Irreclaimably evil. A dangerous liar, a thief! I see, Juliet, that no Christian teaching I can give is likely to reclaim you! I shall write a letter for you to take back to your mama and grandmama—what sort of home life you have at Mallow's Marsh Vicarage, I tremble to think! It baffles my imagination. Wait, wicked girl, wait! Phantom, watch her, if you please! Be careful to allow her no intercourse with any member of my family."

Dr Boisragon walked majestically up the tree-dotted slope to his four-square yellowstone house, where a shaded lamp in Mrs Boisragon's bedroom showed that she was still "resting", and where flickering candles in the dining-room, reddening still more gaily the crimson rep of the curtains, showed that the birthday party was still in full swing.

As soon as Dr Boisragon's back was turned Juliet slapped her flat stomach and said, conversationally, "I'm like a tympanum! I'm as empty as a drum—just you listen!"

She twanged her thin body again. It certainly gave out a hollow moaning sound.

Dr Phantom gave her a very cool, direct look from eyes that hitherto avoided any direct encounter with her own brightly sparkling copper-coloured glance. It was, perhaps, rather the squirrel's tanny coat than its wildwood eye that (as he had at first considered) her lively regard had evoked.

"Not quite hollow," Dr Phantom rejoined with meaning.

Juliet blushed. She really looked quite lovely, her small, Titian-bright head set trimly against a skyey nimbus of Tuscan gold.

"What do you mean?" she asked cautiously.

Dr Phantom leant towards her and took, from a fold in her bib, two or three caraway seeds and a few cake crumbs.

"Dry," he explained. "They were not there when you went up to the house to wash."

"Oh, those? Oh, I just asked Cook Jane for a piece of cake! I was simply starving!" After considering her companion for a few minutes in silence she asked, "Don't you think I took the best line with Uncle Peter?"

"I thought it clever enough."

Looking relieved, Juliet drew closer.

"I just didn't have a chance of thinking it out! We were playing at murdering the Duke, when James suddenly caught sight of the nectarine we'd been hearing so much about, and called out—'First in gets the Holy Globe!' And we all started running down the slope and shouting out, 'Bags I the Holy Globe!' It was a great lark, really, and I got there first; I only beat Victoria McMurthie by the edge of a hair-ribbon as you might say; so I had it, but of course we all shared it. Everyone had a bite! But I had the skin, mostly, and of course that showed more."

"Then all the children were equally guilty?"

"But, don't you see, we don't think it guilty!"

"The fact remains that since you stole something—took what did not belong to you—you have committed a sin against society, and you will have the whole world against you. People think theft the meanest of crimes."

"But Mama brings back a few hairpins every time she goes to her Club, and Papa used to carry home some envelopes and notepaper every time he visited *his* Club, in Sydney, and I wouldn't mind betting, Dr Phantom, that I could catch you out in a theft of some sort if I gave my mind to it."

A mere flutter of dismay, a fraction of alarm, passing across his face as swiftly as the shadows made by the sea-gull's wings on the darkening waters (for the sun was now due west and as red as an apple) told Juliet that she might, as she put it, "be on to something".

Jumping up and down and clapping her hands, the dreadful child pressed home her advantage.

"Will you let me search you? That would be a perfectly fair test!"

She sprang towards him.

He kept her at bay with a grip of iron.

"No! No! I never heard of such a thing! What cheek!"

Dr Phantom shed ten years of his assumed dignity at least, as, laughing and red in the face, he struggled with the lively Juliet.

"A prize! A prize!" shouted that exasperating child, wild with excitement. "I shall find a spoon! One of Lady Mary's salt-cellars!"

The tussle was really incredibly brisk! Juliet's darting attacks, first at one pocket, then at another, were quite spectacular in their success."

"A case book!"

"Mine!"

"A purse!"

"Mine!"

"A pencil!"

"Mine!"

"Bitten at the end!" gasped Juliet, breathlessly, putting it back as she whirled, wriggled, twirled.

"A key! Two keys! Three keys!"

"Mine! Mine! Mine!"

"A love letter!"

"No! No! *A bill!*" He clutched it.

"Ah, ha!" Juliet wrenched herself free, doubled up with laughter. "A prize! A prize! Whose pocket handkerchief is this, you wicked thief?"

As Dr Phantom rushed after her she doubled and dodged round the saplings.

"Whose? Whose?"

"You dreadful child! Give me that handkerchief this instant!"

Catching a moment when her hardly less agile opponent had side-slipped in skimming too quickly round a juniper, Juliet read the name embroidered on the bit of scented lawn, her treasure.

"'Aminta Wirraway!' Oh! Dr Phantom. Oh, you wicked thief! Bad, bad man! I shall tell your mother! Does that poor girl know you have stolen her new Irish linen?"

"Do I understand," asked Dr Boisragon, joining the struggling pair and judging as usual by appearances, "that this depraved child has actually stolen your handkerchief?"

Silence.

Dr Phantom pulled down his waistcoat and re-buttoned his hip-pocket. He looked blankly at Juliet.

"No, of course she hasn't," he blurted out, getting back his breath.

He looked appealingly at Juliet.

She sniffed at the scented square of pink lawn.

"I was just guessing what kind of scent Dr Phantom uses," she said, meekly, "I think it must be Opopomax or Alderman's Bouquet."

"The only perfumes allowable for male use are Florida Water and Eau de Cologne. I myself use Florida Water." He addressed himself entirely to Dr Phantom, ignoring Juliet. "As a bachelor, you might conceivably be permitted a sprinkling of Verbena; it is slightly astringent and not too tropical."

Juliet put the handkerchief back in Dr Phantom's breast pocket.

"Over your heart," she whispered.

Dr Boisragon turned his attention to her.

"Juliet McCree," he announced, portentously, "I have in this letter informed your widowed mother and grandparents of your incredible perfidy. That you, a girl of eleven or twelve, should steal in a house where your lightest request, if not granted, would at least have been sympathetically considered, that you should, when detected in that theft, lie, and that, having lied in the most bare-faced manner, in the plain proof of your falsehood, that you should persist in the most Jesuitical casuistry, in asserting your *innocence*, has so shocked me, so outraged my feelings, that I feel compelled to forbid you ever to enter my house again. My house, or my *grounds*," he looked meaningly at Juliet.

With a humble and gentle expression his niece stepped forward and took the letter he extended to her, at an arm's length.

"Goodbye, Uncle Peter," she said, sadly, and she dropped him a curtsey, the charity bob she had been taught to use when greeting or saying goodbye to her elders.

"If Dr Phantom would be so kind as to send you home in his Hyde Park—should the murderer not object to your company —I should be much obliged to him."

"Oh, certainly, certainly." Dr Phantom was all complaisance. "I will remove everything of value and give my coachman due warning of her weakness. There is a second basket of fruit—"

The trio walked across the shadowed lawn to the Hyde Park which drooped by the kerb in the warm, windless air, for the sea-breeze had expended its energy and a glowing sun, cut across the middle by the twin towers of the church, was pouring its hot rays through the valance and neatly tied-back curtains. Juliet was surprised to find "First Murderer" asleep in the driving seat; she had hardly expected that murderers could sleep, but it was still oppressively warm, and even the piebald Waler in his straw hat snuffled his nostrils and stamped his hooves and whisked his cream tail with less than his usual verve.

"I am sending a duplicate letter by post," Dr Boisragon mentioned to Dr Phantom, intending Juliet to hear. "Should anything happen to my first missive, her poor relatives will hear of her wicked conduct by the first post on Monday morning."

"I think you are so wise," Dr Phantom rejoined, also intending Juliet to hear. "What a disaster it would be for her family if they did not learn what a hardened criminal the child is!"

And in the most ostentatious manner he removed the basket of pears from the vehicle. Their aroma was almost as heady as wine, the heat had brought out their delicious, yet not cloying, fragrance.

"A pear, perhaps, is the most delicate of all fruits." Dr Boisragon's elegant hand hovered. "A *Beurré du Roi*?" He tasted. "Yes I thought I could not be mistaken! The skin paler than the finest champagne! The shape, symmetrical, but slightly squat, if one could apply so bald a word to so desirable a form! Pipless! Indeed the faultless fruit."

With a grave propriety, settling her green checked skirts and folding her hands in her lap, Juliet crossed her neat ankles, in the white culottes, and, at last assuming her straw hat (from China), she settled herself on the box beside "First Murderer", in the Hyde Park, while he, having saluted his master with two fingers, and flicked the piebald Waler's back with his whip, urged that animal to the pace which was, in those days, described as "a spanking trot".

As they were moving off Dr Phantom heard Juliet saying in an easy and conversational manner to "First Murderer": "I am not quite in your class, of course, but this afternoon I have been proved to be both a thief and a liar, and, as one criminal to another, I should very much like your advice, as a more experienced—" He heard no more. He was, however (since he did not care for children), rather surprised to find himself envying "First Murderer".

"At this time of the evening," Dr Boisragon took Dr Phantom's arm, "it is pleasant to sit on the steps facing the water, where one occasionally gets a puff of sea air, and since the children's party is in full swing in the house, let us linger here for an hour before going indoors."

The partners took their places on the step where the basket of mixed fruits still adorned the parapet. Dr Phantom, having set down his own basket of pears by his side, made an incision in a Golden Pear of Xaintonge with thirty-two sharp white teeth.

"I have been thinking over that depraved girl's case," Dr Boisragon murmured, having embarked on a second pear, "I see that her first sin—*theft*—was the cause of her second sin—*lying*—but, delving more deeply into the cause of her crimes, I am of the considered opinion that the child's inability to control her carnal appetite was the primal reason for her downfall. *That girl is a glutton*! Did you notice the way she kept eyeing those grapes?"

"Yes, I did," Dr Phantom rejoined, averting his eyes.

The Rector's Wife Tempts the Bishop with a Brew of Nyppe

SEVERAL BROWN birds, mere specks in an infinitely blue sky, were telling an inattentive heaven what a lark it is to be a lark, while, below them, the tide of Parramatta High Street bustled and flowed, as lively as a Scottish burn in autumn.

Everyone for miles around had come to town. The same people were exchanging greetings with diminishing ardour as they met in shop after shop, every lamp-post was decorated with a nag's head held to it by looped hide, the medley of vehicles quite blocked the road, clarences, barouches, phaetons, landaux, drays, carts, and Dr Phantom's Hyde Park, neatly drawn up beside the kerb outside the chemist's, his groom (whom hc designated Second Murderer) sitting in it bolt upright with folded arms and eyes fixed on space and a spine like a ramrod, and, next to him, the Coachman (designated First Murderer) whose deportment was equally correct.

The cockades on their hats were new. They had something to live up to; for one thing, they felt the power of Miss Juliet McCree's sparkling eyes; she was a critic on style whose opinion they valued, and the Vicarage buckboard was drawn into the sidewalk contingent to the Doctor's piebald Waler. For another thing, Miss Aminta Wirraway, in a stunning pelisse, had stopped—a mere instant—to curtsey to Dr Phantom and to thank him (in a reproachful voice) for the return of a pink lawn Irish handkerchief "taken in mistake for his own".

The lane beside the chemist's had, besides a row of pepper-trees, a spreading camphor-laurel round which scores of Green Fanny and Blue Fanny butterflies were vanning the air, and these did nothing to detract from the charming picture Miss Aminta made as, quite bewitching in olive-green and burgundy, colours that went so perfectly with the curtains of the Hyde Park that they might have been designed for riding in it, she lingered on—a mere fraction of time—to say her few shy words.

"Have you ever known anyone who owned a butterfly?" Juliet McCree asked Dr Phantom as, together, they watched Miss Aminta's elegance, still pursued by butterflies, being as it were, "rubbed out" by scores of rustic figures.

Dr Phantom's level and deliberate gaze met hers, as long, perhaps, as a lacewing settles on a daisy.

"No."

"When you blush," Juliet noted, in an interesting aside, "the red starts just above your stock, and when I blush it begins on my cheek-bones and then goes right through."

The observation did not disturb the flow of her main discourse which she resumed immediately, while Dr Phantom's roving eye followed a flight of starlings bent on keeping a *rendezvous* on the King's School lawn. He did not care for children, but, finding Juliet waiting there, he had, on coming out of the chemist's, stopped to inquire after her "grandfather's lumbago". In asking after the Vicar one picked on any complaint that came handy; he had them all.

"The story about the ravens feeding Elisha and that other one about the widow's cruse should never have been written; they have done a lot of harm. They give people such wrong ideas."

Juliet, who was standing in the gutter, holding her horse's head, took a fresh twist in the reins.

"Look at poor Grandpapa," she continued, her eyes very bright under her "reed" straw hat (from China), "if people did not believe in miracles no one would expect him to live on £90 a year and keep his son's widow and her children—Donalblain and me. Everyone seems to think—and I am certain those stories are to blame for it—that the holier a man is the less he should have to eat, and the shabbier his clothes ought to be, and the more hungry children he ought to feed, and the harder he and his wife ought to work, however old they may be, and give pennies to beggars, and have no other pleasures because being holy is enough reward for anyone, as of course it ought to be."

Dr Phantom made no answer, still, he lingered, his glance tracing the course of a pigeon very high up and as white as snow. It looked like something straight out of Paradise. He felt extremely happy, and he thought, "The earth must be like a pear that has one perfect moment, and this is that moment; the sky has never been so blue, the sun has never been so beneficent, the air has never been so soft, or the trees so golden."

"And you know perfectly well that in any rich household a loaf of bread cuts into eight slices—eight thick slices, for what use are thin ones?—but at the Vicarage it has to be cut into twelve at least."

Dr Phantom looked directly into Juliet's orange-tawny eyes and then withdrew his glance; he made no comment.

"Then—hasty pudding! Have you ever had hasty pudding for breakfast, week in, week out?"

"No."

"I thought not. I suppose you don't even know what it's made of?"

"No."

"Flour and water—just that. Of course sometimes you have a spoonful of milk with it, or a taste of brown sugar, and of course there is simply no one cleverer than Grandmama in making helpings go round! A casket of molasses is very good for growing children—no one denies it—and there is enough nourishment in it to last a month at least, and it is very good for children. Don't you think molasses is very good for growing children?"

"Yes."

"And have you ever eaten 'choke dog'?"

"No."

"Oh, well, that is quite good really, it is made of beef suet and currants and it has a thick sauce made of flour, and when the lemons happen to be ripe it has a lemon flavouring. And a 'Lady Belmore' is quite appetizing, too, and it is made of rice and currants boiled in a pudding cloth, and it has some thin sauce with it, and when it is nicest it is made of arrowroot, and the pattern of the china comes through on your plate, which is interesting really. Only Donalblain, who is four, does not care for it much."

Juliet, with a caressing pat, restrained her horse from biting the nose of the piebald Waler.

"Grandmama thinks the way clothes wear out is a perfect pest, and even the ravens did not bring Elisha a new suit."

She gave Dr Phantom the full benefit of her lively regard.

"Of course, you understand I am not criticizing God in any way?"

"Oh, no, of course not."

"Here comes Grandpapa. He will give you a tract. You could let me have it back, sometime, if the pages are not dog-eared."

The Reverend Phineas McCree (B.A. of Trinity College, Cambridge) at eighty-four was getting a little past his work. So benevolent a countenance as his made many of his parishioners feel reassured about heaven and earth merely by looking at his white woolly hair, his bright blue eyes, his nobly hooked Roman—or Wellington—nose, his red, tremulous mouth; but he supplemented this unconscious influence by an eleemosynary distribution of texts, for he had some difficulty nowadays in speaking; the words did not come easily off his tongue.

Some people thought that he should retire, but, they asked themselves, if he gave up his parish who would feed him and his dependants? It was wiser and more comfortable to beg the question.

Dr Phantom, therefore, was not surprised when Mr McCree making his way towards him by very slow degrees, simply handed him a text without speaking, and then turned away to tackle the difficult ascent of three steps that looked like flattened soup ladles, which made entry into the buckboard easy on a *Lucus a non lucendo* principle.

Handing his groom the leaflet, which bore the title "Is Your Soul a Social Success?" Dr Phantom set himself the task of hoisting the Vicar up, wondering, meanwhile, who would assist him down again.

Juliet had already seated herself in the driver's seat, her whip set at the correct angle, the reins smartly assembled. She looked quite enchanting.

Indeed, she caught the eye of the Governor himself. He was, at that moment, trotting past, helter-skelter, with a great clattering of hooves, as he was driving tandem in his London Curricle.

His Excellency was a descendant of King Charles the Second —as indeed who is not?—and whenever he appeared in Parramatta all women between the ages of sixteen and sixty would inviolably withdraw into hiding until he had passed.

With predatory smiles creasing his distinctly "Caroline", rubicund, yet swarthy, face, he was about to pull up beside Juliet when the A.D.C.-in-Waiting leant across to say urgently, "That is Miss Juliet McCree, the granddaughter of the Vicar of Mallow's Marsh, and she is twelve years old"—and clucked twice (to the horses).

"She is a personable girl for her age," commented Sir Charles, as he acknowledged salutes from Dr Phantom and the Vicar and the small crowd that had quickly gathered, and he moved off reluctantly with a spectacular display of horsemanship.

Dr Phantom stood a moment looking into the crown of his beaver hat, then he said, briskly, "Good morning, Vicar, goodbye, Miss Juliet. I have to return two baskets in the direction of Dural and Hornsby Junction."

Getting nimbly into his Hyde Park he was bowled gallantly away, with four curtains fluttering in the wind of his passage.

Meanwhile, running across the road from the grocer's, Miss Loveday Boisragon detained Juliet to ask after her Grandmother's liqueur.

"Indeed, Aunt Loveday, it is brewing nicely, thank you. Dear Grandmama manages to keep the lid on with three flat-irons. The Churchwardens are taking a great interest in it, and Mr McWhistle has donated—very kindly—two gallons of French brandy and a hogshead of Jamaica rum. The recipe is written in a faint hand in faded ink and it has been difficult to decipher it, but we think the ingredients and quantities are correct."

"And what, dear child, are they?"

"Oh, walnut rinds, oat-malt, beans, fir and birch tree tops, and three handfuls each of *Rosa solia* and *Carduus benedictus*. There are two handfuls each of burnet, betony, marjoram, avens, elder-flowers and bruised cardamom seeds. Then there is a handful of wild thyme. And ten new-laid eggs. Grandmama has yet to add watercress and a generous rasping of horse-radish. Of course the chief things are the milk of two dozen coconuts, three gallons of French brandy and double that quantity of rum. My great-grandpapa, as you know, was a nabob in Calcutta, and we found the recipe in a box of his. There is a note in his handwriting, saying 'This brew it bettered by the addition of a pound of ginger, some sassafras, madder, red sanders and *Enula campana*.' We shall put those in. Another postscript says, 'This Nyppe is strong enough to make a cat speak.' "

"Do you call it Nyppe?"

"The name for it, Grandmama thinks, is 'Nyppa Wine' or wine made from a tree. But she is adding various other things, such as brook-lime and wild parsley, and she thinks it will be more of a liqueur, really."

"I ho-pe," Mr McCree began, in his slow articulation, to which his hearers listened with reverent looks, "that the concoction with bib-beady bub-bubbles winking to the b-brim, will ch-cheer the d-dear Bishop! He c-comes on a p-pastoral visit next month."

Mr McCree looked triumphant.

"Goodbye, dear Aunt Loveday!"

With great judgement Juliet achieved the feat of turning the buckboard in its own length, and, feeling very grand, she whipped the young draught-horse in the shafts to a majestic trot, and the Vicar, bowing this way and that, like Royalty, and sometimes stopping to hand out a text (he had given Miss Loveday Boisragon a pamphlet on "Lessons to be Learnt from the Construction of the Ark"), was borne westwards along the dusty road on which, five miles away, the Vicarage and village of Mallow's Marsh was situated.

In a community where news is so scarce it is not to be thought that information about Mrs McCree's liqueur would not leak out, the Vicarage during the subsequent weeks was besieged by callers; one almost expected straw to be laid down on the road.

Even the Governor, with his dashing A.D.C., rode over one Monday morning, when Tabitha, the housemaid, Cook Teresa, Mrs Cog the laundress, and Abigail the Orphan, who, while learning the laver's art, assisted Mrs Cog with the washing, were pegging clothes on a line.

When, therefore, he visited the laundry, where a large earthen cauldron reposed itself beside the copper, His Excellency was flapped in the face by wet sheets and caressed by other garments, about the ownership and uses of which it would be profane to guess.

Mrs McCree, who at once locked Tabitha, Abigail the Orphan, Cook Teresa and even Mrs Cog securely in the linen cupboard, and was herself closely attended by the Vicar, on affording Sir Charles the privilege of a sight of the cauldron which contained the now golden-tinted liqueur, produced, from a box kept on the copper, a wine-glass and a toddy-spoon, and ladled him out a sup or two of the so-famous "Nyppe".

"It is not yet mature, Sir, of course," Mrs McCree was complacent, "but it will give you an idea of the flavour. Though red sanders, *Enula campana*, ginger and sassafras have still to be added—and a third quart, I think, of French brandy—its bouquet, I flatter myself, is unique."

Sir Charles bent his head and sipped.

A look of extreme and ineffable joy ran like sunlight over his face.

"My dear lady!" he ejaculated.

He sipped, he savoured.

Ecstasy succeeded astonishment.

His eyes shut, with the look of a man in a trance, he tasted, he rolled the Nyppe round his tongue.

He finished the glass.

He stood, vibrating, almost locking his gaze in that of Mrs McCree, his expression one of utter unbelief.

He was then understood to say something like "Shend me sheveral bottlesh"—"Gimme onemorsh"—and the two outdoor menservants and the A.D.C. having assisted His Excellency into the saddle, and handed the horse's bridle first to His Excellency, then to the A.D.C., he was led home by back ways, ecstatically, deliriously happy.

But he was as helpless as a new-born babe.

Mrs McCree with a quiet smile went indoors to let the four maids out of the linen cupboard, and having done so, she put her feet up on the drawing-room sofa and engaged herself, with a somewhat mystic air, in the perusal of a book (perhaps *Crockford's*) which gave lists of deans, archdeacons, canons and prebends of cathedrals, their pay, emoluments, residences, perquisites and privileges, their precedence at banquets and royal levees, and their titles.

The Bishop was expected in about three weeks time.

As a girl Mrs McCree had lived on the Picton Hills not far from the Razorbacks, and this morning, in the intervals of her reading, her eyes looked through her drawing-room windows and lingered on those blue, authoritative ranges. She remembered them in her childhood to have been thatched with trees, now they were denuded; the buff grasses clothing them were intersected with many red channels in which the rains of autumn were accustomed to pelt downwards.

"As a girl," she mused, "I used to look across to Mallow's Marsh and watch the thick mists rising at sunrise from the green fields, and the roads that led, I fancied, to the sea, to cities, to a wider life than I had known."

She dropped *Crockford* on to the threadbare carpet.

"It is true that I adored my home, that there was no one in it that I did not love, no simple everyday happening that I did not value and enjoy. The first apple-blossom! Never shall I forget seeing that! The stunted violets that come before the big ones—never shall I forget how sweet their scent used to be! Ike, the gardener, sitting in the moonlight practising 'Cherry Ripe' on a penny whistle! How mysterious and beautiful it seemed, how clear the faltering notes were! Never, never shall I cease to value those memories! But I imagined that elsewhere I should know a more wonderful life! And here I am at fifty-five looking at two minute, bare churches, one with cows feeding in the churchyard, one with two old horses grappling with the tough yellow grass—the wife of a poor parson trying to live on £90 a year!"

Mrs McCree looked searchingly round the room.

She critically regarded the two owls mounted as fire-screens that stood on either end of the mantelpiece, the silhouettes of her great-grandparents, grandparents, parents, uncles and aunts —so many soldiers, so many sailors, all idealists, no money-makers; the two tea-sets in her china cupboard, one patterned with raised strawberries and their leaves, in a china like pumice-stone, the other sprawled with marsh-mallows and having blue bird-bolts on the back of each cup and saucer. She carefully examined the dessert service, imitating fig-leaves, the glass paper-weight enclosing a cottage on which snow fell if one shook it. Her treasures! Oh, well! They were very sweet, really.

The tapestry covering the Empire chairs was, however, "shrill"; the worn carpet had belonged to her Aunt Martha.

Heaving herself up, Mrs McCree walked to the window, the better to see the hills of her youth.

"Lovely still! Lovely, always!"

"Other people," she told herself, "get more out of life than I seem to have done. What defect in my character has landed me here? What was my weakness? What was my mistake? My apparent freedom has been an illusion! I have had no real, no personal choice in any important crisis. My parents refused my first offer of marriage without even telling me of it—what gay adventures might not that young husband have given me?

"And why on earth did I marry Phineas?

"A poor parson nearly thirty years older than myself?

"Why? Why? Because he looked so woebegone! Because I felt sorry for him! Yes! That was why—I just gave myself away, body and soul, out of charity!"

Another thought struck her. "But was even this marriage entered into of my own free will? At home, as money grew short, I was an extra mouth to feed, I was a burden from an economic standpoint, it was necessary to lighten the family of such a drag! It was a question of having to get rid of me! Oh, I see that! It was taken for granted that I must say 'Yes'. I realized that at the time. Daughters must marry. So I did."

Mrs McCree turned away from the dazzling light.

"My fault has been—generosity! I gave all I had to give—and it has never been enough!

"Thirty years spent in this cramped house. Well, I shall end all this! The consequences? The consequences! I just don't care!

I shall make the Bishop tipsy with my wonderful Nyppa wine, my miraculous liqueur! Yes! I shall! Even if I can't make him give Phineas a deanery! Even if he won't make him an Archdeacon! Or a Canon! (There are several Canons over eighty in the Sydney diocese.) He might at least add twenty pounds a year to his stipend."

Mrs McCree picked up *Crockford.*

With a careful regard for syntax, learnt from Little Mary's *Grammar*, dimly remembering the calamity brought on the man in the mill-pool by a lax use of will and shall ("I will drown and nobody shall save me") Mrs McCree lifted *Crockford* high in the air and acclaimed in a ringing voice (which she hoped her Guardian Angel would hear): "I *will* make the Bishop tipsy, and nobody *shall* stop me!" In case of error she varied this formula by a second declaration of her intentions: "I *shall* make the Bishop tipsy and nobody *will* stop me."

Having done this, throwing her book on the carpet, Mrs McCree to her own complete astonishment burst into tears, sobbing into the silence of the threadbare room, "Oh Phineas! Darling! Wonderful, wonderful man! A gentleman! A scholar! A Saint! Oh, never, never was there such a kind, loving husband! Oh, Phineas! To see you so neglected! So ignored, so underpaid, so overworked! It's a scandal, a perfect scandal! I can't bear it any longer!"

Drying her red eyes Mrs McCree then marched in a resolute way to the laundry, where she poured a third gallon of Jamaica rum into her witch's brew and gave Mrs Cog orders to keep a gentle fire burning in the copper for the next three weeks.

With a relentless and determined face—indeed, she looked more like Lady Macbeth than any actress ever has, before or since—the Vicar's wife re-read her great-grandfather's directions, to make quite certain that no vital, no necessary, ingredient was omitted; tipped yet a fourth bottle of brandy into the cauldron and dropped in a pound of ground ginger and a handful of quick-lime (in mistake for brook-lime), after which activities, and recollecting the effect of one wineglass on His Excellency (a four-bottle man as everyone knew), she buried her face in a damp sheet and laughed till she got a stitch in her side.

The day set apart for the Episcopal Visitation was one of the most perfect Mallow's Marsh had ever known. The sun had very easily dispersed the thick mists, called locally "the pride of the morning". Though cool, the air was not cold. Though warm, the sun was not hot. With the most discerning tact a zephyr sometimes stirred the wands of the pepper-tree, the swathes of the willows, the grey plumes of the wattles, already tasselled with buds. As if merely to display their delicate gradations of colour, ranging through buff and amber to bronze and dun, this subtle wind rustled, sometimes, the long grasses that veiled the Vicarage garden, the unending by-ways; even the main road meandering from Sydney to Picton was fringed with blue grass and red fescue, which swayed this way and that.

Was the sky blue?

It was.

The Vicarage was early astir.

The menu at luncheon was to be—

Roast Pork with apple sauce.
Beans, baked potatoes.
Summer Pudding.
Whipped Cream.
Coffee.

An oratorio of the most heartrending sounds had, two days previously, accompanied the slaughter of the best of the Vicarage pigs. A roomy flagon of Nyppa wine (or "Mrs McCree's Liqueur") had been lowered sixty feet down into the eighty-foot well, to cool off; the most exact calculations having been made to ensure that, though close to it, the bucket in which it reposed should not touch the water.

In the Vicarage every duty allotted to Cook Teresa, Abigail the Orphan and Mrs Cog had been faithfully performed. The garden (the bit, that is, between the front gate and the porch, over which a Maréchal Niel rose was in full flower) was actually neat. A clump of polyanthus (very late) was in bloom by the front steps; there were six clove carnations out.

The service in Church had been most inspiring.

Sixteen sulkies, gigs, buggies and buckboards had brought a congregation of thirty, the Offertory (12/6) had been a record, the organ had produced sounds distinctly resembling music, neither of the choir boys had sneezed during the sermon, which, in its measured cadences, its august prose, its exact, almost poignant scholarship, in the richness of its classical allusions, in the masterly ease with which the Bishop had ironed out a crease in Deuteronomy (or was it the Pentateuch?) and in its dramatic opening sentence, "WHERE ARE THE YOUNG MEN OF MALLOW'S MARSH?", would greatly have impressed anyone able to take it all in. The good Bishop never gave less than his best, even to the most sparse, the most rustic congregations.

Much in the spirit that Art students are sent to Italy, Abigail the Orphan had been "spared" by Mrs Cog in order that she might see the goffered frills on His Lordship's lawn sleeves. She sat in the Vicarage pew beside Juliet and Donalblain. It was hardly to be expected that the ladies from the household where the Bishop was to lunch should appear, but there they were! Mrs McCree in puce surah with a rose in her "pork-pie" hat; her lovely daughter-in-law, who seldom appeared, looked quite ravishing in a Garibaldi-black, of course.

The Bishop seemed to be such a true "Prince of the Church", and his eloquent words so moved Mrs McCree that almost she relented; but her Guardian Angel, a good creature, not very bright, was no match for the old firm, Apollyon, Beelzebub, Mephistopheles and Co.; she refused to weaken; she *would* make that lordly being tipsy!

In her dining-room with its rows of Regency chairs upholstered in red rep faded to magenta, the table positively sparkled with crystal (it really was crystal, three engraved goblets were dated 1683) and glittered with mirror-like silver (it really was silver, mostly of George the First's time).

The green fig-leaves from the dessert service, filled with grapes and hazel-nuts, the immense silver epergne garlanded with yellow roses, and a silver tazza, given to some ancestor who had been chaplain to Her (late) Majesty Queen Anne, made the table look magnificent.

Mrs McCree was proud of it.

"After all," she thought, "only Lady Mary's plate can rival ours," and with infinite care she gently levered the huge glass flagon full of Nyppa wine on to the sideboard. The liqueur was chilled to that clammy yet inviting coldness than only the deep-delved earth can give. Its colour was not bright but treacherous-looking; it had the unsafe look of a bog, strangely unluminous, yet deep-toned. It did not seem to be inanimate! Continually, a kind of subterranean glow radiated from it, its surface would be sucked in, in a thousand dimples, and then, with a sort of sucking sound, released, to flow to the rim of the jug. A volcano that was not in eruption but which was brewing lava would perhaps be a simile that faintly hinted at its mysterious and peculiar qualities; it appeared to be as thick as treacle, but it wasn't! As for its bouquet!

Juliet and Donalblain were having a meal in the Nursery with their mother, for the lovely young widow of the Vicar's son seldom appeared, it was only the Vicar and his wife who bowed their heads when the Bishop said Grace—in Greek.

The Vicar, who was greatly enjoying the company of an old friend of his undergraduate days, had twice already capped a line from Horace with a quotation from Sallust and (let it be whispered) Catullus.

The two outdoor menservants, wearing white cotton gloves, waited at table, Cook Teresa having elected to carve. She could not bear, she said, "to see my lovely leg mucked up". She deftly laid four pinkish, whitish, creamish, fragrant slices of pork on each Crown Derby plate, with its crispish, tannish, delectable-looking strips of crackling flanking them, each with a mound of apple-sauce to add lustre to a perfect mouthful. The beans were strips of chalcedony and chrysoberyl. The potatoes! And the gravy! Oh my dears!

"Ah, yes," the Bishop murmured in his exquisitely cultivated voice, while he waited for the Vicar to be served, "I very well recall, during the early thirties, questions arising in my thoughts as to whether we could really be so cocksure in taking the absolute truth of the evangelical formula for granted. One of the great watchwords was the right of private judgement. We used, on Sundays, to have to find texts to sanction it."

Here a slightly mystic air attested to the excellence of his first mouthful of pork.

"Side by side with our classical work we were obliged to find sanction in defence of Justification by Faith, Sanctification, Total Depravity, Election and Final Perseverance."

"We were taught to look on anyone who did not ag-ag-gree with us with a kind of awful dismay," the Vicar recollected, smiling.

He, too, found the pork very good.

"Of what use were all those glib quotations from the minutes of the Council of Trent?" the Bishop wanted to know.

"There was always a doubt as to whether K-K-Keble was really sound on the more vital aspects of the Christian Faith," the Vicar hinted.

He was quite holding his own.

As the meal proceeded Lucretius Carus wrestled with St Jerome, Epicurus attempted St Augustine, Apuleius, supported by Aemilia Pudentilla, confronted even St Paul himself.

It was a merry repast.

Directly the pork was in play Mrs McCree, rising from her

place, the flagon held in hands that did not falter, said in gentle, confiding tones to the Bishop, "You will taste my little elixir, Bishop? It is made from a recipe left me among the papers of my great-grandfather, Major-General Willing-Toper, of the East India Company's service."

"But, my dear Lady! It is not for you to wait on me!"

Jumping up, and gallantly possessing himself of the jug, the Bishop poured himself out a full glass, using, not the goblet dated 1683, but the hearty Georgian tumbler, with a capacity of one pint.

Returning the flagon to the sideboard, and smiling a faint, almost terrified smile, Mrs McCree went back to her chair.

"My memory is as good as ever," the Bishop remarked, in parenthesis as it were, "and for years, if I am not mistaken, I have addressed you as Jessie—yet, if my ears do not deceive me, I have today twice heard Phineas address you as Lucretia?"

"That is my middle name," Mrs McCree answered, throwing a warning glance at her husband.

Here the Bishop tossed off half a glass of Nyppe.

"Of course, in those days, after the appearance of Tract No. 90, the chief points held out for our consideration were Scripture, the Church, General Councils, Justification by Faith, Purgatory, the Invocation of Saints, Masses, Homilies, the Celibacy of the Clergy and—er—er—other matters of importance."

The Bishop finished his glass and in an absent-minded way got up and refilled it at the sideboard.

Mrs McCree became anxious.

Neither of the menservants had reappeared to take away the plates and dishes. Cook Teresa, ably assisted by Tabitha, was, in rather a flurried way, performing these offices.

"Where are the men?" Mrs McCree whispered, as Cook Teresa removed her empty platter.

"Lorst to the worrld, Mum," Cook Teresa whispered back. "They must have sampled the Nyppe. We managed to drag theer buddies into the scullery. I've covered thim with a blankut, and they look very, very happpy theer. Very happy indade! Abigail is after climbing into a clane gown, and she will be here immejit."

When the second course made its appearance, Abigail proving herself a treasure, the Bishop poured himself out a third tumbler of Nyppe.

"Your elixir, dear lady," he said, turning with a smile (the smile known to the ladies of his Diocese as *his* smile) to Mrs

McCree, "has the three qualities necessary to a good drink. It is cool, it is subtle, it is stimulating." And he resumed his interesting discussion with the Vicar. "It was Tait of Balliol who entrenched himself so ably behind the Thirty-Nine Articles. Did you ever meet Tait?"

"No. No."

"Nor Pugin? Bloxham's 'umbra'?"

"No. No."

"The Master was not pleased with Pugin. He considered he had humbugged Bloxham."

"Ah, yes, so Gooch told me. Did you ever run across Gooch?"

"No, no. But in the May term of 1836 I ran across Bowyer in Athens, and he told me about Gooch. That is, he mentioned him."

Because in their day Englishmen went to Greece much in the same spirit that the crusaders went to the Holy Land, Athens led to Delphi, Thebes to Helicon; there for the next ten minutes they rambled.

"I found the Boëotian plains very striking."

"Ah, yes! As I came down from Cithaeron on the way from Eleusis, they lay before me, rising beyond Asopus into reddish gentle heights!"

"*Helicon, the grey, distant summit, not unattainable!*"

"*The dim, huge, majestic mass of Parnassus!*"

From Mallow's Marsh they looked back on their Heaven.

Mrs McCree, who had been waiting in vain for the return of Cook Teresa, noticed with a failing heart Tabitha's agonized face appearing round the door, and obeyed her beckoning finger.

She was hardly at all astonished, on being led to the kitchen, to find Cook Teresa sitting stiffly on a deal chair, and gazing into space with extraordinary concentration.

"There were a drop or two left in the cauldron," Tabitha explained.

"I brought this on myself," Mrs McCree told herself, beginning to get a little alarmed. Should anything (as she put it) *happen* to the Bishop how could she deal with him? Dear Phineas certainly could not lift him. She peeped into the scullery at the recumbent forms of the two menservants, and remembering a maxim of her great-grandmother's, went across to unfasten their collars; neither stirred, yet they looked happy! She was reassured by reminding herself that a note in her great-grandmother's hand, written in the margin of the recipe had stated: "This Nyppe is good for diseases of the head and for cold stomachs, and nobody can pine away when embalmed in so powerful a preservative."

Not a little comforted she returned to the dining-room.

She circulated dessert.

Tabitha and Abigail brought in coffee.

The flagon was half empty and she noticed with awe that the Bishop was not in the least the worse for liqueur. His noble countenance was decorous, not flushed, his articulation was meticulously exact; indeed, as she entered, he was, with perfect *sang-froid*, asking Phineas if he had "caught this new craze for the cultivation of rhododendrons"?

The word presented no difficulties. His long legs, too, in their elegant gaiters, stepped with their usual graceful precision as he went across to the sideboard and poured himself out an eighth glass of Nyppe.

Sipping at her Mocha coffee, bolstered up with cream, the Vicar's wife, however, felt the first faint stirrings of a real alarm when (Phineas having dropped into a gentle doze) the Bishop drew his chair near to hers, and, with a kind smile, a very kind smile, laid a white hand, wonderfully kept, and given a look of sanctity by the Amethystine Episcopal ring, over hers, and said, lowering his mellifluous voice almost to a whisper, "For some months past I have been hoping to find an opportunity of mentioning to you a subject very near my heart."

"Great Heavens!" thought Mrs McCree, "Is he growing amorous?"

It was a contingency that had never occurred to her.

The Bishop's grey eye certainly looked beneficent.

Was his cheek, perhaps, a little flushed?

"I have not been unmindful of your devoted labours, dear Jessie," he continued. "I have greatly admired the wonderful way you have managed the feminine, the economic, side of my dear old friend's responsibilities in so remote a parish. You are almost, I have noticed, self-supporting! I feel that your gifts should have wider scope. Will you not, dear Jessie, accept the office of President of our Ladies' Auxiliary?"

Mrs McCree had been very well brought up, but she gave a little gasp—was it of relief? Was it of horror? Of disappointment?

It woke up the Vicar, who, looking at his watch, said in his usual direct way, "Th-th-three o'clock! Your man will be at the door by this, I th-th-think."

Rising, he went to look.

Yes! There was the Bishop's Brougham.

And, after the customary ritual common to the departure from a seldom-visited friend's house in the country; the search for the lent book; the borrowed coat, the bestowal of packets of sandwiches, of three pumpkins, two dressed chickens, a sucking pig, a dozen eggs; the assembly of the family: "And—I have added a few bottles of Nyppa wine," Mrs McCree murmured giving them to the groom to stow away in a carriage already packed with gifts. "I have already sent some flagons to the Governor, and to Mr McWhistle and other friends."

The early afternoon had not belied the morning's promise.

The sky was just as blue, the sun was just as temperate, the zephyr as discreet; all nature was keyed to the perfection of an autumnal, a mellow, beauty, as the Vicar, his wife, his daughter-in-law (who so seldom appeared), his two grandchildren, Juliet and Donalblain (who was four) accompanied the good Bishop to his waiting Brougham.

His shovel hat was like a mirror, his gaiters exemplary in cut and fit, his apron quictly orthodox, his handsome face urbane, as with precise, undeviating steps he walked down the narrow path—so sweet with cloves and thyme—and seated himself with his customary aplomb, and a gracious expression of gratitude, in his smart carriage, and was whirled away to his Palace.

"I blame myself, Jessie, I b-b-blame myself." Mr McCree fully realized how disappointed his wife was. "One rather g-g-glosses such things over! Where an Oxford man is concerned, that is! I q-q-quite forgot that Pussy" (for so he called the friend of his youth) "had been at Wadham College. Yes! My dear girl!" the Vicar shook his venerable head, "I should have remembered that the Bishop was a Wadham man. In his day they were all six-bottle men at Wadham."

Donalblain McCree and the Sin of Anger

It was some few months after Aminta's wedding that Donalblain McCree, five yesterday, woke up in his room in Mallow's Marsh Vicarage. He was not, even yet, used to waking up and finding that miracle, the earth, precisely where he had left it when, on the preceding night, most reluctantly, he had closed his eyes.

For this reason he had pulled his cot alongside the window, the better to survey his inheritance, his chin on the sill.

He liked to make certain nothing was missing.

The sun? Ah, there it was! With a sunrise in full swing.

It was an elaborate effort which entailed much flinging about of amber and gold, a particularly happy effect having been achieved by piling cumulus shapes right to the zenith of the sky, then topping these with three cirrus clouds of a bright coral pink which floated like gondolas in a sea coloured a pale pistachio nut green.

Even Donalblain recognized this as a successful experiment. He turned his chin up the easier to observe it and the sun, caprice itself, hereupon sent out a ray that dropped down through steep stairways of cloud to touch the eager face as if to caress it, as if to say (misquoting Baudelaire), "This child pleases me"; while the warm sunshine vibrated like far-off chiming bells to articulate in dancing motes the promise of the sun: "Child, you shall live under the influence of my kiss. You shall be beautiful in my way. You shall love all that I love, the earth, the trees, the sands, all sights, all sounds, all life, rivers, hills, valleys. You shall love through my influence places you have never visited, the memory of scents you have never known shall stir your heart to ecstasy, and my light shall bleach your blonde hair and bronze your white neck, and dye your blue eyes to an eternal blue that will never fade."

Yes, on that radiant spring morning the sun (in his own tongue) said something like this—something of this he said—as Donalblain leaned far out of the window to make sure that the whole of the empyrean was there. Yes, it was. But were such scudding clouds really necessary? Oh, surely not another wet day?

Was the swallow's nest still under the eaves?

Yes, it was.

There was the butcher-bird impaling a lizard on a thorn.

There were the ring-doves who always had the air of falling off a branch before settling on it, pegged, a row of eight on the orchard wall—an erection of grey stones innocent of cement.

Donalblain heard little "Guinea-a-Week" twittering unseen, but piercingly near, and his chirping soul responded.

The child liked everything in the world except Hasty Pudding, but he found the horses too hoofy, the cattle too horny, the dogs too bouncy and barky for perfect companionship; it was the birds he loved. He had even steeled himself to listen without fear to the curlews calling "kerloo, kerloo" as they swept in flocks over the roof on windy nights, or danced on moonlight nights in the boggy paddocks; bald, with patches soaked through with the white gold reflection of water; thatched, with shivery grasses and tussocks of Kumbungi, and extending, chequered by grey three-rail fences right from Mallow's Marsh Vicarage to the Razorbacks.

It is hardly to be credited that the sound made by two eyes opening could be heard all over the Vicarage, yet, directly Donalblain peeped himself awake, every woman in the house was aware of it. His mother, meandering like a long "M" in the middle of a double bed, and, since her husband's death, sleeping with the sheet over her face, would lift a corner of it, smile, and replace it. His sister Juliet in the next room to his would throw her pretty legs over the side of her truckle-bed and feel for her slippers. His grandmama, majestic in a four-poster fringed and curtained in maroon, who, like most old ladies, never slept, would pause in her calculations, her difficult sum in mental arithmetic—"If four new milch cows would bring so many more pounds of butter to be sold in Parramatta market, how long would it take to save the money necessary to send Donalblain to Trinity College, Cambridge, where his grandfather had been before him?" His grandmama was determined he should go there!

The Vicar's wife was convinced that though St Paul might possibly be an inspiration to saints and martyrs, who need not, of course, be people of much social standing, only the classics, only Horace, could create a gentleman. Mrs McCree had no use for "Nature's gentlemen". Indeed, she was really desolate that there had not been, that there never could have been, an Epistle from Horace to St Paul.

On this particular spring morning, all these family manifestations having happened as usual, the three maids who were engaged in turning out the drawing-room were also immediately aware that Master Donalblain was awake. Cook Teresa, smiling, handed her millet broom to Min, the new housemaid, and hurried to the dairy to pour out from the bubbling bucket the glass of new milk, warm, which Juliet, who had found her slippers, was to carry upstairs to her brother. In the interval Tib, the housemaid-emeritus, getting up from her knees, in which posture she had been "lifting the nap"—where there was any—from the Turkey Carpet (already twice swept) with a besom no bigger than a shaving brush, poked a head enveloped in a duster out of a side-window to engage Donalblain in that light badinage for which she had a talent; her undoing. Cook Teresa would allow no such pleasantries as those Tib had engaged in with the new boy, Dan O'Leary; this Tib felt to be unreasonable in a woman who addressed Donalblain as "Young Tinker", "Young Turk", or even "You Limb" (of Satan, being understood).

On the day after his grandson's fifth birthday Mr McCree, who had long noticed that the women spoilt Donalblain, also woke the moment the child stirred, to feel an impression, which had for some time been teasing the back of his mind, harden into a resolution; it was in obedience to this impulse that the old man bent his trembling steps uncertainly to the kitchen, just after eleven o'clock.

At this hour, much like a seagull scrap-fishing in the wake of a tea-clipper, Donalblain was to be found hovering in Cook Teresa's rear. Yes! There he was! Already he had not done too badly! He had accepted with red, moist, pursed-up lips a mouthful of cream, robbed a basin of rich gleanings of yellow batter, cajoled a generous munching of lemon-peel, and, yes, been given, ever so kindly, a whole delicious cumquat in syrup!

There was sunlight in the kitchen.

The room was gay with the rustle of work in progress.

Three maids all in Delft-blue cotton, worn summer and winter alike (for who could feel the cold when active?), and demure in starched white caps and aprons, in which they took pride, were red of face and arm, for the immense stove, roaring up the flues, was in the act of roasting a sucking-pig.

Like salmon in a Scottish fishing-lodge, or bloaters in a Yarmouth cottage, sucking-pig was no dish *de luxe* at Mallow's Marsh Vicarage. There were always so many male pigs, porkers that must not be kept, and, being a glut in the market, could not be sold, born in the six sties in which, this season, six shameless sows had each produced a litter of thirteen piglets—all of the wrong sex—that it was indeed an economic necessity that they should be eaten.

Mrs McCree was well aware that Mrs Noah and Mrs Job must have known a great deal about life that has not come down to us; she was in their class; but—*seventy-eight young hogs*! Oh, even Mrs Noah, even Mrs Job, would have considered this too much! Just the last straw!

In the face of this misfortune the Vicar's wife, quite losing her nerve, had talked with such severity to the man who kept her pigs that he, usually so meek, had rebelled, and, scratching a straw-coloured mop of hair, kept repeating querulously "Phut, Mum, phut had Oi to do with ut? How could Oi help ut?"

Today the grateful smell of cooking pork grew every moment more perfect in bouquet, the sizzling of the crackling, the bubbling of beans in a pot grew every minute more full of promise, as, sitting at the freshly scrubbed and sanded table, Lulu, the between-maid, cut white kitchen-paper into picot-edged flounces, meant to hide the nakedness of the dresser shelves and the high mantelpiece above the stove. Her big curved scissors with the vandyked blades snapped and clapped as the spirals of paper lace increased and the roll of paper diminished. Min, sitting beside Lulu, being instructed by Cook Teresa in the more finicky art of fashioning frills for cruets, cutlets and hambones, plied her small scissors on an accompanying *pizzicato*.

Both maids would have been cooler in the housemaid's pantry, but, no! they preferred the hot kitchen with its constant coming and going of male visitors.

On Mr McCree's entrance all four menservants had sheepishly withdrawn from the open doorway; Cook Teresa was in the habit of giving them all a sup at eleven—nothing much—nothing that would startle the household bills; a pewter tankard of small ale, or penny ale, perhaps, or a glass of sparkling cider—both home-brewed.

In this feminine air of comfort, plenty and security, Mr McCree recognized the enemy of his sex. In this cloying, this enervating atmosphere, this "monstrous regiment of women" the Vicar saw his grandson's undoing; he would become "soft". His manly character would be ruined.

Since the poor child had now no father, his grandfather was determined to warn him, to point out to him the dangers lurking in the society of females, and he took him by the hand and led him out through the orchard to the fallen pear-tree, their usual trysting-place, Donalblain's ducklings following.

Every woman looked out of a window to watch them. Eight faces appearing at the toy-like, white-curtained casements in the old-fashioned Vicarage walls, which were like those of a doll's house, painted to look like red-brick or a cardboard building in a harlequinade, registered the same fear, the same knowledge: "He is going to set the child against us." Intuitively the women realized this—rightly.

Sitting on the lichened trunk of the fallen pear-tree, which had a living branch or two because the tree had not completely pulled its roots out of the soil when it fell, and some remained to nourish it, Mr McCree nipped his grandson between his knees, and firmly held his restless hands, to keep them from fiddling with the ducklings, and he looked intently at the child with his kind, wise eyes, which were yet as blue as those which looked blandly back at him.

"Donalblain, you are five years old," Mr McCree began in his quavering, hesistant voice; he had been made speechless by a stroke a year back, and was only just regaining his power of clear articulation. "I am your grandfather, eighty-four years old. Soon you will be alone, with no father, no brother, and only three women to look after you."

"It is too sad," Donalblain said, tears filling his eyes.

"No, it is not a bit sad," Mr McCree said, testily, "it is merely inconvenient. Well, now, listen well! If a man has land or a house he can leave his land or his house to his sons, or his grandsons. But I have no land, and no house."

"Can't I have this land? And this house?" Donalblain asked, looking round him with a wondering air.

"No. These belong to the Church. They are not mine. When I die they will go to the new Vicar of Mallow's Marsh. Well, now, if a man has tools he can leave them to his children, or his grandchildren. But I have no tools to give you. The only tools I had with which to earn a living have been an old book, and a quill pen and a halting tongue. And it cost my father a lot of money to teach me to read the old book, and write with the scratchy quill, and speak with the halting tongue."

"Mr Noakes, the gardener, has got a pick, a shovel, a pruning hook, a scythe and a wheelbarrow," Donalblain volunteered, as he looked across the neat, gently swaying branches of the trees planted in narrow arcades in the orchard, to where the four men were digging a drain.

"Yes, so he has. And he can teach his sons to use them, but I can't teach you to use my tools because I am too old and you are too young. However, there is one thing I can tell you, and that is this. You are too big a boy to hang round the house with the women all day long."

Donalblain was only half-attending. Working one hand free from his grandfather's weak grasp, he swooped on the duckling which was sipping at his boots, and turned it upside-down. A scientist, satisfied with a deduction, he dropped the boat-shaped morsel of yellow fluff and, slipping his hand into his grandfather's again, prompted, dutifully, "Yes, Grandpapa?"

But his thoughts were with his ducklings. Would they soon lay eggs?

The sun, now quite a fiery affair, was negotiating the bend between the Church tower and the henhouse, and it threw a few diffident shadows across the blossoming fruit trees; across the pears, each bearing a hint of fruit in the last remaining fuzz of vanished petals; the cherries with their dancing and triumphing clusters in full blaze, the red threads left in the peach-branches each shielding a swelling bead that intended to be one of the immense Yellow Mondays for which the Vicarage was famous.

"I have no land, I have no house, I have no tools, I have no money, but I have my integrity," Mr McCree said, and as he watched his grandson's rosy face which blossomed no less radiantly than the blossoming trees, the old man thought, "How can I explain the meaning of 'integrity' to so immature an intelligence?"

"Mr Noakes says I am to avoid women as I would the Devil," said Donalblain.

Hearing this, Mr McCree felt a slight lessening of the burden on his conscience; his burden, it appeared, was to be shared; his grandson was apparently to be accepted into the garnered wealth of the experience of the world of men; he was to be Everyman's son. Every bit of wisdom each man had gathered for himself he would, in all kindness, be ready to hand on to those who followed him. Of course, so it had always been; so it would always be.

The old man smiled, the sweet smile of age, of one helpless yet unaware of his helplessness, and his whole face brightened with that same look of doting fondness which he had so reprobated in the women of his household.

"Yes," the boy continued, "Mr Noakes says, if you meet a girl and a death-adder, kill the girl and cuddle the adder. He says it's safer."

Sitting in his threadbare black cassock on the grey bole of the fallen tree, Mr McCree, who had served his God devotedly for over sixty years, felt that none of his own experiences had brought him any knowledge so salty. He considered, half astonished, the implications of such an attitude. He was, himself, warning his grandson against the deleterious effects of a woman's love; of a woman's affections. But, need one go so far?

"Little dears," he murmured to himself, forgetting Donalblain, and sipping as a bee sips at the memory of some flowering hours. And there was his wife, of course, what a good woman she had been—Still—

"You must beware of women."

"Yes, Grandpapa."

"You must never allow a woman to get the whip hand of you. they are weak creatures." Delving again into the depths of his memories, he added, "Sometimes you must protect them from themselves."

"Yes, Grandpapa." Donalblain was mystified, but he was a polite child.

"You must look after your poor grandmama, your mother, and your sister, and make enough money to keep them."

The Vicar of Mallow's Marsh looked at the small church in which thirty years of his life had been spent, mostly on his knees, where, in all happiness, he had learnt the beauty of holiness and the delight of serving his God. But his had not been a profitable life as regards material things, no, not at all! And when he had passed to his rest, and joined the Communion of Saints (as he was assured he would, meeting, he hoped, several other men from Trinity), the ninety pounds a year with which his labours had been rewarded would cease to support his family—and then? What would happen to them? He had saved nothing.

Sighing, he collected further scraps of experience to dole out, hopefully, to his grandson.

"You must have faith."

"Yes, Grandpapa."

"You must be a man."

"Yes. May I begin now?" Donalblain looked eagerly up. "May I have a catapult? May I shoot at the birds, and keep them from eating the seed?" He had often asked this before, but he saw that his grandfather was in a yielding mood. "I would not hurt the birds! Only frighten them. That boggart Mr Noakes put up is no use at all."

There is nothing that so becomes an orchard as ecclesiastical black, however faded it may be, and Mr McCree's cassock, swishing across the green springing orchard grasses was a telling contrast to that amazing medley of cumulus clouds, the exulting cherry-trees.

His rosy face, bright with the animation of coming manhood, hopping along to avoid the persistent, nibbling beaks of his ducklings, Donalblain McCree, in his blue smock, chattered away to the old man in the easy confidence of an equal. "I see your point," he said, "Sir"—this was his first claim to the status of an adult. "I will stand on my own feet (as you tell me to) and hang by my own tail (as Mr Noakes advises). I will be careful about women, too, Grandpapa!"

"*More wheat*
More to eat!"

the child chanted, in sheer joy of being alive, as they joined the four men, working at the drain. "That's a poem," he cried out to them gaily.

Everyone there, Mr Noakes, Boy Bob, Man Jonathan, and Dan O'Leary, the new hand, all agreed that it was a good poem, and putting their picks and shovels and mattocks aside, they combined in the manufacture of a catapult, contrived from the fork of a cherry-tree, a piece of garter elastic and the thumb of an old glove. Everyone there tried the sling out and gave Donalblain good advice, and each man had his own theory about the art of flinging a stone.

Standing beside Mr McCree, who looked on, smiling, Dan O'Leary, the new man, said in a humble, ingratiating voice, "Indeed, Surr, it's a privilege for us poor folks to spake to the Quality. It does us poor folks good, Surr, just to see the faces of the High Folks."

He gave a sort of scrape with one foot, and his bold, handsome face took on an expression of gentle humility.

"Why did you wink at Mr Noakes, Dan?" Donalblain, who stood on the far side of the boy, asked, interested.

"Wink, is ut? It was a tear, Master Donalblain. I've had a sad life an' all, and it's new to me to be stepping alongside the gentry, that it is!" And he slid a fierce, angry look sideways at the child.

The other men kept wooden faces and no more was said.

Donalblain, then, with his new catapult, went off to the wheat-field, to drive the birds from the newly-sown seed. He was proud and happy. He could see all the other men at work, and he, too, was at work, and he, too, was becoming a man, and, what was more, his grandfather had promised him a fourpenny-piece, a Joey, as a reward for his labours.

So he sent stones as high as he could, standing under the larks that hovered, pouring out their full hearts, near a heaven that was entirely blue from one horizon to the other. Resplendent, two Wampoo Pigeons, birds of passage, bound for the scrub, rested a moment on the arms of the scarecrow, the boggart, that had been there so long that inkweed was growing out of his hat. A family of "grey jumpers", called "The Twelve Apostles", next came hopping over the ground, and when Donalblain, taking careful aim, flung a pebble their way (but not too near) they flew to the branches of a tree in the edge of the wheat-field, ascending from branch to branch in a series of leaps, all the time calling out indignantly and harshly at the disturber of their meal. These birds gave Donalblain lots of fun, and he would break off work sometimes to tell his ducklings how silly they were. And he would refresh his love for his ducklings by rubbing their soft yellow down against his cheeks.

"Do not think, darling, that little scissors-grinder does any harm, because he eats only spiders, my pet," Donalblain told his eldest duckling, and he did not shoot at these birds when they came chasing their tails over the ploughed clods of earth. But when a whole flock of lorikeets came sailing and swooping in their scalloped flights to assail the cherry-trees, the child had moments of great activity; he thought of nothing else, rushing to the borders of the wheat patch for pebbles, making his ammunition of the smallest he could find, so that they could not hurt even the tiniest bird, and slinging stones wildly about.

"Jerrygang! Jerrygang!" he shouted in the exuberance of his joy, and he rolled about in the grass, and the sun shone, and the faintest of zephyrs disturbed the tranquillity of the older blossoms, and wafted their discarded petals about like snow in the warm, soft air that smelt more of honey than of anything else. The Vicarage wall-flowers were out in the Vicarage garden, and their scent came puffing over the field in fragrant gusts of heavier air.

Far off the Razorback hills were a deeper blue than the sky. Nothing stirred in all the waving miles beyond the Churchyard, for the larks had all left the earth, preferring heaven, and the cattle, since it was noon, were out of sight, preferring the consolation of the river and the lower ground, where the cool water ran thinly over the flattened rushes. The men had gone to their noonday meal. There was not a soul about and the sunlight purred like a cat.

It was then that Donalblain noticed Dan O'Leary standing on the far side of the field, watching him. There was something threatening about his still figure, in its three-flounced cape coat and tall hat, and he looked very big. In that flat country even lambs looked like Leviathans. In that beautiful hour the child felt some misgiving in his heart. He hoped that Dan would go away. He pretended that he was looking for stones close to the orchard wall, and that he did not see him.

Donalblain had hoped all along that a big bird, a bird so large that he would not hurt it if he hit it, would come along, and now his wish was fulfilled, for a whole tribe of currawongs, whistling and wailing and behaving in their usual noisy abandon, came rioting down from the hills. They walked and strutted about, picking up sticks and looking coy, and setting their black heads on one side, in their indecorous courtship. "Let us build nests" was what they were saying to one another, and the cachinnations of the older birds at some shy first-nester were amusing to hear.

Donalblain forgot Dan O'Leary.

He had a handful of stones in the pockets of his Nankin breeches—new yesterday—(and with straps that went under his jemimas, his elastic-sided boots—new, too), and he was fitting a stone into his sling when he saw that Dan, unseen, had come round the orchard wall and was standing not two feet behind him.

"Oh, hello, Dan," he said, to disguise his trepidation.

"Hello, young master," Dan said, amiably. "You are learning very fast to use your catapult, aren't you? But you don't seem to hit much, I notices."

"I don't aim to hit the birds, only to frighten them away."

"You don't seem to have frightened them currawongs."

"I've only just begun to frighten them. I scared away the Twelve Apostles, and the lorikeets."

"They never stay long. They were going in any case."

Dan was a very handsome lad with curly black hair and dark brown eyes that were apparently black, for their pupils had no light in them; they looked flat, and had no depth in them, and reflected nothing back; and his nose was tip-tilted, and his ears pointed, and his arms, Donalblain noticed, were so long that his fingers, as he stood there holding his bundle, reached his knees. Though he smiled with his big, curled, hungry mouth, there was a wind of fear that seemed to blow about him; he was a figure alien to the calm and peace of that happy hour.

Donalblain felt nervous. He fitted the stone which had fallen out of its place back into his sling, and let fly, to miss a sitting currawong not ten feet away.

Dan laughed heartily with a show of good-fellowship.

"Come, young master! I'll teach you how to hit a bird!" he said, and stretching out a large, hairy hand, he took the catapult, and, stooping, picked up a stone, and said to Donalblain, "You watch me hit that currawong! I'm a dead-sure shot, I am!" He drew the elastic well back, twanged off his missile, and the eldest duckling, quite in a different direction to the big piebald bird at which he was aiming, fell dead, with its head hanging almost off its neck.

Dan clicked his tongue.

"Dear me, now! Isn't that misfortunit? To hurt your duckling! That was the last thing I wanted to do!" Dan said, watching the child's face fade from red to white.

He would have run over to the bird but Dan put his foot on the child's foot, and said, smiling, "Wait a bit, little master! I must aim better next time!"

"You are hurting my foot, Dan," Donalblain said, trying to pull it from under the big, heavy boot.

"Am I, indade? Oh, no, master, I wouldn't for the world hurt the likes of you, indade an' I wouldn't! Why should I?" He pressed his boot harder down on the small resisting foot under his heel. "It's mistaken entirely you are!"

"Just you watch me," Dan continued, fitting another stone into the catapult. "I'll hit that currawong over there—beyond the scarecrow! It's a long shot, that—just you wait."

The second duckling flopped about, with the soft embryo of a wing trailing on the wheat blades.

"Tut an' tut! Sure an' isn't that the Divvle an' all? Where's my cunning gone to, ava? I'm ashamed of meself—to shoot that wide!"

Dan stooped, to look directly into Donalblain's smarting eyes.

"I'd best put the poor thing out of its misery, now."

Dan knocked the third duckling out with his next stone.

Then the fourth, the fifth, the sixth.

"I hope I am not discommoding you with my foot, Master Donalblain?" he asked in a gentle, polite tone. "It's the difficulty I find in aiming straight, that's what it is, that makes me lean so heavy on your toes; shall I lift me foot?"

"Yes, please, Dan," Donalblain said, setting his lips.

Dan lifted his boot and then stamped it hard down on the child's small foot.

He made an exclamation of annoyance.

"Now, aren't I the fool of a man? I thought I was stamping on that snail there, Master Donalblain. I don't know what's come over me this noon, that I first kill all your ducklings when I aims at them blasted currawongs, and then I hurts your foot—stampin' on it—like that!" He ground his heel on the child's instep.

"Does that hurt, little Master?"

"Yes, Dan."

"With its new boots an' all!" Dan murmured softly into Donalblain's ear. "Would the other foot be feeling it less?"

He brought his foot down.

Donalblain stood, his lips set, looking at his ducklings.

The one with the broken wing still struggled, bleeding, to get out of the trough of earth into which it had fallen.

"Don't you think it would be kinder to put that duckling out of its pain?"

"Yes, Dan."

"Come over here, then, just stamp on it with your boot, that will give it comfort, like. You'd like to be kind, wouldn't you, young Master?"

"I don't want to hurt my duckling."

"Oh, it's being cruel to be kind, that's what it is, just like me! I'm teaching you something, that's what I'm doing, but I'm just a clumsy oaf, just a poor man, Master Donalblain, and I don't rightly seem to have the gift of it, like my betters. They can thrash my back with a cat-o'-nine tails, and do me good, see? Because they're the Quality, and can't go wrong. But I'm no hand at it."

Dan walked across and stamped on the duckling.

It was said, in medieval times, that a man in the paroxysms of an overpowering rage had white eyes.

When, for instance, King Arthur ran "wood-mad", Mallory tells us he had white eyes, and Langland gives "Ira", anger, white eyes.

What was so dreadful to see in Donalblain, a child transported by rage, was just that same alarming manifestation. When he saw Dan stamp on the wounded duckling, in his fury his eyes became white; the pupils turned inwards, as it seemed, and slewed round out of sight like a Medium's eyes in a trance. His vibrating feet stamped up and down on the grass, in a swift staccato tattoo, a rapid churning! Up and down! Up and down! Donalblain's legs moved so quickly that they were difficult to see, like flails on a windmill, or like a man trying to keep his place on a treadmill. They whirred up and down. And he thought not at all of his bruised feet which were next day to show black and blue.

The child's hands beat wildly in front of him, sawing the air in a demented fashion, threshing it, hitting out with all his might when, running over, he got close enough to batter Dan O'Leary's knees—he could reach no higher. And the tears fell in immense bright drops, a clear, incredible torrent, pouring down his now flushed, now scarlet face, round which his yellow hair stood out almost on end, and a sort of high keening noise, a most curious whinnying sound came whistling out of his wide-open mouth, moist and dripping with saliva.

It was a noise so piercing that it seemed impossible that he could be making so strange, so clamorous a shrieking; an animal braying, a primitive echo from the first abortive transports of man.

Dan O'Leary was amused and gratified.

At that moment he almost liked Donalblain.

He stuck the catapult back in the little boy's breeches pocket and started tickling him.

At this last outrage the inverted eyes came back into focus.

Donalblain turned and ran back over the ploughed field, over the once-hopeful arena of his first initiation into the service of his fellows, racing back through the shadowy orchard, where so lately he had stood, a happy child between his grandfather's knees; he ran pelting back, still screaming at the top of his voice, past the laundry, the kitchen door, along the narrow strawberry-beds, scream-screaming, screaming in that high ass-like bray of sheer terror.

Every woman's face again appeared at the Vicarage windows.

Eight alarmed, compassionate women, leaving those points of vantage, rushed out to meet the child, and even his mother, throwing aside her novel, jumping up from her rocking-chair, after one wild look from her bedroom window, rushed downstairs so quickly, her white spotted wrapper streaming out behind her in the wind of her swift passage, that she was the first to reach him, and Donalblain flung himself into her open arms, that maternal refuge, and cried till he slept.

Like that first Dove sent out from the ark, Donalblain had come home. Of the death of his ducklings, of the knowledge of evil, of cruelty, which he had gained in that moment of his initial experience of the world outside the nursery, he spoke never a word. He answered no questions. Instinctively he conformed to the masculine code.

There is nothing so mysterious as the way that the seeds of the future germinate in the character of a child.

It is a miracle like that of the bud, which has, folded in it, the uncurled petals of the rose.

It is time's triumph, like the fashioning of the cone, the brass cone, which is to be the trumpet, silent until breath animates it, till breath blows the fanfare for which, from the first casting of the instrument, preparations had been made.

On that spring day the child Donalblain's destiny was made manifest; it was made coherent on that spring day when, on waking, he approved of the sunlight, when his teeming heart was united with the singing bird's, when he and little "Guinea-a-Week" sang their psalm together; when he was happy among the women of his grandfather's household, when (with the eyes of a scientist) he studied his duckling, and with the eyes of a dutiful child he looked up at his grandfather to learn, without speech, the meaning of the word "*integrity*".

On that spring noonday when, without rancour and being for the first time conscious of a sense of duty to others, of the pleasure of service, of a male desire to protect the weak, when he drove the birds from the patch of wheat; his family's bread; and then, seeing the death of his birds, felt in his young, untried heart the anger of the Saviour unable to save, of the pitiful soul unable to exercise the virtue of pity, or to save the helpless, the suffering, or to master (with his puny strength) the evildoer; in that moment, when Donalblain realized that he was helpless in the presence of cruelty, of wickedness, his fierce emotion operated like a dye, like woad, like murex, to colour his whole nature. Like a piece of cloth, dipped in a vat, to come out purple, he was metamorphosed, by that moment, to be then what he was always to be, at that moment, at every moment of his childhood, his youth, his manhood, his age.

Yes, Donalblain's character was stabilized by all that he suffered then. His experience on that bright noonday made him the child, the youth, the man he was always to be; the crisis of that encounter, the agony of that defeat, which taught him he was not omnipotent, that he was powerless in the presence of sin (it is a lesson all must learn), stood like a peak in the accumulated sensations of his whole life.

Like a child he cried himself to sleep. Like a child he accepted the comfort of his mother's embrace, but deep in his heart he had learnt all he was ever to know of man's capacity for grief beyond the reach of consolation.

He had exhausted himself in this knowledge.

That night the moon, caprice itself, looked down on Donalblain, sleeping by the uncurtained window, sleeping with his cot drawn as close as he could get it to the wide-open window, and the moon said (misquoting Baudelaire), "This child pleases me."

And the moonbeams dropped down through gigantic stairways of parting cloud and streamed, unimpeded, through the panes of glass, the doubled panes of the pushed-up window, high above his head, and touched his face as if to bless it, as if to caress it, to print on it the splendour of the human knowledge of good and evil, of sorrow, or joy, and this radiant light became articulate with the moon's promise:

"You shall live under the influence of my kiss. You shall be beautiful in my manner. You shall love all that I love, water, clouds, silence, darkness and the illimitable sea."

And from that day and that night, the sun was Donalblain's brother, and the moon was his sister, and in his long, useful and distinguished life, though love informed him, he cared to make no nearer relationships.

But Tib, the housemaid-emeritus, the girl of sixteen, knew nothing of such depths when, after the moon rose, she slipped out from her attic to join Dan, who was waiting for her behind the orchard wall in his three-tiered driving coat and rakish hat; clothes which Mr Noakes had called "a nob's togs", and had asked him how he came by them.

Tib had her neat carpet bag, bright with roses as big as cabbages, which had enclosed in it the wardrobe which the Duke of Wellington himself had chosen for female emigrants; a mixed bag of eight calico garments (in the selection of which the Duke had portrayed a singular innocence) and two pocket-handkerchiefs, and one Huckaback towel; she wore a dress of grey linsey-woolsey, and a coal-scuttle bonnet, into which, with great daring, she had stuck a rose.

The child had a month's wages—the twelfth part of two pounds—tied in a corner of her handkerchief, and she was not afraid of anything that might happen to her.

Though man's inhumanity to man may make angels weep, Nature shows a singular and impartial beneficence, bestowing on king and tinker alike the best earth has to offer; Dan, walking in that soft moonlight night through the orchard with Tib, the simulacra of last year's apples, the dust of last autumn's toad's-meat crumbling and dispersing under his footprints, was triumphant.

While the lovers trudged the long miles into Parramatta his

voice murmured untiringly, as he told Tib all he had suffered and all he meant to achieve.

And they delighted in each other, the strong, handsome young man in the pride of his manhood, and the innocent young girl in the beauty of her budding womanhood; and they had no fear of each other, or of the future.

And peering out through the white muslin curtains of her bedroom window, Donalblain's mother, the young widow, watched them go, and her tears fell faster than Widow Dido's, indeed they did.

Peronel McCree, and the Sin Called Pride: the Arch-sin

"WE SHOULD HAVE more Faith in Fate!" Peronel McCree told herself, not two days later when, just as she despaired of all joy, just as she believed her life would flow on, and on, in the drab security of her mother-in-law's rule, something did happen! Actually!

"Of course your dear Mama must accept His Excellency's Invitation. It is a command."

The Vicar of Mallow's Marsh voiced his agreement with Juliet's impulsive "Oh! Mama must go! How beautiful she will look!"

Every member of the McCree family was gathered in the shabby morning-room at the Vicarage, into which sunlight was streaming, wholly unimpeded by the threadbare curtains.

Mr and Mrs McCree, their widowed daughter-in-law, Peronel, whom in the sanctity of the maroon fourposter they would sometimes refer to as "Peronel Proud-heart", and their two grandchildren, Juliet and Donalblain (aged five), were opening the mail, scarcely five minutes back delivered by the red-coated, white-helmeted "Postie", who was now being regaled with small ale and baps in the kitchen.

Cook Teresa naturally offered sustenance to a man who had walked five miles to deliver two letters, and since every other client on his beat also entertained him with rum, peach-beer, cider, penny-ale, mum, or any other liqueur that came handy, the road that seemed so straight and flat when he started out from Parramatta at dawn, was apt to seem hilly and curly as he trudged home after a round of fourteen miles.

Today Postie had brought to Mallow's Marsh Vicarage two letters, one of which had a gold crown embossed on the flap of the envelope.

This was addressed (in very bad writing) to Mrs Augustus McCree (who had, "Oh, my dear, been nobody, nobody at all!") and in it was a gold-inscribed card which begged, in dispirited prose, for the honour of her company at a ball, to be held at Government House, Parramatta, on November the 5th. "Is it for Guy Fawkes?" Donalblain wanted to know.

Mrs Augustus McCree (who had been nobody) could easily have made a fourth when the three goddesses stood up for judgement on Mount Ida. Paris would certainly have awarded her the apple, for she had less flesh than Juno, less intellectual acidity, less string in her limbs than Minerva (who was never in the running, for she was not his sort, anyway), and her supple figure, her patrician yet delicious face, with its short upper-lip, its cherry-red, bee-stung lower lip, its desolating cheek-bones, which seemed to have known such sorrow, and which quite contradicted the Mona Lisa-like ambiguity of the inviting eyes (so full of sly caresses), certainly outvied the beauty of any known and authentic portrait of Venus herself.

Yes, Peronel McCree was even more beautiful than Botticelli's shell-borne migrant, or Titian's roaring girl, or Giorgione's almost perfect sleeping "Queen of Love".

A bloom of ineffable youth far excelling theirs veiling the rose of her cheek, a luminous quality in her milk-white skin causing it to glow as if seen through an alabaster lamp, her rich fan of most curious hair flaming round her small, proudly poised head like a torch, Peronel was altogether lovely.

This young Mrs Augustus McCree had for a Guardian Angel a somewhat battered Custodian of great ability but debatable piety, really rather a Trollop (if female) or Gamin (if male), if the truth must be confessed, who was capable of leading her in any mischief.

"Guardian Angels are bound to vary in merit just as ordinary people do," Peronel had assured herself on first realizing this charming creature's limitations, "but who am I to expect to have allotted to me the most efficient Angel in High Heaven? I must make do with the one appointed to me."

And did he (or she?) lead her a dance?

Or she lead him (or her?) a dance?

It was difficult to say.

As for the indeterminate sex of such a heavenly visitant, Peronel called her Guardian Angel "he", it sounded more dashing.

Mrs Augustus had the habit of standing with wide-open eyes fixed on some spot just beyond the orbit of vision.

With the crested envelope in her hand, so she stood on this sunny morning, her white-spotted muslin wrapper (resented by every woman in the house) clouded by a hundred goffered frills, green bows decking it from neck to instep. Wide bows, these, accentuating at five-inch intervals the titillating undulations of her sweetly inflated body.

The question, of course, was—what should she wear?

About this everyone was most helpful, though "a drawback, really", as Juliet said, there was absolutely no money to be spent—not a penny.

"If you unpick Juliet's bridesmaid's dress, the cream nun's veiling she wore at dear Aminta Wirraway's wedding, and eke it out with an extra yard or two of red plush, you might contrive a most striking toilette at the cost of a dozen eggs, which I will give you dear," Mrs McCree offered kindly.

"I think the curtains off Grandmama's Fourposter would make a unique and magical dress! They are watered silk, of such a beautiful shade of maroon, almost a magenta, really—though one likes to forget about the blood, for I think Magenta comes from the colour of the earth after that battle was fought," Juliet interposed. "But you may have my dress if you like, Mama. I can easily re-sew it, without the plush, for my confirmation next year."

Speculation often glinted in Juliet's eyes when she looked at her radiant Mama. Like the rest of the household she did not quite trust her, though to do her enterprising Guardian Angel justice, the young widow's conduct for the first six months of her widowhood had been exemplary, impeccable; remote, certainly, but as far as the watching women who surrounded her were aware, blameless.

An absence of privacy is the chief drawback of family life.

Remarking on the shifts that the reader of a love-letter may be put to, even Boccaccio has commented on this disadvantage. The unblinking limelight of affection was a sore trial to Peronel and her Guardian Angel. Both, therefore, were delighted when at breakfast, a week after the acceptance to the Governor's invitation had been dispatched, Mrs McCree announced that her whole family must attend a party of reconciliation planned by her brother, Dr Boisragon (who had been somewhat estranged from her), in Parramatta. On the strength of her own absence she gave all the servants a holiday.

Peronel, protesting the Penelope-like task of unpicking and resewing the nun's veiling, to be her ball-gown, stayed at home.

She waved gaily from the front door as the buckboard, the young draught-horse Ruby between the shafts, lurched off down the long, straight road and disappeared behind the turn by the Church tower, the only twist, the only building, between Mallow's Marsh and the metropolis.

How delighted Peronel was to be alone!

For awhile, merely to be in the sunshine, she wandered about without purpose in the garden, and punished the insolence of Nature by stamping on a daisy. From the arbour of Passion-vines, from the ripening orchard, the field of green wheat, the drilled rows of corn, the innumerable wooden sheds dedicated to the procreation of domestic life, which had sprung up under the ward of Mrs McCree till they surrounded the Vicarage like mushrooms, right to where the blue, entrancing Razorbacks shaved the sky, the stillness was complete.

The hens clucked not, the cows lowed not, the river chuckled not; all was silence, all was sunshine.

Behind the Vicarage no buxom women laughed with the men-servants; indoors no high-piping childish voices argued about this and that. Every window and door in the house stood wide open. "Not even a thief is to be expected." Oppressed a little, Peronel strayed inside.

She bent her steps first to this room, then to another, enjoying as she went some intimate and revealing conversations with her Guardian Angel, with whom she was scarcely acquainted (he was new), and whose wings, she now noticed, were slightly singed; but she had no misgivings, they suited each other, they under-stood one another perfectly.

Both agreed that in this isolated spot, in this barebones of a house, so threadbare, so niggardly with the joys of this life, so lavish in its promises of the next, there was no scope for either of them, no, none at all.

How they laughed together at the absurd picture of Boadicea with her two girls in a chariot on the snuggery wall; at the statue of the Winged Victory in the linoleum covered hall; at the coloured engraving of the Duchess of Devonshire kissing a butcher ("for political reasons", as the text explained); and at all the smug daguerreotypes and washed-out miniatures infesting the drawing-room wall.

The woolwork flowers under the glass dome!

The beaded footstools!

The S-shaped conversation sofa meant for flirtations.

The antimacassars tied on every chair-top on which no bache-lor's pomaded head had ever rested!

"Is this to be my home for the rest of my life?" Peronel demanded, dramatically.

"No, indeed!" answered the Guardian Angel indignantly.

"Am I, Peronel McCree, to go to the Governor's ball in my daughter's cast-off clothes? In a perfectly hideous dress?"

"No! No!" The Guardian Angel was positive. "Indeed you shall not."

"With no money, and just a dozen pullets' eggs to sell, how can I get a better dress?"

To Peronel this question was purely rhetorical. She had then no hope of getting a better; but her Guardian Angel looked sly: evidently he had something up his wing.

Obviously the house offered her no alternative to re-making her daughter's dress. There were no curtains to be taken down, no hidden lengths of silk to be purloined. But it was three o'clock before Peronel, weak with laughter (Oh, her Guardian had a pretty turn of wit), settled herself at the antique sewing machine in the morning-room that was, so easily, the shabbiest room in the house, to pedal vigorously away at a wrought-iron treadle whose activities depended on a rubber band that slipped continually off its wheel. To snip! To tear! To tack! Though she hated such work she had a genius for it. Since she was one of those people who never give less than their best, the *toilette* (at the word she laughed again) began to assume quite a Parisian air. "Certainly," she told her soul-mate, "it dashes, as well as nun's veiling can ever dash."

She was standing draped in loops of the fabric in the room which faced north-west, so sunlight still streamed into it, and the motes still danced in the yellow beams that fell on her, had she known it, with the dramatic effectiveness of the rays in contemporary pictures of Victoria's Coronation, when, looking across to the door, she saw a young man looking in.

He made a low bow, a most distinguished salutation, his black, low-crowned hat—a shovel-hat with its rough nap, not at all like the headgear worn in Parramatta, sweeping far back as his eyes fixed themselves, with intensity, on his boots.

"Of the Great World!" Peronel realized at once.

She nudged her Guardian Angel to let him know she recognized his handiwork, and he hopped through the window, and flew off to settle on the orchard wall; he was no spoil-sport.

Peronel's visitor wore a red coat cut rather short at the waist in front, but having longer skirts at the back. His waistcoat was of red-and-yellow striped cloth, his breeches were white, with straps buckled below the knees, and his mustard yellow gaiters were buttoned over Wellington boots. Or were they *Hessians*? And were "Hessians" boots or were they gaiters?

Peronel was vague.

But she was not at all vague in her perception of her visitor's good looks. He was remarkably handsome. The chin that asserted itself above the white stock showed him to be a man of character; he was no mere dandy.

The young widow looked into his blue eyes and thought she had never seen anything so blue. Her caressing gaze took in his aquiline nose, the tanned skin that made his fair hair almost white by comparison.

Peronel had never in her life seen so glorious a being.

Glancing out of the window she perceived that her Guardian Angel looked smug. As she opened her lips in greeting a shower of pins fell on the carpet, but she inclined her head in stately recognition of his civility.

"I could make no one hear, so I tied up my nag to the veranda-post, and tracked down the whirr of your machine." He smiled. "Are you at home?"

"Not at home!" she answered sadly. "Mrs Augustus McCree is not receiving this afternoon."

"What a bore," the young man remarked, as he entered and took a chair beside the sewing-machine, removing, as he seated himself a froth of flounces. "I was so looking forward to making her acquaintance."

"The whole family have driven into Parramatta."

"I passed them on my way here."

"Oh?"

Peronel again seated herself at the sewing-machine.

"And what were you looking at so intently on that part of the wall where I see nothing?"

"At my Guardian Angel," Peronel returned, stooping to place the rubber band on its wheel.

"Is he having the afternoon off?" There was a note of hope in his voice.

"No. I keep him within call."

"I expect he leads a busy life. What is his name? What is he like?"

"His face is a bit like a swan's—it has that sideways look. He is very fair, a white-winged angel (of the Wyandotte family, I dare say) and he has a magnificent spread of wings—these, unfortunately are a little singed. My last Guardian Angel left in a hurry. I had not a good word to say for him." She bit a thread. "In fairness to others one must be truthful, don't you think, even when writing out a reference for an Archangel?"

"What was the trouble?" The blue eyes met hers.

"Just want of speed on my part. I simply could not keep up with him. However, one hardly realizes the troubles an angel may have."

"Yes?" he prompted.

He was certainly very good-looking.

"He said it was hard in this flat, treeless bit of country to find a decent place to perch. He said he had to hover over the clothes line, for there wasn't a safe bough up to his weight in the orchard, and the wall was too low to give him a good take-off. Yes, poor thing! He had to hover so much that it tired his wings, and in that tired, that fatigued state, he found Heaven too far to fly to on his evenings off, so he took to dropping in on Hell. It was sad, really."

Her vis-à-vis was now holding one end of a flounce while she fed the machine; there was a sociable air of work shared.

"You feel you can trust the present fellah?" He expressed a real anxiety. "Feel you can depend on him at a pinch, and all that?"

History has not vouchsafed a portrait of Paris. Did he have a perfectly proportioned body which was the acme of masculine strength? Was he endowed with an athlete's grace of movement? Did he have a head like Phoebus Apollo? If so, looking at her visitor, Peronel felt she could guess what Paris looked like. And Narcissus, now? There was no authentic portrait of the youth who died for love of his own reflection, but Peronel rather wondered that this self-assured young man could tear himself away from the mirror. Looking at him she had an inkling of what Narcissus might have been like.

It has not been customary for poets to hymn the beauty of the male, a strange inhibition, suggestive of what? Of what, indeed! Few portraits, even those of the heroes of antiquity, are meant to emphasize masculine good looks merely; fewer still portray the wit that may lurk in a wanton blue eye. Exposed in her helpless state to the full appeal of such devastating enchantments Peronel behaved with perfect propriety. Her Guardian Angel would have been disappointed in her.

Her caller, on his part, having felt her eyes caress him, their touch, as they rested with a moth-like lightness on his face seductive as the brush of thistledown, presently went off, bewitched. Pleased with his own sensations, he gave no hint of what he felt, but he booked the first six dances at the coming ball.

"And may I take you in to supper?"

He might.

"And may I drive you home after the dance?"

"Perhaps." She was demure. "I must ask my Guardian Angel about that."

When he had bobbed out of sight behind the pear trees, vanishing as Peronel had watched Dan and Tib vanish, only last week—why! It was only ten days or so back! Three days? How long ago it seemed!—Peronel realized that she did not know his name. But *had he a name*? Had he, in fact, any reality of person? Was he a wraith born of her own imagination? Or had that dismissed Guardian Angel, by way of revenge, sent one of his less reputable friends to lead her astray? He was, she reflected, quite capable of playing her such a trick.

Peronel trembled.

Doubts assailed her.

Temptation followed in the train of her misgivings.

Quite suddenly and with an absolutely firm resolution she decided then and there that nothing—nothing—would induce her to wear the nun's veiling dress at the ball.

What! Be a laughing stock to such people? To such people as *his* friends!

What! See those china-blue eyes rest with amusement on her finery? Her *rustic* finery?

What! Find him cutting *his dances* with her? For shame of being seen with her?

At this last thought Peronel knew she was ready to commit any crime in order to get a dress that would make her the most fashionable, the most alluring siren, in all Parramatta. Yes! She would sin, if necessary! And when her Guardian Angel rejoined her, a little dishevelled, for a wind has risen, a strange cold wind for a summer evening, she told him so.

He did not seem at all surprised. He was most helpful.

"Yes, yes," she murmured, listening to him in great excitement, her head bent close to his tempting mouth. "Yes! I catch your drift! I will finish the nun's veiling as if I meant to wear it, and then—at the very last minute! Yes! Yes! I understand—*As late as possible!* As late as it would be safe to leave it! Oh, what a marvellous idea!"

There was a further whispered suggestion.

Peronel was shocked.

"Oh, Guardy, I couldn't!" she gasped.

But during the coming night she weakened.

"After all," she asked herself, "what harm could come of following one's Guardian Angel's advice?"

Peronel spent most of the night leaning out of her bedroom window and watching the sullied and shrivelled moon slink, sulking, behind banks of cloud, while flocks of curlews flew inland, whistling over the Picton hills. Like the Naxian widow, deliciously disarrayed, her eyes violet-ringed, she watched the sunrise, unaware that she had not slept a wink.

Early in the morning she harnessed Ruby into the sulky and drove herself into Parramatta.

Usually, of late, she had avoided seeing people, but today she stopped to talk to everyone she met, to gossip, to ask questions.

"He is *not* a nincompoop," Dr Phantom remarked on being questioned. "They say he fought at Delhi, and Lucknow."—So the Chemist.

"He was in the Sandbag Battery, in the Crimea," Dr Boisragon was affable for once, when Peronel encountered him in the Chemist's.

"*His name*?" No one rightly knew.

"Well, dear," Mrs Wirraway said, after confessing that she missed Aminta, "he's staying at Government House. He went out riding this morning with that pretty girl, Lady Mary Something-or-other. The Governor's niece. Such a lovely young creature with a complexion of milk and roses. She wore a bottle-green habit, trailing almost to the ground, and a top hat with a flowing veil—yards long, just like the Queen's when she reviews troops. She rode a lively chestnut cob which she managed perfectly."

"I never saw so handsome a pair," Miss Loveday Boisragon exclaimed. "They are perfectly matched."

Such was the tittle-tattle Peronel picked up.

She spent the price of a dozen pullets' eggs on three-quarters of a yard of cheap plush and drove home—disconsolate!

But she was not inconsolable. "*He exists*," she told herself. "Nameless or not, he is a real person—not a myth, as I feared."

She was utterly resolved to take her Guardian Angel's advice: she would wear at the ball the most magnificent dress ever seen in Parramatta—oh! in all New South Wales! Sin? What is sin? It is merely an experiment made in pursuit of happiness. And an experiment may be a success, or may not—who said "The end crowns all"? Ah, who indeed.

On the evening of the ball, which was to commence at nine o'clock, Peronel dressed herself in the nun's veiling and was duly admired by the whole family at Mallow's Marsh Vicarage.

The dress was beautifully sewn. Everyone allowed that.

It was made with a plain bodice in the hour-glass shape then fashionable. The red plush was folded back, a few inches below the waist in the style called "a fisher-girl saque". Below this frills fell to the instep, and *lissé* pleats showed below them. The neck was cut in a modest square, much frilled. The elbow sleeves were also frilled, and finished with red plush bows. Peronel's sole "jewel" was a plaited bracelet of her late husband's hair. She flirted a black satin fan on which was painted a kitten looking out of a top hat, rumoured to be the work of Winterhalter. A white woollen cape, flowing from neck to hem, completed her outfit.

Everyone saw Peronel wearing this dress.

Everyone crowded to the gate to see her drive herself off—a bit early—in the sulky. They watched the young mare, Ruby, trotting gallantly in the middle of the rut-holed road, the light vehicle swinging from side to side. They saw the elegant figure of the lovely Peronel sitting in the centre of the trap in order to crush her frills as little as possible.

But—*they did not notice the basket under the seat.*

But—they did not see the Guardian Angel behaving with complete abandon as he swooped, soared and circled in the sky above his charge.

He was in the highest spirits.

It was a fine night, warm, yet not too warm for dancing. The moon, free of all cloud, beamed down from a starlit vault.

There was no wind.

The mare knew the road and required no supervision. Peronel was at liberty to watch her escort, who always charmed and amused her, and he was in the act of swinging up-sky after a triple somersault when, in the brilliant moonshine, she saw an expression of complete dismay overcloud his face.

They were being followed! This Peronel at once realized.

There was that on her conscience which told her, immediately, what her follower would be like. She had not the slightest doubt that his scarlet garments would be designed to hide a forked tail and that his peaked cap, with its cock's feather, would be widened to conceal a horned head.

Fearfully looking round she found her conjecture to be right. The Foul Fiend himself was hot on her tracks.

"How efficiently his office must be run," she reflected.

For a sinner, even a sinner poised on the brink of committing her first really walloping sin, Peronel had plenty of pluck. Consoling herself with a riddle ("When is a sin not a sin?"—"When it is merely a peccadillo")—she drove calmly on.

Her competent custodian, having called to his aid several friends who were enjoying an evening off, soon had a white-winged bevy circling round her; a cordon of Angels. They kept her persistent pursuer at bay. Though athletic, musical and good, as all their kind must, of necessity, be, these angelic volunteers came, naturally, from the lowest strata of Heaven, they being creatures not quite good enough on the harp, and possessed of voices perhaps a little off-key.

The clop-clop, clup-clup, of old Ruby's hairy heels ringing on the steely road were the only sound to be heard except for the frou-frou of wings and the twitter of a few late, sleepy larks. In that flat, croppy marshland, where not a house or a tree punctuated the miles, the trotting draught-mare assumed gigantic proportions; she looked like an immense chocolate animal, buttered, for the sweat poured down and darkened her quivering flanks. Her mane was tied with red tape into scores of double-backed plaits (Donalblain's labour of love), her hearty tail was also rolled double and tied into a blob with tape. Yet the moon shone down as if nothing out of the way was happening when lovely Peronel in her white cape, a choir of angels swooping round her, a devil lurking in the rear, her light vehicle swaying behind the gigantic mare, romped through the great gates of Government House, Parramatta.

But, why, Oh! why, did she immediately turn off the driveway?

But why, Oh! why, did she tie up the sulky, and dragging behind her the basket she took from under the seat, disappear into a thicket of oleanders?

The angels, naturally, turned their backs.

There was always a difference of opinion at Mallow's Marsh Vicarage as to what time Peronel returned next morning.

Cook Teresa said "Five o'clock", because she was just getting up, and she always rose at five. (She said.) Juliet said "Six" because she always woke up at six. (She said.) The Vicar said "Seven" because he always went across to the Church to conduct a service of prayer and praise at that hour. And he really did. And they all heard, at these stated times, old Ruby's trotting hooves as they rounded the church tower, from which point they would first have been audible.

Peronel herself could not be questioned as she had dropped into bed at once, pulling the sheet over her face. Though everyone trooped in to look at her no one dared to wake her to ask her how she had enjoyed the ball.

The first gust of the coming gale, the first hint of trouble, came from some words let fall by Miss Loveday Boisragon, who, as her brother had a patient to see in Mallow's Marsh village, had driven over with him; she was anxious to congratulate Mrs McCree on her daughter-in-law's brilliant success at last night's ball.

Sitting with the assembled family in the morning-room, she laid her bouquets at their feet.

"They are all saying that Peronel was the most beautiful woman ever to be seen in that ball-room."

"Did she get all her dances?" Her family had been anxious on that score.

"Every dance! Perpetua Thistledew says there was such a crowd round her the whole time that it was hard to see whom she danced with. His Excellency, apparently, took the first three."

Juliet, sitting in the arm-chair by the window, had taken her brother on her knee. While listening with half an ear, she was giving Donalblain a lesson in the multiplication table.

She kissed him first on the lips.

"That is *one*! Twice one is *two*." She kissed him on each cheek. "Twice two is *four*." She kissed him on cheeks, chin, and on the tip of his nose.

Donalblain kissed her on the mouth.

"That is 'Amen'."

"The kiss to end all kisses."

Donalblain had been warned against women. He could not think why. For himself he could see nothing wrong with them.

It was at this point in their play that Juliet heard Miss Loveday, a little bewildered, repeat—"*Red plush*!" She gazed round the circle, "But no one mentioned red plush."

"Mama did have red plush on her dress. Cotton-backed plush, for pullets eggs fetch so little—"

"This week all the eggs are being pickled—" Mrs McCree broke in.

"Oh, I know! But it was such cheap stuff that I helped Mama to lift the nap with a steaming kettle—"

"I am certain that dear Perpetua mentioned no *plush*!"

Miss Boisragon rose to go. Her brother was waiting and must

not be detained; without a word said everyone realized this; and hurried her off.

"I suppose, in that crowd, Perpetua didn't really notice Mama's dress."

The rest of the family agreed with Juliet; they thought no more of the matter. But, that afternoon, while Peronel was still sleeping, Perpetua herself drove over in the Gander's Pond barouche, a coachman and footman on the box.

It appeared that Dr Phantom had also got to see a patient in the village, he had broken his rule. He had brought over a pretty girl, Bathsheba Wirraway, who was so overcome by the adventure that she sat silent the whole of her visit.

"Oh my dears! Never, never has anyone created such a sensation as Peronel created last night! All Parramatta is talking of nothing else! Her beauty! Her radiant happiness! Dr Phantom said it was more infectious than measles. Wherever she went one noticed there was laughter! Her grace! In the Lancers! In the opening Quadrille! The gallopade! There was a round dance—*not* a waltz, of course—but after supper there was a perfect riot, and we danced 'Sir Roger de Coverley'. I thought Lady Mary looked down her nose at that. I hardly dare tell you! We ended up with the de Alberts! 'As if this was a *barrack-room*!' I heard Lady Mary say! Of course, early on, we had done 'The Dashing White Sergeant'. That's all the rage! Peronel danced these dances with such enjoyment that half the men in the room stood round the wall to watch her. And *then*!" Perpetua put down her empty cup, "My dears! Her *dress*!"

The assembled family looked complaisant.

"Dear girl," murmured Mrs McCree, "she made it herself, out of Juliet's bridesmaid's dress, the nun's veiling she wore, dear Bathsheba, at your sister Aminta's wedding!"

"And I helped her raise the nap on the red plush."

"*Nun's veiling? Red plush?*" Perpetua was amazed. "Peronel wore no nun's veiling or red plush."

"You cannot have noticed."

"Notice? Of course I noticed! Peronel's dress was of cream brocade, a most exquisite Italian brocade. I stood quite close to her. I even fingered it."

"Did it have elbow-length sleeves tied with red plush bows?"

"It had no sleeves."

"But it had! We saw her!"

"No, indeed. I was standing quite close to her when His Excellency brought her back to the dais after her third dance with him.

I heard him say, 'I used to believe that a white camellia looked white, dear lady, until I saw one against your snow-white bosom and marble shoulders.' And he pressed even closer to her. Peronel backed away, and said (so sweetly), 'I look better from a distance, Sir.' And she sailed right across the room and His Excellency dashed after her (you know his way, he's a descendant of King Charles the Second), but, *fortunately*, just at that moment one of the *aides* brought up the Mayoress of Doggett's Patch, and Peronel escaped—luckily!"

"But her *dress*!" everyone breathed, astounded.

"Marvellous! Of cream brocade, with a pattern of gold leaves and grapes! Just round her shoulders—which were bare—she wore a circlet of white camellias. Oh, it was exquisite. A full skirt—like those crinolines the Queen wears! Nothing could have been more fashionable. She made every other woman in the room look dowdy. Though Dr Phantom—who danced four dances with her—*did* say that my poor little pink rag looked just as nice on me as her gorgeous raiment did on her! But none of us begrudged Peronel her triumph! It was an honour to the whole sex. I told Dr Phantom we felt like that."

Perpetua chattered on into a silencc as deep as a well.

Mr McCree had been quieter, even, than usual as Perpetua rattled on. Usually he liked the women of his household to sit in dumb adoration round him as he told them about the Hittites or the Jebusites, or elucidated some knotty point, which (he thought) may have been troubling them, in the Apocrypha, then almost a best-seller.

But this afternoon, after listening, as it were, under protest (these women will still be talking), a glint came into his blue eyes, an expression difficult to fathom. It seemed as if he had caught sight of the tail-end of a fabulous monster just whisking round a door. He looked incredulous. He looked horrified. He debated within himself as Nebuchadnezzar may have debated when he saw the writing on the wall.

Presently, with a determined air, he rose, hoisting himself out of his deep arm-chair, and quitted the electrified gathering, which still argued about Peronel's dress.

"*Where could she have got it?*"

Like the Wiltshire farms that lean up against the great house, so narrow a margin separating them from it that, they say, the noise of the threshing-flail is, in the drawing-room, always in the ears, the church had been built up against the Vicarage. A few paved paces, bordered with St Barnabas's Thistles and St John's

Wort, brought Mr McCree into the Vestry. There was in one corner of an inside wall a chest, a sort of bureau, in which were stored the Church vestments, the one extravagance for which the poor Vicar saved up all his pennies. He opened the top drawer. To his astonishment (he had not expected it), the cope he wore at festivals was there. It was a cope of cream brocade patterned with gold grapes and grapeleaves, and it was said to be a length which, rumour elaborated, had once belonged to the Borgias. He had bought it in Italy in his youth. In spite of its origin it was well-behaved; it did not wear out or crumple; but Mr McCree thought, was all as it seemed? Doubts disturbing him, he shook out the gleaming fabric, and freed it reverently of its silver-paper wrappings.

In the bright light that streamed in through the Gothic windows, which faced west, even the Vicar's tired eyes could see the needle-pricks along the edges of the front panels.

Was that a tacking thread?

He decided it must be.

To all appearances, the cope had been unpicked, re-made, and, yet again, unpicked and restored to its original shape.

It was the sun's last rays that were so generously expending themselves in the vestry. The summer evening was dwindling into night. Every blade of grass in the far-stretching landscape that rolled from Mallow's Marsh to the sea on the one hand, and to the distant Picton Hills on the other, had its gold-tipped shadow. The hens had gone to roost. The men had milked the cows and carried the foaming buckets into the dairy. Except in the old Vicar's heart all was peace.

Life, indeed, was slowing its tempo when Dr Phantom, driving in his smart Hyde Park, rattled up from the village and leaping gracefully out, while his new groom held the horses' heads, ran lightly up the flagged path from the front gate, to stand by the French window, looking into the lamp-lit drawing room. It is hard to guess for whom his eyes, with so much love in them, were searching.

Coming towards the Vicarage from the Parramatta road, a horseman, who, for the past half-hour might have been discerned trotting thitherward—one saw for miles in such a low-lying terrain—arriving just after the young doctor, and just as the sun was staging one of the most spectacular sunsets in all its history—had anyone known it—tied his mount to the fence, and ran, with an ardour equalling Dr Phantom's, to take his stand, at the second

French window, peering into the lighted interior. He, too, looked with love-lit eyes at some compelling magnet, not to be identified.

The brocade cope over his trembling arm, Mr McCree had entered a moment or two before the young men took up their stations.

There are, in old Bibles, steel engravings of Sarah standing half in shade, listening, close to the door, while Abraham interviews his angel. So these young men stood gazing in, while Peronel, dressed in her widow's black ("never was under cloud black so fair a star"), entered at the fatal moment when her father-in-law, displaying the brocade cope, was asking Perpetua, "Is this the pattern you noticed on Peronel's dress?"

"Yes!" Astounded, Perpetua rose to her feet, to finger the rich material. "Yes! The gold thread! The mellow parchment-like colour! The damascened pattern of grapes and their leaves! Oh, glorious, glorious! Of course it's the same."

She threw an agonized glance at Peronel.

"I did not mean to be a tell-tale, dear Peronel! The question took me by surprise!"

"Dear Perpetua! Of course you didn't! But, naturally, I meant to explain that I had *borrowed* the cope for the evening—for the honour of the family! How could I possibly have appeared in that brilliant gathering—the elite of Doggett's Patch, Dural, Hornsby Junction, Parramatta, Gander's Pond, and even Little Peeping in the Inlet—Oh, everyone was there! How could I have worn, at such a function, my *daughter's old dress*? One everyone had seen at Aminta's wedding? Everyone would have recognized it—everyone!"

Fairer than Cressida, in her widow's weeds, Peronel looked her loveliest as she spoke. (Though Cressida, possibly, was not expected by an exacting mother-in-law to cover her hair with a widow's cap of white *lissé*.)

Staring in through the two French windows the young men on the veranda had intended to enter, but delight in her beauty held them immobile.

Mrs McCree, in her maroon rep, sitting upright in a high chair, her hair parted and plastered down on each side of her neat head, her hands on her lap, her feet (as directed by the *Young Ladies' Intelligencer* of 1839) laid one across the other at the instep, her usually rosy face white with emotion, could only gasp, "Oh what wickedness! Oh, what wickedness! Oh, what desecration! Oh, what sacrilege! Oh, my dear girl, what possessed you?" A murmur that went on like a bee droning, whatever anyone else might be saying.

Juliet, low in her basket chair, clasped the sleeping Donalblain in her arms. It was not for her to criticize her beautiful mother.

But the Vicar, his voice again stuttering, asked. "D-d-do you mean to say you took this sacred vestment and wore it at a b-b-ball? As a *d-d-dress*!"

"Yes, I did!"

Remembering her triumphs, Peronel smiled.

(But where did that whisper of "Sin!" come from? Certainly not from her Guardian Angel, whom she saw peeping wistfully in through the side window. He had approved her action! He had advised it! Was that still, small voice her awakening conscience? Oh—she *hoped not.*)

It had lately been ruled by the hierarchy which attends to such matters that it was not necessary for the elder members of the McCree family to have Guardian Angels. A little nightly attention from Matthew, Mark, Luke and John, a few minutes on guard duty round their four-poster, as a compliment, merely, was considered all that was necessary for beings so naturally good as Mr and Mrs McCree.

That Peronel should have needed a mentor was an admission of her frailty. The whole household was aware that she had one; no one, therefore, was much surprised at her reference to such a personage when she continued, "I don't admit that I was, personally, to blame in any way. I did it on my Guardian Angel's recommendation."

Looking across at the side window she saw that *cher confrère* nod and smile. He was quite prepared to take the knock himself.

"What!" Mr McCree cried out, warmly. "Do you mean to tell me that such an act of sacrilege was committed on the recommendation of a Heavenly Being? I am appalled! What a scandalous charge! How shocked, how surprised, everyone in Heaven must be to hear you!"

"Indeed, Heaven will not be in the least surprised! If it was considered wrong of me to borrow a Church vestment—why did Heaven *allot me a Low Church Guardian Angel*? Tell me that now!"

Though Mrs McCree here went off into peals of laughter, though the Vicar smiled a slow smile of appreciation at her neat point, Peronel lost her nerve.

Looking her loveliest, she tore off her widow's cap, with its fluttering *lissé* lapels, and threw it on the floor, and crying out in her delicious voice (her eyes full of tears): "Oh, darling! Don't let them bully me!" she flung herself through the open French window into the wide-open, the waiting, the welcoming, arms of one of the young men.

Though the lamps were lit in the room, it is a bit tantalizing that it was too dark on the veranda for the onlookers to see into whose arms she so gracefully, yet so impulsively, rocketed.

Murder!

Dr Phantom, the most eligible bachelor between Mallow's Marsh and Hornsby Junction, did not admire women, he did not really care about children, but, since his manners were perfect, being the product of a kind heart, not of the etiquette book, on seeing Miss Juliet McCree (though, being sixteen, she was a mélange of both his abhorrences) balanced on one knee on the highway, her horse's hoof resting on the other knee, he drew up to ask whether he could be of any use?

"My horse is quite lame! The hairpin buckles every time I get it under the stone in his shoe!" Juliet explained, lifting a glowing face. "How I shall find my way to Mallow's Marsh I can't guess, and dear Grandmama McCree has given me a Charlotte Russe (it has two glasses of Grandpapa's best port in it) to take to the new Rector's wife. Beside, it is St Agnes' day! I have to dress the well."

"Dress the well?"

"In thanksgiving for the *particularly* good drinking water we have at Mallow's Marsh. It's delicious, really. Last year we dressed all six wells, but this year I have just brought some daffodils and tinsel, and a figure of St Agnes, and I shall do the Rectory well, if they let me."

Standing up, Juliet gave Dr Phantom the benefit of her lively regard.

"Oh! You are driving your Tilbury," she exclaimed, enchanted. "I am so glad to have the chance of seeing it without having measles, mumps, whooping-cough, or scarlatina! I found a four-leafed clover as I was leaving Carefree Farm—you know my Grandparents live there since Grandpa retired? His son-in-law, my step-papa, bought it and gave it to him!"

"Oh, yes! I'd heard—so generous a gift!"

"When my horse went lame I was afraid the clover was proving a complete failure as a luck-bringer, but no! I do call it a piece of good fortune to meet you and see your new turnout."

Leading her horse, Juliet walked round the vehicle.

"An osier-cane body! Gold as a guinea! Japanned wood wheels!

Picked out with yellow! Striped like a wasp, really. A hood you can hoist up and down!" She felt its supple texture. "Leather!"

"*Russia* leather!"

"I believe you! And what a picture your new mare is!"

The mare was indeed a wayward beauty.

At one instant she would stand on two elegant legs to look at the blue, distant Razorbacks, and another she would waver and tittup sideways, backwards, forwards, perversely seeing in the hedges or ditches meandering giraffes, elephants, or all that a horse most dislikes. At the same time she flecked gobbets of foam from her churned bit, rolled her treacle-soft eyes till the whites showed red-veined, or pricked her fidgety ears backwards "in the most adorable way" as Juliet pointed out.

Dr Phantom was beginning to wonder whether he had bought the right animal, one which the vendor had promised "could do everything except wait at table". He felt, therefore, a little comforted by Juliet's praise of it. This extreme nervousness might, perhaps, be an endearing trait? He twisted the reins round a hook on the mirror-bright dashboard, while his groom, his "Tiger", wearing a neatly belted green uniform and a cockade in his black top hat, jumped down from his perch hidden behind the hood, and ran to hold the mare's bridle.

Dismounting briskly, standing beside Juliet on the red spongy road, Dr Phantom looked with a minimum of enthusiasm at her unkempt colt, and, having taken a clean duster from the Tilbury, he lifted the debatable hoof with fastidious care, to pronounce that no remedy was possible without the aid of a smith.

"I heard that you had put down the Hyde Park," Juliet said, still lost in admiration, "*that* was smart enough in all conscience, but this positively whistles with splendour!"

Indeed, the slim precision of its craftsmanship evoked memories of an ant's waist, or a spider's web or any other such naturally spindly miracle of nature. It was a superbly attenuated vehicle.

Dr Phantom looked complaisant.

"Yes! My partner, Dr Boisragon—it's hard to imagine him as your uncle—coveted my Hyde Park. And you know what he is?"

"Do I not!"

Dr Phantom looked away from her shining regard.

"I found it more restful to let him have it. I got the coachbuilder in Parramatta to make me this Tilbury, which needs only one horse and a boy instead of two horses and two men. Directly he saw it—if you please—Dr Boisragon asked me to exchange it for the Hyde Park!"

"Now isn't that just like Uncle Peter! He thinks he has a right to get everything he wants! Not only what he *needs*, don't you know?" She raised her eyes again to eyes that immediately withdrew their gaze. "He has never spoken to me since that awful day—I was twelve, then—when he accused me of stealing his Red Roman! He told Mama I am a thief and a liar. He thinks no sin too bad for me to commit. But, quite frankly, Dr Phantom, I know, in reality, very little more about sin than Moses did. And in his knowledge of it (judging by the *paucity* of the Ten Commandments) he does not go very far."

"Don't speak so slightingly of Moses! You shock me."

"I'm praising him, really, for his innocence of heart. Don't you always feel that he has to eke out his experience, rather—there is so much that he leaves unsaid?"

"Absurd child," Dr Phantom said to himself, "she is too thinly clad for this raw spring day! Her grandmama brought that family up on starchy food, hasty-pudding and choke-dog, as Juliet called their 'treats'! Charity child dishes! And as for that flighty, selfish mother of hers—off to Paris with a brand-new husband!" Pity shook his heart! He held out a hand from which he had stripped a pig-skin glove.

"Hop up, child. I'll drop you at Mallow's Marsh."

The saddle was bestowed under the seat. The horse was turned into Farmer Salter's paddock among the grazing cattle.

Dr Phantom climbed into the driving seat beside Juliet; the Tiger, who had been swinging like a bat from the mare's bridle, let go, and, like the wind, off they flew, the boy having flung himself into his perch as they went.

It was a perfect though astringent morning in early Spring.

The sprouting grass, unbrowned by frost, showed through the mirror-like surface of a thousand puddles in which grey ibis fished—for frogs? Every grazing beast had its chirping retinue of wagtails. Whitethorn and Traveller's Joy caressed every sliprail. The wide, almost treeless, emerald plain was greedily devoured by a man-eating sun, ardent as a beast of prey.

High above the gay equipage flew a milk white dove.

Looking up, Dr Phantom remembered to have seen just such another bird, flying in a paradise all its own. When was it? He followed the glinting wings, thinking, "Yes, I was happy, four years ago, when I watched that other white bird! I was standing beside Juliet then, too, in Parramatta High Street. Yes. That was the time! I remember thinking—so I did—that earth is like a pear, that has one perfect moment!" He felt some stirring in his singing heart, he thought again, "Yes! Life brings moments when one feels superbly happy—for no reason that one knows of!"

He saw, laid out like wax flowers in a glass container, the small symbols of an earlier flame; a pink lawn handkerchief, a regurgitated nectarine (a Red Roman), and he recognized a lost illusion without regret.

He and Juliet, bowling along the shining roadway, were both happy; time had candied (as it does) their griefs.

"I wanted to go to Scutari, in the Crimea, to join Florence Nightingale. She was taking thirty-seven nurses out, and would have welcomed another doctor! I may manage to go, yet, though my partner has so far refused to relax the terms of our agreement. He won't give me a year's furlough."

"The war with Russia will soon be over." Juliet attempted consolation.

For some minutes they progressed with a crablike movement along the rutty highway, the mare only sometimes remembering that the earth was her proper element.

"I find," Juliet remarked, after a thoughtful silence, "that a group of people in a particular place has a peculiar reality all its own. Away from that place, parted from each other, such people are different. That is why I dread going back to Mallow's Marsh, where once I was so happy."

"Yes." Dr Phantom glanced at her serious profile. "A Curate in your Grandfather's place—that will be sad to see!"

"Do you remember such a group in your own life?"

Dr Phantom was cautious.

"I remember one day, when I was lying with my brothers under a wattle-tree in flower—I still see the yellow against the blue sky—and, I remember, that we decided all we were going to do when we grew up—that might be vivid because it's a collective memory—one they remember as well as I do?"

"Life is made up of a succession of such groups."

"Life is peculiar. Look at the way some people keep on coming into one's life."

He stooped to look under Juliet's hat brim, but her eyes evaded his.

"Yes, indeed!" She, however, heartily agreed. "Parties now! People who have never met before—how their destinies get entangled!"

A light spring cart drawn by a handsome dray-horse had been lumbering and jolting towards them for the past quarter of an hour.

"Why!" Juliet, watching it, exclaimed, "I do believe that is the Rectory cart with old Ruby in the shafts, and that Man Thomas is driving it! We left it for the Curate's use!"

To her delight it proved to be none other.

Since in that neighbourhood no one dreamt of passing without exchanging the time of day (a lost phrase, that), the Tilbury drew up by the side of the road, and got as near to stopping as the mare allowed. Man Thomas very easily chirruped old Ruby into immobility. He and the dray and the mare looked just the same, Juliet radiantly noted. Brass earrings as big as bracelets gleamed through the frizzy hair of Man Thomas's unshorn locks. His beard was Byzantine, certainly, its waves stiff and deep as the furrows of a Babylonian King's. A Mithridates returning from a lion hunt—some such carved frieze his presence evoked.

And now he came charged with news.

He knew his manners. He asked, first after Juliet's grandparents, her brother, Cook Teresa, and every farm hand and animal at Carefree Farm, with a persevering fidelity. But his hearers, all the same, sensed the bringer of tidings.

"Sims like," Man Thomas said at last, "Sims like as Curate has murdered his wife."

"What!"

"Sims like."

"Whatever makes you say such a thing?"

"Disappeared, she has."

"Oh, come!" Dr Phantom was amused. Juliet's delight at meeting such a bizarre friend had touched him, still—

"She's not in Church, she's not in Rectory, she's not in Mallow's Marsh—I'd swear to that."

"When was she last seen?"

"Saw her myself, I did, the day Curate arrived. I passed her, walking on the road to Fisher's Ghost Crick."

Man Thomas fanned himself with his hat. "English, she were."

"How could you guess that?"

"Too tall, flat chest, big feet, nose like Mr Nosey Parker's, and talking through it like a blackbird, she were. I knows an Englishwoman when I sees one."

"Has no one seen her since?"

"First or last. Granny Peachy says she's in the Ottoman. I holds she's in the well. Churchwarden, he asked the Curate right out, 'Where is your wife?' And the Curate laughed. Laughing all the time, that young gentleman is! But I be going for to fetch the police."

"Are you, and Granny Peachy and the Churchwarden the only people who suspect the Curate of this crime?"

"Mid not have been a crime—"

"Oh?"

"Mid have been a necessity, like."

Dr Phantom knew dismay. Could he leave Juliet at the scene of so recent a murder? Yet, his patient, he with the ruined stomach—it was the usual complaint hereabouts—beyond Fisher's Ghost Creek, he could not be neglected.

"Yes," Man Thomas continued with relish, "whole of Mallow's Marsh knows as he murdered her. If not—where is she? That's what we asks! We've looked under the culverts and bridges, in the ponds and cricks, we've combed every nook! We done it thorough. And all the time, there was His Highness, a-peeping at us from every window in turn—doubling up with laughing. All he does is laugh!"

Man Thomas said "Hup" to Ruby, who, waking out of a doze, broke into a wilful trot that caused the cart to sway from side to side, and soon carried Man Thomas on his way to the Police Station in Parramatta.

"Grandpapa and Grandmama both like the Curate. Even Grandpapa (a Cambridge man, as you know), said, 'For an Oxford man he is an exceptionally harmless type.'" Juliet re-tied the ribbons of her hat. "Would Grandmama have sent me to take a Charlotte Russe to a man capable of murder? *She* would have seen at once if he had been at all eccentric!"

Dr Phantom guided the dancing mare over a bad bit of road.

"Personally I was surprised that she should have sent you so far on such an errand—"

"She meant to console me."

"Console you?"

"Mama had sent me a present from Paris."

"Then why 'console'?"

Juliet hid her face below her brim.

"She sent me a doll."

Dr Phantom burst out laughing.

"Grandmama says she must have gone out shopping with some young admirer, and so might have wanted to appear very young! So she sent me a doll, and Donalblain," her voice faltered, "a set of corals."

Dr Phantom stopped laughing.

"Grandmama immediately went off to the dairy and made a Charlotte Russe—a most expensive one! As she stirred and whipped and poured in one valuable ingredient after another, she kept saying, most indignantly, 'A child? Juliet with a doll? Oh, yes, my fine high madam! I'll teach you what kind of child your daughter is!' Dear Grandmama very seldom loses her temper, but when she does—Oh! She's dangerous!"

"Dangerous?"

"She acts!"

"I see," Dr Phantom remained thoughtful.

Mrs McCree was angry with her daughter-in-law, not for marrying again—apparently she had approved of the marriage—but for sending Juliet a doll—well! That was understandable! But how did the pudding sent to the Curate's wife provide an answer to that?

He had a lively tussle with the mare, who wanted to leap a three-rail fence—on either side of the road, she did not mind which—then he observed, "If I do not set you down at Mallow's Marsh Vicarage, I may be spoiling some plan of your grandmother's. She is a woman who knows what she is doing. I'll drop you at the gate, and pick you up again on my way home."

"Frankly," Juliet laughed, "I don't believe a word of Man Thomas's story."

Half an hour later Juliet waved goodbye to Dr Phantom from the Rectory gate, and opening it, walked up the long-familiar path.

"There is the polyanthus—in full flower. There are the clumps of clove pinks. But how bare the windows look. No curtains. And there's no mat at the front door."

She knocked.

Steps sounded on the bare boards upstairs. It seemed that someone slid down the banisters, then the door was opened, and the "new Curate" (now Rector) stood before her.

He was incredibly fair. His hair was almost flax-white, his complexion pale as milk; his eyes however, were not an albino's, but as blue as cornflowers.

"My Grandmama, Mrs McCree, has sent you a Charlotte Russe—for your wife.

He appeared to be convulsed with mirth.

"Impossible!" he laughed, "Mrs McCree *knows*."

Absurdly amused, he led his visitor into the morning-room, which overlooked the orchard wall, and the well in its patch of long grass shaded by a wattle bush, now in flower. Far off the Picton Hills gnawed at the sky.

There is one thing in this deceitful world that can never be hidden; that is poverty. Even the usual palliatives, soap and water—and sunshine—though they may adorn it, cannot conceal poverty. The Rectory had never looked opulent. It now shrieked of indigence. As Juliet had already noticed, there were no curtains to the windows, no carpets—one chair; the ottoman, she was amused to see, stood by the window. The wallpaper showed faded patches where the two prints, "The Fair Trespassers", had hung.

Her host sat on the famous ottoman which may or may not have hidden a corpse.

Juliet handed over the pudding in its basin; she sat on the one chair, facing him, as he kept ejaculating, "Impossible—a pudding for my wife! *She knows*!" He stopped suddenly. "How old are you?"

"Sixteen."

"Heartfree?"

"That is one of the questions I never answer."

Dazed, but hungry, the Curate brought spoons and plates, and together they embarked amicably on the Charlotte Russe, which was delicious, as both agreed, Juliet's protest—"But, surely your wife should have it?"—only provoking further amusement.

Looking round her, Juliet said, in her usual direct fashion, "An empty house is sad, isn't it? Don't you find it depressing?

She had forgotten about the missing wife.

"Did your Grandmama tell you to say that?"

Juliet looked astonished.

"No. Why should she?"

"Did she tell you to mention the patter of little feet?"

The young man began laughing again.

"No. Why ever should she?"

"Can you tell me the name of any character in history who died of laughter?"

"St Hilarious?"

"Call me Hillary."

"My name is Juliet."

He left the obvious unsaid.

"Tell me," he asked, "have you heard that I am accused of murdering my wife?"

"Oh, yes," Juliet responded, cheerfully.

"Do you belong to the school which says I killed her with a cleaver and hid her in the ottoman? Or to the school that says I threw her down the well?"

"If you are the bloodthirsty type, delighting in slaughter for its own sake, you slew her with an axe, and hid her in the ottoman. If you are one of those tender-hearted people who cannot bear to see others suffer—you threw her down the well." Juliet gave him a wide smile. "I do not know you well enough to guess your type."

"Let me know when you make up your mind."

"Yes. I suppose you know that Man Thomas has gone for the Police?"

"Man Thomas? Oh. You mean Ahmen Hotep? Or Thutmos the Tenth? That one?"

Juliet did not often laugh, but a chirrup escaped her.

"He is such a nice man, really."

"So are they all nice men, all Egyptian assassins."

"Well. You have been warned." Juliet rose. "I shall go and decorate the well. I have always dressed the well on St Agnes' day. I have brought a saint—such a pet—and some paper roses—"

They went out together.

That was how it happened that Dr Boisragon, driving past in the recently bought Hyde Park, saw his niece and, as he considered, a murderer, putting a wreath of roses on the well-head; the well in which he knew the murdered wife to lie; for Granny Peachy had just told him the whole dreadful tale; and the Churchwarden had affirmed it.

"Ho! Ha!"

Dr Boisragon drove in through the stable gate, and leaving his vehicle, stood watching the young people.

By this time the sun was declining westwards, and long level rays caught Juliet's red hair, making it radiant. They shone gaily through the paper roses with which the well, rope and bucket were now garlanded. The light danced through the flowering wattle. Behind her, the Curate, listening to her chatter as he dangled a foot over the well, was so much absorbed that he did not hear the clink and clatter of the Hyde Park.

"Yes, I quite agree," Juliet was saying with her usual complete unselfconsciousness, "as you remark, a Curate *is*, perhaps, the most vulnerable form of bachelor. Other men can entrench themselves behind a facade of whiskers, brandy and rank cigars, and feel reasonably safe. But, a Curate—"

Looking up, Juliet saw her Uncle.

He had been to a funeral. His handsome figure was encased in black, crêpe banded his top hat and was looped in a "weeper" round his right arm. His gloves were black; his cane, ebony. His stern, classical face was set in its usual lines of regret for the sins of others. How familiar Juliet felt with that air of reprobation for erring humanity!

"Once again, you abandoned girl, it is my duty to reprove you! At twelve you were proved to be a thief and a liar. That, I understood, on reflection, to be the outcome of greed! You were a *glutton*—theft and lying only pandered to that vice! I find you now satisfying even baser appetites."

"I only took my fair share, Uncle Peter," Juliet said, in a small, nervous voice.

"*Your fair share!* What! You can stand there and admit your trespass—and *justify yourself*!"

Dr Boisragon walked close enough to tower above the shrinking Juliet, who was entirely bewildered, while the Curate, too, was too much astonished to move.

"You can stand there beside your paramour—that murderer—whose poor wife's body is lying, I hear, drowned in that well, which—with what profane intention I cannot guess at—you have actually decorated with the roses and raptures of vice—oh, you Jezebel! Do you mean to tell me that you had only taken '*your fair share*'—your fair share—*of what?*"

"Of Grandmama's pudding," Juliet answered, trembling. Yet she was mystified—whatever had she done this time?

"Of Grandmama's pudding! It is the first time I have heard such an expression applied to such a sin—Eve's apple—yes! But, Grandmama's pudding! You wicked girl—is that meant for wit?"

Dr Boisragon really did seem quite astounded.

It was at this opportune moment that the Police, led triumphantly by Man Thomas, joined the group.

The two mounted policemen, to show their zeal, jumped the hedge. Magnificently uniformed, with superb mounts, they made a dashing entrance, and leaping from their foam-flecked horses, they stood on either side of the Curate, whom Man Thomas, elated at being "in time", pointed out to them as "the murderer".

The Churchwardens, who had driven over with Dr Boisragon, and had, with Granny Peachy, been lurking in the safety of the stables, now took their places round the well, while all the inhabitants of Mallow's Marsh (six men, three women and twelve children) peered over the orchard wall.

The scene was set.

The sergeant took out his note-book and licked his pencil.

"From hinformation laid," he began, "I 'ave to hinform you as you are under suspicion of 'aving murdered your wife. Name?"

"Hilarious."

Juliet gave her small chirrup.

It affronted everyone more than words can say.

"—Orlando Furioso—"

Again that irrepressible chirp of laughter from Juliet.

The Police were shocked. Even in their unimaginative minds, "the girl", as they termed Juliet, was assigned to the position of "the Murderer's paramour".

"Yes?" The Sergeant again licked his pencil point.

He scorned to ask how Furioso was spelt.

"Surname?"

The Curate stopped laughing and said, soberly, "As a matter of fact my name is Plumtree, sometime Fellow of Oriel College, Oxford, and Rector designate of this parish. I am the Bishop's nephew."

Visibly shaken, the Sergeant stuttered, "Name of late wife—Sir—if you please?"

"I have not got a wife."

" 'Oo is the murdered lady?"

"There is no murdered lady. I cannot think how this absurd story started. Unless one of the maids at Carefree Farm, where I dined with Mrs McCree a week ago, may have overheard, and misunderstood, a conversation I had with Mrs McCree."

"Better ask Man Thomas."

Man Thomas in his simple way was a seeker after truth.

He stroked his glossy crenellated beard and pondered.

"Yes, yes," he murmured, "it might be so. Yes. It were Abigail at Carefree Farm as told me new Curate had a wife, like, so she did, so she did! And when I sees that Englishwoman in the lane, I thinks, 'that's Curate's wife'—so I did. And when no one seed the lady to Rectory—well! I draws my own conclusions, like, so I does! Well—'twer natural to think as Curate had put her away—now, wasn't it? And everyone agrees to it. Churchwarden and Granny Peachy—" Man Thomas gave a great guffaw of laughter, "I sees the joke! I sees the joke!" He slapped his tough thighs and laughed till the tears made watercourses down the furrows and channels of his beard, and the Curate, glad to have found a soul mate, laughed, too, while Juliet gave her small chirrups and spurts of gaiety, as sweet to hear as a thrush's song.

At first the Mounted Policemen did not see the fun, but the Rectory cellar being better stocked than the larder, and, Granny Peachy being an adept drawer of penny ale, they soon relaxed over brimming flagons in the kitchen, they, and every man in

Mallow's Marsh, and it was a convivial party that broke up over an hour later.

Dr Boisragon, who made no apology to Juliet, drove away alone in his Hyde Park, which somehow looked less magnificent under new ownership, for the horses were not well groomed, and the curtains not pressed, and the wheels unwashed, and Dr Boisragon, upright and unsmiling, caused no hearts to beat faster.

While unbuttoned mirth rang out from the kitchen, Juliet strolled through the orchard with the Curate.

The almond blossom, always the first to flower, was punctual; the next trees to flower in a normal year would be the damsons; they were punctual; every bough appeared to be crystallized.

One apple was out. Six quinces were early. Against all precedent the cherries, usually the last to flower and first to fruit, were ineffably a month too soon.

Though the sun was sinking, and reasonable larks might have felt at liberty to drop down to the chirping tussocks below, they were pouring their full hearts out still, in unpremeditated bliss.

In a stuffy study in England a scientist, about this time, was penning the words "*Propinquity acts as a liberating stimulus to instinct*". Two young people in the orchard (had they known it) were proving the truth of this axiom. Juliet, growing aware of her Grandmother's outrageous matchmaking (for the pudding was to introduce the Curate to his wife to be), forgave her. Orlando, who had come from a college which managed to exist without women, who had found Mallow's Marsh an anti-climax to his dreams of preferment, grew aware of the meaning of the words of Martin Tupper, the great Oxford poet, about "twin-souls" and the "ecstasy of Being".

It would be premature to say that the young people left the orchard "engaged". But by the time the first constellation took up its position north of the Razorbacks (quite unaware that it was a well-known star, and had been much "written up"), they were certainly in love.

Dr Phantom, calling for Juliet so late that every star was in its appointed place, and an unintelligible moon rode in the zenith, looked once at Juliet's revealing face, and knew the answer to a question he would never put.

It was, however, eleven months later that Mrs McCree wrote the letter that had been simmering in her heart ever since Peronel had sent her children those infantile toys. To write it, she put on her best dress, a lavender silk affair, bustled like Gibraltar and pleated to the limits of perplexity. With a fresh quill pen she wrote, triumphantly.

"My darling Peronel,

By the time you get this, *you will be a grandmother*! Dear little Juliet keeps very well, and Orlando makes a devoted husband. The Bishop has promised to christen the little stranger—I know you will rejoice—" and so on and so such!

No letter had ever given a prospective great-grandmother greater joy to write, and Mrs McCree drove into Parramatta in her new basket-work Victoria and posted the letter herself. It was a delicious revenge!

The Love-nest; or, Which Sin Is That?

THE TIDE OF LIFE flowed very briskly in those regions, and there was a great deal of conjecture about a new dwelling at Little Peeping in the Inlet, a cove until now uninhabited, and used merely by such small ships as put in to fill water-casks, or land merchandise on the beaches that flanked the river mouth. For the river here joined the sea.

It must be remembered that in Parramatta and its sparsely populated neighbouring villages at this period (the Crimean War was not yet over) there prevailed a general idea that the good were poor, and the bad, rich, and that money, in short, was not to be accumulated in any great quantities except by the enjoyment of the Devil's own luck or cunning, and by nefarious means.

The very reasonable sum represented by an income of two hundred pounds a year was regarded in such circles as being quite sufficiently "warm" (enough) for the godly, or even the demi-godly.

The appearance, therefore, of violent and ebullient prosperity expressed by the almost audible chink (reported to have been heard by passers-by) of spondulix, Golden Joeys, Happy Dicks, Yellow Boys, or guineas, or any other term by which money was then designated (a sovereign in particular being considered hardly "nice" enough for open reference), obviously tainted the lustre which shone like an aura round the cottage, reared up practically under cover of night, above the estuary of the river, a couple of miles below Doggett's Patch.

In local eyes its flamboyant well-being immediately invested it with the effluvia of sin; whether mortal or venial sin remained to be proved.

The radiant dwelling faced that estuary by means of which (of course clandestinely) contact might be made with the Pacific Ocean (here hardly wide enough, Miss Loveday Boisragon felt, for all that so palpably "went on" there); and the fact that the minute building with its singing canaries, its muslin curtains waving like flags through every opened window, was so sweet, so gay, so airy that it might have been constructed of sugar-cane instead of cedar, further conduced to its recognition as being a love-nest, a place to be personally and religiously avoided (but nevertheless watched and gossiped about) by all decent Christians.

It was Victoria McMurthie, now seventeen, who first reported to her family the surprising existence of this debatable dwelling.

Victoria's father, Captain James McMurthie, was a shipping magnate poor enough to be considered virtuous. He owned various little ships of sixty tons and under, which sailed to Mauritius for sugar and cocoa, to Van Diemen's Land for apples and potatoes, and to "the Islands", to garner in whatever they might yield; a certain reserve was shown in the enumeration of such cargoes.

The *Rose*, a brig of forty tons, carried the London trade, and since she was not passed by the Port authorities as being perfectly seaworthy, Captain McMurthie usually sailed her himself. She was, at the moment, a month overdue from Rio de Janeiro.

These vessels had all been named by the McMurthie family in full conclave as they sat round the red-clothed, lamp-lit table in their two-storied wooden house some way out of Parramatta.

The brig *Victoria and Alberteena* was named as a tribute to the two eldest daughters. The *Edward and Elias* was a tribute to the two eldest sons. The *Henry and Alice* in this domestic navy represented the youngest members in a family of sixteen; all hungry.

The *Fruitful Hannah* celebrated the virtues of an exemplary wife, of whom the Captain was very fond (she had been baptised "Téméraire"); the ketch *Dainty Jane* he had himself singled out for honour; no member of the McMurthie family was called Jane.

The daily lives of these nautical children were so wrapped up in the comings and goings, the crews and cargoes of their beloved vessels, that they felt every change of weather even more acutely than the indefatigable man and girl, labelled "wet" and "dry", who popped in and out of the Swiss Chalet set above the dining-room mantelpiece.

Bunches of seaweed, swelling or wrinkled furbelows, dried-up scraps of arrow muzlets or dahlia wartlets, nailed to the veranda posts, reflected the emotions of these sea-changed young people as faithfully as they, in their turn, were influenced by the humidity or lack of it in the atmosphere; such things were kept for their prophetic qualities.

Should a cow lie down, or a swallow fly high, or a spider spin a web before noonday, such apparently trivial happenings would be reported as news; a black nor'-easter would keep Victoria awake all night; a southerly buster would prevent her from eating a bite of breakfast; a fair wind would send the whole McMurthie tribe scattering like gulls to watch the Heads (having begged lifts into Sydney) or inspire them to organize riding-parties to some vantage-point along the coast.

It was on one such excursion that Victoria had observed the "Love Nest", which was not, of course, supposed to be known to her by so opprobrious a title; yet she had heard the name applied to it.

She and Miss Loveday Boisragon returned to this same view-point one afternoon towards the end of winter. Having followed the rutty track that dropped down to the sea-shore from Doggett's Patch (they were staying at The Devil's Tail), they reined-in their horses on a convenient headland just facing the cottage, but on the far side of the river, and stopped to discuss it.

It was a Monday.

That most revealing of all betrayals, the washing, on which a curious coterie from Doggett's Patch, Hornsby Junction, and even Dural had kept an hebdomadal watch for months past, was waving in the sea-wind that, every afternoon, blew inland.

It was by this time well known that, as a rule, every Monday two sheets would wanton in the breeze for some three weeks on end; that every so often four sheets would make a snowy and irregular appearance. Very strangely, everyone thought, no saveloy-like bolsters filled with wind would flounce about on the clothes line, as they might have been observed to do in every other household. Even more strangely, during those months in which a watch had been kept, sometimes as many as twenty sheets—sometimes even thirty—would flutter in the Love Nest wash.

"As for night-shirts," Miss Loveday had reported to her sisters, "the effect of scores of them all prancing about in mid-air was unnerving, quite. All Mallow's Marsh, Doggett's Patch, Hornsby Junction—even Parramatta itself—could hardly have produced so many."

Loveday had several times been down to peep at the cottage and today, talking to Victoria, she again expressed wonder.

"As a revelation of the number of occupants of the cottage the number of sheets, naturally, should be perfectly revealing."

She waved a horse-tail switch which kept the flies off—sometimes.

"But I find the whole affair baffling! We can only go by averages. As far as I can make out, one person lives there. Sometimes a second person stays a few nights—under a week—and every two or three months the permanent resident entertains a house-party which would tax the accommodation of St James' Palace, or even Government House, Parramatta!"

"But so many people change only one sheet every week, on each bed," Victoria protested. "The lower sheet is put to the wash, the old upper sheet takes its place, and a clean sheet is put on top of it? Don't you agree?"

"You completely amaze me!" Miss Boisragon spoke with energy.

The astonishment in her charming voice was reflected in the grey regard which dwelt with penetration on the glowing, youthful face beside her. Victoria's eyes, sloe-black, were so shallow as to be without light; even her brothers admitted a resemblance to boot-buttons. Devoid of candour, they told one nothing of her thoughts. Her mouth, however, extremely sensitive, having one corner curled up more than the other, was always illuminating; it gave her away.

"You know so much! Yet your knowledge has not contaminated your mind. Someone in the Apocrypha says, 'The knowledge of wickedness is not wisdom.' Yet there seems to be, my dear child, nothing you do not know. What freedom your generation is allowed!"

Miss Boisragon sighed.

"Was that want of freedom your tragedy, dear Aunt Loveday?"

"Indeed, yes! Yet times have so changed that I can speak of it without a blush—and to a girl of seventeen!"

"Tell me."

"One Monday, long, long ago, I was so unmaidenly, and, as they thought, so depraved, as to read our family washing-list. I was sixteen, admittedly an 'awkward' age. My parents, my dear father in particular, could not bring themselves to forgive me."

"Oh, how terrible!"

"Yes! They could not forgive a trespass so degrading. It was the reason, too, that I never married."

"Oh, surely not!"

"Indeed, yes! The story got about. So lascivious a curiosity was considered to be 'fast'. The fastidious gentleman who had been paying his addresses to me would not, could not, trust me."

"You have lived it down?"

"Yes. I think I have. But I have never forgotten *him.* I did so adore him. I can never dip into a blue eye without anguish."

Sadly the pair looked across the swirling waters, now sliding backward into the sea over rocks and sandbanks; the tide was on the ebb. It was a neap tide.

It was now at that mysterious hour of the late afternoon when the shadows, darkly crepuscular, appear to be longer than normal; when a rosy light brightens the tree-tops, emphasizing the red veins in each pendant eucalyptus leaf, outlining each hissing wavelet—so fatigued after a long day's work—with a warm crease behind each breaking crest.

The gulls were wheeling far out to sea. The clouds bunched round the declining sun were apricot. Stretching beyond the estuary to a limitless horizon, the ocean, heavy, inert, as if stirred by every seventh wave, alone was placid in the Greek sense, when the word means depth as well as quietude. Its colour was so ambiguous as to call to mind the phrases Amaranthine purple, Tyrian blue, or other such designations that admit of no exactitude.

There was a breeze; but it was fitful, it allowed for moments of inanition as pregnant as the silence of lovers.

"A cherry-tree in flower is lovely," Victoria ventured, her soul visible in her tremulous mouth, "a pear-tree, too, in moonlight! How bewitching! A chain of hills—how adorable!"

She paused, looking with an absent eye at what might have been a seagull on the blue slowly-heaving ocean. A bird? Yet it seemed not to be!

"Yes? Dear child? You were saying?"

"But a ship! A ship! Aunt Loveday! How can I explain to you all that a ship means to me? A swan? A ship is lovelier!"

"Yes. Man has invented nothing. He improves. He copies. He sees a swallow's nest and builds a palace. He sees a swan, as you say, and creates a ship."

Victoria re-established a shining top-hat, heavily veiled on her thatch of vital, short black hair.

"Yes. Man does copy Nature. He does improve on Nature. His ship makes a swan look blowsy. Oh! But do turn quite round!"

Miss Boisragon turned, horse and all.

As they looked seaward their heads were neatly inserted by their drooping mounts amongst the tops of blackened saplings and she-oaks. Three years back the bush had been burnt out and the few standing tree-trunks and even the rocks wore widow's weeds. Like figures on a Japanese screen, aunt and niece watched a small vessel which, hitherto unnoticed, except perhaps unconsciously, as being, perhaps a ship, perhaps a bird, had rounded the blue bay's furthermost island.

"It blows up the estuary like a lily before the wind."

"How utterly I agree!" Miss Boisragon was herself excited. "He, dear, whom I shocked so much—he was a sailor!"

A girl came out of the cottage, a girl whose possible good looks were not to be deciphered, quite, at such a distance. She stood waiting.

"A ship sailing into an arm of the sea, into a purple inlet where a gay, gay cottage, its veranda-posts made of Edinburgh Rock—"

"No! No! Of barley-sugar! No! Of something rarer—say of Marzipan!"

"Of Marzipan, then—where a girl in a pink dress is waiting for her sailor lover! Oh, what could be more romantic!"

"Romantic? Yes! I agree. But I cannot profess to guess why local opinion so insists on the *riches* of the inmates of that charming sugar-plum!"

"Man Thomas and Ike Peachy came down from Carefree Farm to have a 'look-see' as they put it, and they told me with awe that they saw a bunch of bananas *as large as a chicken-coop* hanging up on the veranda to ripen! There's riches!"

"Pink, somehow," the tone was disparaging, "is such a plebeian colour."

"A bit. It appeals to the masculine taste too brazenly."

Was the ship a sloop? A brig? A ketch? A cutter?

It finally revealed itself as being a sloop, with a single mast, a fixed bowsprit, and a jib-stay—a stay running from the masthead to the bowsprit-head. She flew towards them, steering her proper course under easy sail.

The sun had dropped lower, to shoot almost vertical rays of light through the clear water. The breeze had freshened.

"She is well handled for so light an air of wind."

Victoria spoke sagaciously. She knew a great deal about ships, having been permitted to sail her own *Victoria and Alberteena* (in which her sister, being younger, was hardly allowed to share) from Sydney to Newcastle and back.

"She's a sloop, possibly a Naval tender of some sort," Victoria decided. "Somewhere, out of sight, there may be a larger vessel."

Still watching, she expressed dismay.

"They cannot be so foolish as to anchor just there, while the tide is running out, and the sand, as they must know, shifts about in the channels. The wind is freshening, too, and I think it is working up for half a gale. We may even be in for a black nor'-easter."

But, riding with a steep shore on her larboard bow, a rock and shoal extending on both hands, the foolhardy sloop did drop anchor, with a rattle and splash, into a few fathoms of water, which, as Victoria well knew, would momentarily lessen.

"That boat will be high and dry in half an hour."

The name *Amiable Nelly* was now to be made out on her stern, she had swung-to almost below their eyrie.

"Hail them and tell them so."

"They would not hear! How queer the men look, foreshortened and hopping about like Jacks-in-a-box."

"Sailors use their arms and their lungs more than their legs, don't you see, so in any case they would have chests a bit too big for them, you might say, but of course they stand firmly—don't, as people say they do, roll in their gait. Do you notice? They stump about. They spring about! They are so lively in movement, aren't they?"

"How romantic the sound of masculine voices carrying across the water! Oh, I do think we are enjoying our afternoon, don't you?"

Victoria listened, a pleased smile widening her delicious mouth. "They are singing 'Abel Brown'! We are too far off to hear the words, but I recognize the tune."

"Oh Victoria! That shocking chanty! Why, it's never been printed! It could *never* be!"

"Tra-la-la, Aunt Prunes and Prisms! Nowadays girls are not prudes!"

"It's the little man who seems to be ordering everyone about. He is very brisk."

"They are putting some bundles into the dinghy. The two young men in coconut dungarees are evidently going ashore."

Looking at the two well set-up young men, so handsome, so lissom, as, with an older man, they embarked in the dinghy, Victoria had a moment of exasperation.

"It's really not fair that men, who have everything—*everything*—who are so clever and brave and wonderful generally, should have such good looks as well! Consider their splendid physique! Their muscles! Observe, dear Aunt Loveday, the backs of their necks, even!"

"Beautiful!" Miss Loveday unbent. "It's the splendour of perfect health and strength."

Victoria made a decision.

"We must prevent such superb beings from adorning a ship that's high and dry on the rocks! Will you come down to the beach with me?"

Their horses slipped and slithered down the boulder-strewn, pebbly, almost precipitous river-bank. It was littered with so many broken boughs and burnt trunks of trees that their progress took some time, and when they finally arrived at the water's edge they found that the tide was indeed running out.

Yet the two men left in the sloop, leaning on the rail, were talking in perfect unconsciousness of its peril. They were quite absorbed, one oldish, blue-eyed, the other younger, brown-eyed, ruddy under a deeply burnt-in tan. They were obviously sailors—sea-dogs, almost—quite caked with salt.

Just as at a review, at some grand parade, a cur will appear from nowhere, and, running before the troops—say the Household Brigade in all its glory—bring an unwanted touch of comedy to a splendid occasion, so, apparently, to judge by their remote air, their indifference to all attempts at communication, were these two sailors, accustomed to find women springing up under their noses, unwelcome beings, to be snubbed, to be ignored, like dogs at a review.

Obviously aware of the fair equestriennes who so persistently hailed them, they scorned to reply.

"Really, they are too ridiculous! But a sloop is a sloop. Left as she is our *Amiable Nelly* will certainly be damaged when the tide drops even five or six foot lower. I'll edge Buttercup along to that spit of sand nearer the ship.

Miss Boisragon, amused, waited on the sandy point a hundred yards, perhaps, from the sloop.

Victoria, forcing her mount into the river, guided it along a shallow ledge until she was a few yards—twenty or so—from the *Amiable Nelly*.

"Hi!"

No answer.

"Hey, you!"

"Ahoy!"

Victoria, raising her clear treble, became more nautical in her appeals. They were unacknowledged. Regardless of a fashionable habit that trailed from the saddle to the ground, she let her mount wade further across the deepening rocky shelf until the river flowed strongly against her stirrup, until her face was level with the averted eyes of the chatting men, who scorned, it seemed, to pay tribute to her presence by shifting their positions.

"Really!" Three yards from them, Victoria voiced her indignation. She was, after all, not only a sailor's daughter but the owner of a brig. "Really! My good men! Unless you bestir yourselves and get into deeper water, the tide will leave you high and dry. I know this river! I tell you frankly I would not give a silver sixpence for your little tub in half an hour's time! Tide ebbing! Wind freshening! What on earth are you thinking about?"

Indeed, a strong air was now a little abaft their starboard beam.

The blue-eyed man, the small, briskly-moving one, who had, as Miss Boisragon had noticed, been "ordering the others about"—one of those fussy people who can let nothing alone—glanced an instant at the swirling water (superficially the river looked wide enough for a safe anchorage), his companion, too, glanced; dismay was registered on his face, anger on his companion's.

"How soon do you expect the crew back?"

The three men who had toiled with their bundles up the hill to the cottage were now within doors, out of hail.

"The bosun, who knows the passage" (he had, indeed, voiced his misgivings), "may be an hour. I'll get the anchor up and work her alongshore into deeper water."

The tall man sprang from his lounging position on the ship's rail.

"Thank you for your warning," he exclaimed.

The blue-eyed man, without thanks, was slackening a rope. The sails had been furled.

"I had better take the wheel—I know the channel well!"

The *Amiable Nelly* rode dangerously close to a rock that terminated sharply in deep water, and by venturing with some intrepidity to its limits, the river almost to her saddle-flaps, Victoria, leaning far out, was able to clutch a rope, gain a hanging ladder, and helped by the strong arms of the taller sailor, make the deck without disaster. Her mount, freed, was caught by Miss Boisragon who, guessing her niece's intention, had followed her along the shallows which had befriended her purpose. Withdrawing to the sandy spit of shore, where she waited with the two horses, Loveday Boisragon, having several times searchingly observed the blue-eyed man, had ceased to look amused.

"Get those sails set—and hurry up, man!"

Like a Pirate who had captured a prize, Victoria began giving her orders, and she ran gaily down the spotless deck, her dripping habit scarcely impeding her flight.

The little man obeyed her, sourly.

The anchor was weighed, with two to do the work enough sail

was set to bring the sloop down-stream, and, Victoria at the wheel, a safer berth was found in deeper water. Here the sloop was again made fast under the lee of an islet, to await the dinghy's return.

"After all," running a caressing hand along the smooth, worn surface of the mast, Victoria was gracious, "you two work better than I had expected of you, after you had made so foolish an anchorage! I took you for a pair of guffies."

Engaged in watching the colour of the water as she steered the sloop through a dangerous passage, Victoria had yet been dimly aware that the taller of the two men laboured under some suppressed emotion. This impression had not clearly registered itself on her attention. She had been too much absorbed. Now that she was less engrossed, however, she realized that he was agitated by suppressed laughter.

"Your skirt is trailing on the deck, Madam."

The blue-eyed sailor spoke without suavity. Though he drew nearer, his manner was even more distant.

Unaware that his deck, not her habit, was his anxiety, the young interloper, as she became conscious of being, reassured him with a bright "It's Dreadnaught! It's waterproofed serge! My father buys a bolt or two every year from a naval quarter-master he knows."

Her answer brought no responsive smile.

By this time the sun, about to bed down for the night, had, like a Nautch-girl, shed its last cloud. A bright red ball of light, it stained the water's gold, splashing a dazzling glory over the ship's mast and stays and rigging; making its ropes gold, its deck agate. There was an exaltation past expression in the beauty that renewed each object on sea and shore with a parting benediction.

Miss Boisragon, sitting her drooping horse with a lissom grace, was a gold statuette, something precious from Tanagra, as she waited patiently on the radiant sands.

"Who is she?"

Leaning by Victoria's side on the rail the brown-eyed man was friendly. He had got the impression that the child was "peaked". She was, in fact, anxious about the *Rose*.

"It's my dearest aunt, Loveday Boisragon. Isn't she a sweet little pouter pigeon? She's always as neat as one of those wooden figures of Mrs Noah in a toy Ark."

"When that cormorant frightened her horse she handled him well."

"Oh, she's a wonderful rider! She's a marvellous person. But, of course, she's old." Sweet Seventeen was cruel. "She will be twenty-nine next birthday!" Victoria squeezed the water from a dripping skirt. "But nothing daunts her."

And Victoria being that kind of girl, and used to taking part with her friends in free discussions on the characters and idiosyncrasies of her acquaintances, a diffuseness rendered harmless by a general goodwill, by an instinct that recognized the basic untruth of everything everyone said, the victim of such gossip being endeared rather than otherwise by the imaginary failings laid bare, immediately embarked on the tale of Miss Loveday's broken heart.

"And, do you know," she wound up, "that utter idiot, who was a sailor, and sailors don't usually, do they? sheered off, just because, at sixteen, she read the family washing list? Yes, she was pierced to the very marrow of the heart. She loves him still, she says—she will always love him! To dip into a blue eye, Aunt Loveday says, is anguish! Anguish! It brings him so clearly to her mind."

Victoria found no difficulty in catching her companion's brown regard, which remained glued on her shallow, unshadowed black eyes. Eyes as unreflecting as slabs of chocolate, and seeming, too, to be all pupil and no iris. Indeed he was most flatteringly attentive, his manner being in direct contradiction to that of his shipmate, who, from the first, had betrayed a dryness of manner, a disharmony, rivalling that, say, of a Gapelet, or even an Opelet, jettisoned on hot sand by an unkind tide; he was very stiff. Used to a neighbourly world, Victoria could not make him out.

"Oh, oh, oh! She read the family washing list!"

The brown-eyed man had found a pretext for laughter. How he laughed!

Though still standing near, the blue-eyed sailor gave no sign of having heard, though he loitered, he did not move out of earshot.

"Of course she could have married. There was a widower, for instance, but—"

Was she being indiscreet? Victoria wondered.

"About that widower?" She was not to be let off.

"It was the horsehair sofa that spoilt that match." As Victoria explained her companion took notice of her dimples. "When he came courting every Sunday afternoon at three o'clock, sharp, he and Aunt Loveday and the little boy sat on the horsehair sofa, and the little boy, don't you know, always cried. So Mr Tovey felt, he told my grandfather—Colonel Boisragon of the Madras

Army—that perhaps the child had taken a dislike to Aunt Loveday, and he married Miss Augusta Wirraway instead."

"Did your Aunt regret it?"

His young friend appeared to give the question her deep consideration.

"A choice that might be said to be made between the Devil and the deep sea—between making a dull marriage and living a spinster—is always difficult to make, but it rather stands out that Aunt Loveday, who perfectly well guessed the reason for the child's tears—the pricking horsehair—did not disclose it. She tells it now as a joke."

At this moment the boat, manned by the two handsome young sailors (the Bosun, apparently, had waited with his wife) was rowed briskly round a bend, and came alongside heavily laden.

"We came down today," Victoria remarked watching the men make the dinghy fast alongside and begin dumping the baskets it had carried on to the deck, "to peep at the Love Nest—that cottage on the hill about which everyone is so curious. Something *very wicked*, as far as I can make out, is going on there."

Again the hearty laughter.

"Nothing more wicked than the Admiral's washing! And sometimes, too, the wardroom washing of any other ship in port. The bosun's wife lives there. She washes for us. And, of course, the man gets leave sometimes to wait a week with her. It's more convenient to send a boat in here than to go into Sydney Harbour."

"Oh! Have you a ship of your own?" Victoria breathed.

"Certainly." He was not communicative.

"Has *he*?"

No answer.

Victoria had slowly become aware of a sinking of heart. Were the two men whom she had so unceremoniously ordered about people of importance? Men she had criticized! Not reefers! Not Jack Tars! Not—above all—"*guffies*"? Not chewers of Bonded Jacky? Singers of Abel Brown?

As, trembling, Victoria mused, she looked about her at the shining brass, noticed afresh the deference of the sailors who had just come aboard, who smartly saluted, it seemed, each time her first friends drew a breath or cast an eye about them; she then observed that the trail of smoke, which had been for some time apparent as a black indignity on the golden air of evening, had chuffed itself fully into sight.

"A Man O'War!"

Her delight in it brought an answering smile.

"H.M.S. *Grasshopper*."

"Oh! Your ship?"

"My little ship."

Together they watched the newcomer, smart as paint, of course! A funnel as tall as her two masts, elegant paddle wheels, adorning an iron hull.

"Oh! Have you chased the Barbary Pirates?"

"As a midshipman."

"Have you defeated the Russian Fleet?"

"Oh, yes."

"Have you seen the Sea-gypsies in the Selung Archipelago? My father lost a ship there three years back!"

"We have attended to them!"

He laughed at Victoria's eagerness.

"Come and say 'goodbye'. It's time we left."

"Oh! Will you row me yourself?"

"Naturally."

The blue-eyed sailor was no more cordial when Victoria gave her hand in saying "goodbye".

Instead of taking it, he put in it a silver crown-piece, and said, frostily, "With my thanks."

"Thanks?" Victoria was bewildered.

He said no more, but turned away. The series of accidents that had led to the miscarriage of his barge and had necessitated his transport to the *Grasshopper* in so menial a tender as the *Amiable Nelly* was going to make life difficult for some unhappy midshipman, that was certain. The disgrace (as he considered it) of being caught out by a girl of seventeen in making so dangerous an anchorage (for the bosun had hinted at its dangers) he knew he would never live down. In an imagination that did not usually function, he pictured the wardroom laughter—behind his back—yes—but he would be well aware of it. Remembering, too, the talk he had overheard about his first-love, Loveday Boisragon, delighted though he was to have escaped so degrading a connection, he stuck his nose in the air, he ground and gritted his teeth.

The dinghy put off, Victoria steering, and in the Seventh Heaven, her new friend (as she thought him) rowing.

They found Miss Boisragon walking the horses up and down the sand, less a woman than a silhouette outlined in a fading gold that, as the three talked, became dusk; a dusk washed with silver from a rising moon, a dusk that was the airy hunting-ground of some sort of moth—or an Evening Brown, perhaps—that, softly and quietly as an owl, now stirred in a neighbouring tree, would brush, sometimes with the most elusive of kisses, their cheeks.

The river, a moving tide, still had its facets of light, a blink, here and there, of phosphorus; sometimes a fish jumped.

"Look, Aunt Loveday! A present! A silver crown for saving a ship!"

Victoria laughed outright at the "tip" as the man with eyes of a colour not now to be determined lifted her into the saddle.

"No one ever gives me a present."

Loveday Boisragon was wistful.

The sailor standing beside her, taking a small hand offered in farewell, said, as if he meant it, "I will bring you a present. Should you like a canary? A parrot? A length of Chinese brocade? A Spanish fan, an ivory workbox from Golconda, a phial of rose-attar from Persia? Any of the things we poor sailors bring back from sea?"

Looking mischievous, Miss Boisragon leant from her saddle to smile in the luminous dusk into his eyes and say, "I should like a canary, a parrot, a length of Chinese brocade, a Spanish fan, a workbox from Golconda, a phial of rosewater *and* a coral locket."

The poor woman could not actually ask for a wedding-ring but the question which then hung in the air between them later resolved itself; he gave her one.

As the *Amiable Nelly* put out to sea to join the *Grasshopper*, which was beating off-shore, Captain Jahleel Brattle (whose eyes were brown), leaning in talk against the rail with a blue-eyed Sir Jason Popham (Admiral of the Red), ventured on a criticism.

"Should we, perhaps, er—" he changed his text. "Was it entirely right, do you think, to tip Miss Victoria McMurthie five shillings—for saving the ship?"

"Perfectly correct." Sir Jason had regained his assurance. "That girl was a person of no family. You may trust me to be the best judge of that."

"Oh?" Captain Brattle dared say no more.

"Yes. Did you not notice? She said my '*father*' instead of my '*papa*'. Evidently a girl of no social training!"

Captain Jahleel Brattle at this moment made out the *Rose*, hull down, on the starboard bow.

Which Proves It Is Cheaper Not to Commit Adultery

FAIRY MARTINS had established themselves on the ferry which plied across the Lanterloo River, just above Doggett's Patch. Quite a colony of them were nested on, or under, the deck-ledge of that contraption of wire and cedarwood.

Today the wide, deep river was in flood, but in any case it was almost always yellow with mud and rucked-up into wavelets that, even in a morning light, were backed with orange.

Like ideas clothed in feathers rather than birds of flesh and blood, the twittering Martins flittered over the Lanterloo on such intangible wings that they had the substance, merely, of butterflies or moths; yet their moist and polished iridescences of rusty red heightened the river's buff tints a tone or two, and thus seemed to relate them more intimately to the ripples below them than to their own colourless element, the air. The water's beauty was burnished by their ubiquitous wings.

Tenants of the ferry, they gave themselves the status of owners. They would thread their way almost invisibly between the horses and vehicles on the punt, or dart about the heads of the standing passengers as pertly as if they resented infringements of rights so palpably their own.

Just there seldom used, the ferry might stand idle for weeks, its tip resting on the clayey ramp. It had been this immobility, one spring day many years back, which had led the pioneer Martins to mistake it for a bridge. Their nests were already chirping when, to their astonishment, the pontoon had groaned and whirred, jangled and clanked its way across the turbulent stream to the opposite bank, attended by how furious a flight of parents!

On this particular spring morning, accustomed to their domicile's mobility, the birds accompanied the ferry much as doves and sparrows are shown to circle round the chariot of love in some classical design. The air was full of the scent of pear-blossom from the orchard that abutted on to the track on the far side of the river, the sun shone, the deep-dyed Lanterloo purled and purled, knitting its wavelets into an interminable pattern—make one, drop one, knit two together; and there was absolutely no reason why anyone should not be glad to be alive, just there and at that delicious moment. The Fairy Martins plainly rejoiced, and the very beautiful young lady seated in the white basket-work phaeton behind two dashing cream Arabs evidently shared the general glory of the earth and sky with them. Her face wore a most alluring expression of content as she waited, at ease among her red and white striped cushions and curtains, her "Tiger" in his seat behind her.

She was utterly enchanting, yes, she was, and to those who watched for it, her equipage grew daily smarter; the two cream ponies (whose flowing tails almost touched the ground) now wore straw hats (with ear-holes) bound with red, a rose adorning each; the "Tiger" (as such boyish grooms are called), had also a rose.

Truth to tell, Babette d'Entrecasteaux, Her Excellency Lady Willing-Toper's "French" maid, had once been charmed by just such another turnout as her own, which had been driven through the Champs Elysées by a lady who was now her model, her ideal. An indulgent mistress humoured her fancies, for Babette was the only woman she had ever had who really understood her *toupée*.

The tall young man who ran the ferry was bronzed and bearded. He limped a little, for he had lately returned, wounded, from the Crimean War. He left his cuddy, his wheelhouse, the shelter where, secure from the weather, he turned and turned and turned the winch that drew out, or reeled in, the twisted copper cables that bridged the river, and along which the punt wallowed its loopy way, and went to offer his help in getting the two ponies to face the awkward boarding of the tip.

However, another vehicle, a very smart Hyde Park, drawn by a pair of bays, and driven by a cockaded coachman attired in a uniform of mustard and green (as was the groom seated beside him), had trotted briskly up; Dr Boisragon from Parramatta, looking very handsome—in the manner of the *earlier* Roman Emperors—though still in deep mourning for a wife two months dead—sprang out and took charge of affairs.

"We have met before, dear Lady!" Dr Boisragon exclaimed, joyfully, standing, hat in hand, beside the phaeton. "On the day of His Excellency's arrival in Sydney, when you landed on the wharf at Hunter's Hill!"

"A boat from the *Surinam Merchant*, in which I had travelled from Madras, had brought me there."

"And your delightful carriage was there to meet you! I had the good fortune to restore to you a fan you had dropped!"

"Indeed, Monsieur, I remember pairfectly! It eez a fan I cherish."

Dr Boisragon pulled down his black waistcoat and looked even more handsome. He became protective.

"Is it safe, Mademoiselle, for one so lovely to journey unattended in this remote neighbourhood? There are rough characters about."

"I haff my leedle groom—my 'Tiger'—and my wheep.'

The "Tiger" by this had left his perch behind the red and white striped awning of the phaeton and gone to hold the horses' heads. He was small for his age (twelve); to be a jockey, to ride races in Hyde Park, or along the Parramatta Road—*that* was his tremulous ambition!

"As white as a snowflake!"

Dr Boisragon tenderly regarded the hand that held the carriage whip. He noted with relief that its fellow was defaced by no wedding-ring, and leaning gracefully across the basket-work shielding the wheel he ventured on a conversation.

"The ship? . . ." "Her journey! . . ." "How privileged the sailors! . . ." "India, land of spice, the coral strand!—How blest the land! Her birthplace? . . ." "Never, in the course of his whole life, so meaningless until he met her, had he seen such loveliness, such . . . ?

The colloquy, though the lady responded merely by dazzling smiles, or down-bent eyes, proceeded along the usual lines.

Meanwhile the loose-limbed young ferryman was busy with the Hyde Park.

One of those agnostics whose scepticism appeared to be all-embracing, the cool appraisal of his regard had the cynical air of seeing through all those disguises, those subterfuges, which veiled the conduct of his fellows; and a cold derision was inherent even in the smile which (so seldom) displaced the soft thatch of his chestnut beard to disclose his white teeth and full, red lips. A short-shrift-giving character, who reinforced the edges of peremptory speech with a brisk whistle or a snapping finger, he now, with one of those shrill bids for attention, opened communication with Dr Boisragon's coachman, and with various expressive clicks of his tongue, sibilant breaths expelled through shut teeth, and snapping, irritable fingers, got the Hyde Park past the phaeton and on to the punt.

The Hyde Park itself was weeping. Black crêpe was tied over the four carriage lamps. The whip, upright in its holster, bore a black bow. Even the bays had black rosettes on their bridles. Everyone agreed that Dr Boisragon had done the thing handsomely.

The two menservants in their bottle-green livery with its mustard facings, their left arms saddened by crêpe, their top-hats shadowed by bands similar to the one that subdued the brightness of their master's "stove-pipe", stood at their horses' heads discussing him.

"Clean bowled over, 'e is!"

The coachman indicated Dr Boisragon by a gloved thumb.

" 'E goes a hunner miles a week out of 'is way, 'oping to meet 'er."

"Too proud to harsk 'oo she be."

The men laughed slyly—they knew.

"It's a serious case. 'E sent 'is childer and their Auntie off to Gander's Pond."

"To leave 'is 'ouse empty for a bride, like."

With knowing looks at the fair occupant of the phaeton, who was cutting out, as they said, Miss Fragrance Thistledew, the reigning beauty of Gander's Pond, the men laughed again.

Here the Ferryman carelessly touched one of those "forage-caps" worn by most of the lads who had returned from the Crimea; from the slaughter-yards of Inkerman, Balaclava and Sebastopol, the Redoubt, the Sand-bag Battery; from the charges of the Light or the Heavy brigades; actions in that never-to-be-forgotten struggle, in the defeat of Russia; about which, getting together in groups, the returned soldiers talked interminably, as if such sacrifices mattered; and said, briskly, "Ready, Sir, if you'll be so good!"

"Oh, carry on! I'll wait and escort the lady across."

"Sorry, Sir!" The Ferryman invented a rule. "Owners must travel across with their own conveyances."

"We can't carry four horses, certainly not those barbs and the bays," he added, hurriedly, anticipating Dr Boisragon's next suggestion.

A scene was to be deprecated.

Dr Boisragon, with good grace, bowed his adieux.

"May I not call? Can we not meet?"

His tone was urgent.

"Hélas!"

He was given a snowflake.

A smile dismissed him.

"I shall live in hopes."

Gallantly saluting his fair Incognita yet once again, Dr Boisragon took his place in his Hyde Park. The ferry groaned and clanked its way across the swiftly-flowing yellow river, the Fairy Martins whirring round it, and, the Hyde Park duly decanted on the opposite bank, it returned, with such celerity that even the Martins were left lagging behind.

Instead, however, of leading the perfectly placid Arabs on to the punt, the limber-limbed, debonair young ferryman leant, as Dr Boisragon had done, on the white basket-work splashboards protecting the wheels of the phaeton, and fixed its delicious occupant with a cool, derisive stare.

All the fluttering airs and graces, the demure smiles, the downbent glances, the controlled dimples, her whole armoury of wiles dropped (together with "French" accent) from the lady as she greeted him; a hard stare, equalling his own in its bold, impersonal intensity, met the ferryman's unwavering gaze.

That mysterious charmer Mademoiselle Babette d'Entrecasteaux, became, in one instant, a girl of his own class; she knew, instinctively, that, as far as this admirer was concerned, their love affair was to be a fight with the gloves off; he was not to be kept at bay by guile.

Still meeting his teasing eyes (even more blue than usual backed by the yellow river) Babette stretched out two fingers and, fishing in the breast pocket of his open shirt, she brought out a packet of conversation lollies; in those regions, and in such circles, the badge, it might be called, of the courting male.

The derisive smile with which he had waited for this manoeuvre, though hardly softened, became slightly triumphant as he put his own large hand over the white morsel—the snowflake of Dr Boisragon's compliment—and took out a sweetie.

"Read that!" he commanded.

"Kiss me harder, dear," Miss d'Entrecasteaux read, her dark eyes, devoid of expression, fixed on his.

Such was the legend, as the ferryman perfectly well knew, that was inscribed in red letters on the pink disc.

The ferryman took off his lady's coalscuttle bonnet (of green velvet, shirred and lined with a coronet of white moss-rose buds) and put it on the seat beside her; then, kiss her he did, quite oblivious of the wide-eyed "Tiger", the flitting Martins, or the pink pinafore which was hanging out clothes on a line further down the river.

This task done, and done in a manner with which even the inventor of the conversations on the lollies could have found no fault, the young ferryman took back the paper bag and bestowed it in his pocket with a complacent smile.

Stepping back, Babette's brusque admirer whistled to the "Tiger" to lead the ponies on to the punt, just stopping, as they went off to give his lady-love two peremptory taps on the shoulder and say, coolly, "Meet me by the church clock in Parramatta at eight tonight, and don't be late this time. You are not to keep me waiting—understand?"

"I couldn't help it, Willy," Mademoiselle d'Entrecasteaux said in a gentle humble tone. "My lady kept me."

As she tied on her flighty bonnet she thought, "He talks to me exactly as he talks to his horse or his dog," and her heart beat happily and proudly. She was very young.

Edging himself back into his box the derisive youth turned and turned and turned the winch, whistling, meanwhile, with coloratura variations, the popular tune—

When Cardigan the Fearless
His name immortal made,
He charged the Russian army
With the gallant (tweet, tweet, tweet)
Li-i-ght Brigade.

The punt slapped and staggered its way across the surging river, the Martins joyously escorting it, until the other bank was reached. Then the tempestuously flowing waters that made so wide a setting for the minute cottages, and the Inn—the Devil's Tail—at Doggett's Patch, were left behind; the gay little phaeton vanished out of sight.

But not out of mind, in many cases!

Not only did the ferryman brood over the image of its fair driver; not only did Dr Boisragon, trotting hither and thither attempt, in vain, to brush her lovely features from his heart; but at Government House, where, in due course, Babette turned in (at the stable door), two equally distinguished admirers were thinking of her.

His Excellency, as he waited for his carriage on the front steps, was wondering whose kiss it was that had been pressed on his hand from someone below, as it slipped down the banisters, on his descending, that very morning. Was the unseen trespasser Babette? Or was it only Harriet, the Second Housemaid?

He pondered, a smile on his lips.

In the servants' hall, too, where the mid-day meal (an unheard of thing) had been kept back for ten minutes on her account, Babette's breathless entry caused a stir.

The circle round the table, seated in their customary ranks, included the cook (at the head), the butler (at the foot) and ranged round them the four footmen, the five or six house and parlour maids, the sewing maid and other upper servants, who were being waited upon by servants of lesser degree, such as kitchen and scullery maids, vegetable girls, pantrymen, boots and buttons. Besides His Excellency's valet there were several visitors, too, at the high table.

As he pulled out her chair for her (next his own), the butler asked with jealous eyes, "Are we to have the honour of knowing, Mademoiselle, where your morning has been spent?"

"Indeed, yes! I drove to Doggett's Patch!"

"For the tenth time in a fortnight. And tomorrow? Doggett's Patch again?"

The butler carved the roast.

"Oh, no! Mr Ponting! Tomorrow I go to Gander's Pond. Miss Fragrance Thistledew has promised to show me the new way to whip net."

The butler was so good-looking, so well-groomed, and had so important an air that, in London, he had frequently been mistaken for a Duke, and even Cupid had so far respected his dignity. But, now. Oh! Sorrow! Sorrow! Mr Ponting had found himself to be but mortal. He was aware that, where Babette d'Entrecasteaux was concerned, he was behaving like a fifth footman. Yes, indeed! All that he had determined upon, in bestowing his heart, when the right moment came to dislodge it from his immaculate bosom, he had thrown by the board! He was in love. He contemplated making a *mésalliance!* What! Marry a French maid? He had tried to fight his passion but, Oh, the flesh was weak! Today, to see the engaging little creature come rustling in, almost rosy from her drive, her glorious eyes alight, her voice seductive with undertones of greater richness than ever before! Oh! Oh! Oh! Inevitably he would have made a "declaration", except for one thing; that was the presence, in Government House, of the Duke of Dustboreham (pronounced Duttum) himself.

(And the Duke had come on a very important mission; on most intimate family business; very.)

Since their august presence was (naturally) felt to be a brake on the inborn gaiety of the lower servants, below-stairs etiquette dictated that, after the first course had been served, the butler, the cook, and the Lady's Maid should withdraw to the housekeeper's room, to partake of the "Sweet". That lady joined them at table. They were there waited on by other underlings, who would presently eat a scratchy meal in the kitchen surrounded by a perfect marathon of dirty dishes.

The housekeeper's room was cosy.

It was the repository of all the Empire furniture recently discarded by Lady Willing-Toper, and formerly treasured by her predecessor, Lady Mary. The present Governor's wife had introduced the new mid-Victorian mode; the *curate*, the stand that held three tiers of cakes, the *conversational sofa* shaped like an S, the *daisy-picker's sociable*, on which six people sat back to back, without any possibility of addressing one another.

Just as the previous Governor's wife had banished her predecessor's (an earlier First Lady's) things—the Gothic trifles in the Strawberry Hill manner—so had the still earlier Vicereine bundled out the "hideous" Hepplewhite and Sheraton chairs which her own predecessor had installed. And in due rotation, now, all the late-Georgian, or early-Victorian "rubbish" was discarded to make room for mid-Victorian "coy" pieces; chairs just wide enough not to hold two people, and so on. The housekeeper's room was the repository, the museum, which housed many of these banished treasures.

In this maroon retreat, then, the butler had, for the past two months, been growing more daily subject to Babette's spell.

It was here that the housekeeper, Mrs Perks, the cook, Mrs Greenhill, the butler and Babette, gossiped in the most delicious intimacy and discussed from every angle the Duke's strange activities.

Every morning at ten o'clock the Duke would stroll into the A.D.C.'s room and seat himself at the desk which had hitherto tabled nothing more important than invitations. His Secretary and the Solicitor who had accompanied him out from England would produce immense ledgers and work would commence.

The ten or twelve men or women, or a mixture of both, who each day waited in the ante-room, shyly and silently, but regarding each other with a concentrated curiosity, would be singly introduced into the Duke's presence. Pens would fly. Money would clink. Oaths would be taken.

His Grace, in fact, was straightening out a tangle left him by his father, the twelfth Duke. He was interviewing those members of his family who had been born, as they say, on the wrong side of the blanket.

The Duke was verifying their claims.

He was also disabusing the mothers of these children—now adults, with families of their own, for the most part—of the notion that jumping over a broomstick when the moon was full, even when in company with a Duke, constituted a legal form of marriage. (The late Duke had been of a whimsical turn of humour.)

It had been the Twelfth Duke's grand-seigneurial habit to dispatch to the colonies such contributions as he had made to the human race. Very properly, he had been most generous in his provision for them. He endowed them, not only for the first generation, in which he had taken so beneficent (if casual) a hand; but he had made provision even to the fourth and fifth generations; he would never have it said that the Dustboreham (pronounced Duttum) nose was to be met with in the gutter; even in an Antipodean gutter.

So his children and their mothers came out, liberally endowed, to Port Jackson.

The coterie in the housekeeper's room found much to amuse them in all this. They laughed gaily at the medley of vehicles arriving at the "official" entrance, through which only the Chief Justice was supposed to come and go. One lad had arrived driving, with a great cracking of a forty-foot cowhide stockwhip, a wagon-load of wool drawn by sixteen bullocks, which had waited for hours in the drive and was thought to have been responsible for an almost Egyptian plague of flies.

"In that lad came," Mr Ponting related, having himself admitted him, "and shakes hands with His Grace as bold as brass. There they were, the very spit and image of each other—allowing for the difference in age, of course! Even the Duke got a shock. I could see that."

"They all have the family nose, with wide, cut-back nostrils, and a high bridge that runs up between the eyebrows, it's unmistakable!"

Babette, with a finger, was drawing an imaginary shape beyond her own lovely nose, when the third footman entered, bearing two notes, folded into cocked hats, that seemed to be sailing across the silver tray like yachts; he presented one to Babette, one to Mr Ponting.

No one could fail to see that they were inscribed in the Duke's own generously rambling hand.

A hush fell.

The notes (permission being asked of the housekeeper) were opened and glanced at.

Mr Ponting turned white as a lily.

Babette blushed red as a rose.

"His Grace requests my advice about a small matter." Obviously extemporizing, Mr Ponting, rising hurriedly, left the room.

Babette, after a few minutes of dazed silence, went dumbly out.

"They, too!"

"*On His Grace's family list*!"

"Babette—of the Duke's kin!"

"*And* Mr Ponting."

The cook told the housekeeper she would never believe it. The housekeeper told the cook *she* would never believe it.

Meanwhile Mr Ponting duly presented himself in the A.D.C.'s room, extremely dignified, and much alarmed. But dignified; oh, yes!

He found His Grace with the immense ledger open before him. The last three names on his list were plainly to be read.

Dr (Peter) Boisragon. (Milly Weaver.) £20.

Ebenezer Ponting. (??) £7 (arrears).

Babette d'Entrecasteaux. (Mary Jones.) £5 (this month).

Mr Ponting read these names rooted to the spot.

The Duke had his own kind formula for greeting the applicants for his father's bounty. He rose. He shook hands heartily. He said in a cordial, high-pitched voice, "It's always a pleasure to me to meet one of my own kith and kin. After all, blood is thicker than water. Do sit down."

"Thank you, no!" said Mr Ponting, firmly. "Your Grace is under a misapprehension. I can acknowledge no relationship with the Twelfth Duke!"

"Oh, my dear fellow! Come now!" The Duke pushed the ledger sideways so that Mr Ponting could read it clearly. "There is your name as plain as a pikestaff! You can see it for yourself! Mr Peck and Mr Pool are still away, lunching out, but this record is kept with meticulous care."

"All the same, Your Grace, my name, and Mademoiselle d'Entrecasteaux's are certainly there in error. She was born in Madras."

The Duke realized the delicacy of the situation.

"My father was Governor there—seventeen or eighteen years ago."

His Grace could have no knowledge of the pain he was inflicting. *Babette* his sister! *His sister*! Mr Ponting could not credit it. He refused to believe so bizarre a tale.

Babette—*his sister*!

In his youth Mr Ponting had been personal footman to a Queen. He had been entrusted with the Royal Teapot, the early cup of tea. He had a poise, a dignity nothing could shake.

"Your Grace is entirely mistaken in both cases. Permit me to withdraw. The subject is one I do not even care to discuss. I have my work to do."

Bowing, the butler moved towards the door, which was flung suddenly open and Babette came in.

At all times an alluring sight, Babette now sparkled like live lightning, and though she was in black, her crinoline making a black blot all round her, both men had the impression that a rainbow had suddenly entered; she radiated such a glorious fury.

She took Mr Ponting's hand and faced the Duke. The book lay on the table before them, the fatal entry, as she stood there, was plainly to be read, and read it she did.

"Do you dare to tell me that I am illegitimate?"

"Oh, my dear young lady!" the Duke cried, shocked, "do not put it that way, do not, I beg of you. I acknowledge you as a sister (in a way) and I have come out from England to see that you are not in want. *Pray* do not be so easily affronted."

The Duke had the intention, directly his work was finished, of going up to his bedroom and putting his head out of his window to enjoy a cigar; for smoking was not allowed in Government House. He wore, therefore, his smoking cap of red plush, gathered into a deep band of crocheted wool. His smoking jacket, too, was of red velvet, frogged with gold braid. Otherwise he was in pearl-grey; a grey hardly less ethereal than his white whiskers, which, of the pattern known as "Mutton Chops", had the lustre of spun glass. His face was pink. His eyes were blue, his whole expression kind in the extreme.

His manners, of course, were delightful.

"My Papa was Riding Master of the Green Bays! In Madras! Her Excellency knows him. She can prove your story is quite untrue!"

The snowflakes, beloved of Dr Boisragon, were lifted high to Heaven.

"I swear it."

Mrs Siddons as Lady Macbeth, Malabran as Desdemona, Wilhelmina Schroder-Devrient as Leonora, Pauline Viardot-Garcia as Orpheus, though (to heighten the pathos) they would have worn tights (except, perhaps, Lady Macbeth), even in their greatest hour could never have raised such a tempest of emotion as Babette did now, pouring out a torrent of words in an unknown tongue. She was superb.

The Duke, who had seen the greatest tragedians of the day, was spellbound. Mr Ponting, who, to the role of butler brought the soul of an artist, felt an extraordinary revolution of feeling.

"Could, by any chance, this glorious being be my sister?" he asked himself with a fast-beating heart. "My own sister! A *sister*! God's most glorious creation? And, perhaps, the least expensive of human relationships?"

He pictured himself introducing her, "My *sister*!" He pictured himself leading her up the aisle, the bride, he, her *brother*, was to give away.

To gain Babette as a *sister* would he even acknowledge the Duke's untrue aspersion? (For he knew it to be untrue; he could prove, he felt, that point.)

Mr Ponting debated the problem, his eyes never leaving Babette's face.

Mr Ponting had known no family ties.

"To have Babette as a *sister*."

This refrain kept singing through his heart.

A pride! An ornament! And *no expense*! No responsibility.

He fell in love with the idea.

Meanwhile both men listened to the melting tones of Babette's oratory. She spoke (but how could they tell?) in the "Gond" language, with which she had been familiar in childhood. Doubtless she was eloquent. Certainly she was supremely beautiful, mesmeric, musical. Her hearers were both enchanted, if bewildered.

She had reached, it seemed, her peroration, when the door again opened and in walked Dr Boisragon. The fresh shock brought Babette to her senses.

She stretched out a hand and pulled him into line with herself and the entranced Mr Ponting. She said, in the tones of Phaedra, "The Duke says I am illegitimate. He says you are illegitimate. He says Mr Ponting is illegitimate."

She closed her eyes and threw back her lovely head.

She resumed. "He says *you*, Dr Boisragon, are my brother. He says *you*, Mr Ponting, are my brother—*neither eligible*!"

It was the wail of "Sophonisba! Sophonisba! Oh!"

Dr Boisragon was, naturally, a man of the world, yet he was, after even two meetings with her (as one could so easily be) in love with Babette d'Entrecasteaux, whose name he did not know. He had come, suspecting nothing (for he had heard nothing of the Duke's strange mission), in response to a message from the A.D.C.—"Could he step in when passing?"

He looked at the Duke.

"Would you, my dear Duke, explain? I am utterly bewildered."

The Duke explained.

Dr Boisragon examined the entries of the book.

He seemed, however, to be less dazed than might have been expected.

Babette, too, peeping over his shoulder in a calmer mood, had the appearance of seeing a glimmer of light.

Here the A.D.C. entered, in the full-dress uniform of the Bombay Horse Artillery, which, it may be remembered, included a brass helmet hung with flowing strands of horse-hair, dyed red and white, thigh-high top-boots over white breeches, a scarlet, blue and gold coat, behind which hung a second jacket, edged with fur and frogged with gold braid, its sleeves dangling loose, and various impedimenta in the shape of a clanking sword, a sabretache embroidered in gold thread, gold aiguillettes, and a tasselled belt. The young man had been with His Excellency to a Mothers' Meeting Conference, at Little Peeping in the Inlet, and he had been standing for three hours in the sun; his face was brick-red, but still had an almost girlish prettiness, enhanced by golden "Dundreary" whiskers.

He was looking for something, it seemed.

" 'Pon my Soul," he exclaimed, wandering round the room, searching here and there, "Her Ex. came in and asked me to jot down some housekeeping expenses, bills to be paid—why, Bless my Soul!—*there they are*!"

He was about to take up the ledger, which was just like any other ledger, when Mr Pool and Mr Peck, with the furtive air of men returning from a good lunch, entered and stopped him.

"Not so fast, Captain Fortesque-Montmorency-Boodle-Stammers-Quint!"

"Hey?"

"That is our ledger."

"No. No. My account-book. Bin lookin' for it everywhere."

"It is the Duke's private—very private—property."

"*So it is*! And I have jotted down my memo in it, and increased His Grace's family by three!"

Mr Peck and Mr Pool, the Duke, and Dr Boisragon were not amused; but Mr Ponting and Babette were; they suffered excruciating agony in refraining from laughter, and stood there looking wooden and not daring to meet each other's eye.

The A.D.C.'s sufferings came from excess of laughter.

Finally he caught Dr Boisragon by the shoulder and propelled him into the adjoining room, his office; he had to give him, by Lady Willing-Toper's directions, a cheque for twenty pounds, for attending Milly Weaver, whose name, since she was the daughter of one of the gardeners, was not familiar to the indoor staff.

Babette, however, on saner reflection, realized that "Mary Jones" was her own sewing maid, and due to get five pounds for some shopping expenses incurred on Her Excellency's behalf.

The sum entered against Mr Ponting's name was his weekly bill. Just that.

But, Babette had lost two admirers.

The mere idea that she might have been his sister, one might say, had made her sacrosanct, tabu. Neither Dr Boisragon nor Mr Ponting would ever again think of having her in any closer relationship.

Mr Ponting would presently ask her to be a sister to him; he would, very proudly, on her acceptance, hurry into Parramatta to buy her the first of many gifts: a pair of garnet ear-rings; he was even to have the honour (already envisaged) of giving her away when she married. But the second housemaid, Harriet, whose devotion to him had outlasted many years, she whose kiss had been pressed on His Excellency's hand by mistake, she it was who was destined to be Mrs Ponting.

Looking out of the sewing-room window through the first green leaves of the acacias, and their pendant cones of privet-white, Babette saw Dr Boisragon drive away. She heard his directions to his coachman—"Gander's Pond". She knew what that meant.

Babette realized, too, Mr Ponting's change of heart (but how often, in the succeeding years, was she to lean on him for some help or kindness) and she felt her lonely, forsaken state very keenly; yes, she did. Tears were not far from the lovely eyes as she noticed, idly, a Fairy Martin threading a dizzy way among the ineffable green fronds of the acacias. A second came. She soon could not count the flash of circling wings, so moist-looking in their rust-red plumage, so ethereal, giving in their softness, their airy persiflage, a hint of butterfly's downy, powdered beauty.

This phenomenon, which autumn might have brought, but

never spring, had hardly inspired her wonder when the clop-clop of a rough-swaying trot was to be heard approaching from the stable avenue, and in a piercing strain, the popular tune, "When Cardigan the Fearless", whistled with bravura, like an overture before a rising curtain, resolved itself into the sight of the gallant young ferryman himself, who, immediately, and with a lover's eye, caught sight of the pale, wistful face set among the flowery acacia boughs—but what he said to Babette, reining in his hairy-hooved mount under her window, is nobody's business.

Is Arson a Sin? or a Peccadillo?

It was a day of unparalleled sunshine, Spring, Summer, Autumn and Winter had met, it seemed, for a promiscuous dance of the happiest hours of the year 1857.

Oranges ripened in the orchards, in the vineyards grapes voiced their promise of warmth and cheer, white sheep nibbled the grass on every hill, cattle roamed the pastures, nursery gardens flourished as never before, the borders in every cottage rivalled the storied wealth of the Hesperides, every bird was as busy as a bee, and the Parramatta and District Royal Horticultural Show was in full swing.

People for miles around had flocked into town.

In addition to the local inhabitants of Parramatta and its ring of villages, the whole population of Dural, Hornsby Junction, Mallow's Marsh, Gander's Pond, Doggett's Patch and even Little Peeping in the Inlet was packed as tightly as eggs in a cod's roe into the yellow marquee in which a dazzling display of fruit, flora, and gigantic vegetables was up for judgement.

These last-named exhibits were mostly pumpkins, marrows, water melons, and cabbages, and though a tray of rainbow-hued mangel-wurzels as big as footballs held pride of place, trite turnips, and carrots, immaterial lettuces, and the third bundle of asparagus to be grown south of the equator lent variety and charm to the stand.

The new-fangled tomatoes, which, when they had been called "Love Apples" had been vetoed as "poisonous", made a primal, dubious appearance, but they were hardly considered to be human food; they made a shy showing labelled "Give them to your poultry".

The Hokey-Pokey man's Gondola had trundled its way from Balmain, from the Capital itself, as a sure sign of the importance of the occasion. With its polished brass standards, twisted like sticks of barley-sugar, supporting the gayest of awnings, the Gondola was backed into a position just outside the tent flap; children were swarming over it while the Italian proprietor warbled, tunefully, "Hokey-Pokey, Penny-a-Lick!"

Sir Jeremiah Willing-Toper, the most popular Governor New South Wales had ever had, was unfortunately away reviewing the Sydney Volunteer—just one—in Hyde Park; but to the satisfaction of everyone except her own relations, Lady Willing-Toper, who during her two years in office had greatly endeared herself to the Populace, was to open the Show and make a short speech.

True, the Wirraways, McCrees, Boisragons, McMurthies, Phantoms and Thistledews trembled in their neat babouches, elastic-sided Prunellas, or Hessians, for "Corporal Cora", as she was called in her family (it will be remembered that she had been born a Thistledew from Gander's Pond), was so tactless that it was impossible to guess what she would say next; but who were these people—a mere handful—compared with the teeming citizens of a growing colony? Who, indeed!

What a crowd there was!

The countrymen, in their Nankin breeches and woolly beaver hats, had their beards—frizzy black, crinkled and crenellated gold, or flowing chestnut—brushed and pomaded till they shone. They wore, as often as not, blue or unbleached linen smocks, with bandana handkerchiefs round their necks and gold or silver ear-rings in their ears. They were quite as brightly bedizened as the women; more so, really, for the colours being worn at the moment were subdued, ladylike tints of lilac, dove-grey, lavender or white, and though each Poke bonnet or Coalscuttle had under its brim a wreath of artificial flowers, these adornments did not show from the back. It was too hot to wear a Kashmir shawl, or even a ring-wallah. Every lady carried a fan. Waist-long gossamers flowed from every bonnet, Dolly Varden or Pork-pie hat.

As for the merinos, the dandies, the exquisites!

Since Parramatta gave itself the airs of a capital city the Jeunesse Dorée were indeed the glass of fashion and the mould of form. Oh, absolutely! They had such glossy curls, such sparkling ruby rings, such tailored waists—as slender as a girl's. They displayed such flexible hips, such wide shoulders, such adventurous chests! As for their mutton-chops, their feathery Dundreary whiskers, their yellow kid button boots, their thick gold watch-chains! Oh, even Sydney itself on a gala day scarcely rivalled them! And they were so handsome, too, not merely mannikins; many of them had but lately returned from enduring the hardships and horrors of the never-to-be-forgotten Crimean War.

The young Ensigns and Lieutenants of the Fighting Fortieth, then passing through Sydney, were on their way to India, where there had been a great deal of fighting lately, and they quite outshone the flowering auriculas on dear old Mr Phineas McCree's table (he was now ninety-nine, and restricted to work only in a greenhouse).

Compared with the stalwarts—so sunburnt—of Parramatta, how blond were the English soldiers! One of them, squiring Gussie Thistledew, was heard to say, "I don't, my deah, care a Joyey for the wild beasts of Bengal, or the wild men, either, but I am quite terrified that in that climate I might fweckle."

Arrangements were perfect!

His worship the Mayor of Parramatta had attended to all details himself.

Three trestle tables, a few feet apart, ran right from the small raised platform at the end of the tent to the tent flap. These carried the exhibits. Flowers were on the left, fruit and ferns on the central panels, and vegetables were arranged on the right. The avenues between these tables left just room enough for two people to walk abreast.

It was easy to see that ferns were a favoured hobby, and that daisies, pelargoniums, auriculas (late-flowering, and grown under glass) and fuchsias were the fashionable flowers. Of course the show of camellias was outstanding. Dr Boisragon had even managed to coax a few final flowers from his almost legendary "Countess of Orkney". It had raspberry-striped petals, alternating with white bands flecked with pink. It was much admired. Everyone also admired the exhibit sent by Mrs Peter Boisragon (neé Georgiana Thistledew). She staged six named varieties of pinks. "Master Tuggie, His Princess" was reported to have been brought to this country by Mrs Macquarie. There was an equally rare "Red Halloo".

"With two sets of twins in the nursery (such bouncing boys). I wonder that dear Georgiana Boisragon has time for gardening!"

"And she has also undertaken the care of three delicate stepchildren."

"I consider young Mrs Phantom's Marvel of Peru a much more stylish effort."

"Dr Phantom himself has a small exhibit of goanna eggs."

"Is it wise to leave the eggs so long in that hot corner?"

Victoria McMurthie and her cousin, Bathsheba Wirraway, passed on the arms of two personable young sailors from the brig *Rose* (of forty tons, just returned from London, via Rio de Janeiro) and they stopped to curtsy to Mrs Wirraway and Mrs McCree, who were watching Hiram Thripp (who was simple) and his mother (who was not), for this mysterious pair were paying great attention to a mammoth watermelon, and the ladies (knowing them) were wondering "*why?*"

Victoria's jetty, expressionless eyes had their usual air of being black currants or boot buttons, but her sensitive mouth held the tremulous promise of spring, and she, with her blonde cousin Bathsheba, the blonde of all blondes (her nickname was "the Junket"), who had a sweetly silly expression that went straight to the heart of every male observer, were being looked at with even more attention than the Thripps by the two sailors. Poor boys! They knew that the two vivid young faces would presently, as a memory only, blot out the Pacific, the Spice Islands, the clouds, the stars; they knew that Bathsheba's blue eyes would presently condemn the Arafura Sea; but, with infatuated eyes, they gazed and gazed, determined to lose no nuance, not one perfection of detail; yet they had been warned against the perils of the deep.

"Mr Guerdon, the undertaker, not his brother, Mr George Guerdon, the butcher, has sent in an excellent pottle of strawberries." Sophia Thistledew loomed up out of the press, her lips stained red. "Such delicious berries! *Do taste*!" She was carrying the straw pottle round with her.

"Ah, well!" Mrs Wirraway's fingers hovered. "Perhaps one would not be missed."

Mrs Wirraway was tempted. Mrs McCree took three.

"Straw is no object to Mr Guerdon. It's in great demand. All that he has sold to lay down on the roadway, he carts away—after the accouchement—or the funeral! As I drove down the High Street just now there was either straw or tannin bark laid down before no fewer than four houses! That! In one street!"

"Young Mrs Wirraway, young Mrs Septimus Phantom, dear Georgiana Boisragon, and, of course, dear Juliet, are all expecting. They have such devoted husbands that nothing is begrudged them!"

"I never knew Peter Boisragon lay down straw for any of poor Letty's twenty confinements! He spoils Georgiana!"

"Yes! He does pamper her, doesn't he? But, truly, dear, the noise increases! The thunder of the traffic gets worse and worse."

"Indeed, yes! Dr Phantom's cabriolet does clatter on the cobblestones, now that he drives tandem. Dr Boisragon's Hyde Park is the worse for wear these days, it jingles, jingles, jingles! After they had both passed me Farmer Truscott's dray lumbered past with a load of hay, for the Governor's stables. Oh, we are quite a metropolis. *Sophia*!" Mrs Wirraway broke off to exclaim in shocked tones, "*Not another strawberry*! You'll leave NONE!"

"I've only eaten two and nibbled five. As Honorary Secretary of the Ferns section, I deserve some perquisites! Take another?"

"Thank you." Mrs McCree took two.

"I have a conscience."

"I forgot to mention that the Rectory Buckboard, from Mallow's Marsh, was jogging down the High Street, too. Juliet should be here by this."

"Has she the family with her?"

"Not all. Just five boys and the baby. The elder girls and the twins have the measles."

"There is an idea getting about that measles may be catching as they call it. Catching! A new phrase!"

"What? The measles *not* a Heavenly Visitation?" Mrs McCree was shocked. "What profanity!"

Sophia Thistledew, however, still lingered, sated, it appeared, for she had replaced the pottle of strawberries (bolstered up with straw, the nibbled strawberries placed good side out) on Mr Guerdon's stand.

"Mrs Thripp, the Toll-keeper's wife," Sophia observed, "is what I call a comfortable body. Her poor benighted son carries a lighted lanthorn wherever he goes, and she takes it so naturally—quite as a matter of course."

"What with that tasselled peaked cap and that tight Norfolk jacket, it's hard to guess whether Hiram Thripp is a child dressed as a man or a man disguised as a child." Mrs Wirraway turned her blue eyes on the Thripps who were bending over a magnificent basket of Hare's foot ferns and maidenhair. She rearranged her gossamer. "And that *peering* look! while he holds the lanthorn right against one's nose. It's unnerving, quite!"

"Yes, that lanthorn might be a pipe or a malacca cane, his mother bows so casually to his right to carry it, in broad daylight through the streets of Parramatta!"

Mrs McCree retouched a sprig of caraway at her own table where six bouquets of herbs were arranged in unstoppered attar-of-rose bottles that still held in them traces of attar.

"Mrs Thripp sees to it, I'm thankful to notice, that today her foolish son is not a danger to the community. He carries a hurricane lamp, I notice. Anything else, in this inflammable tent, would be too risky."

"That boy's temper is notoriously uncertain. He set fire to Mrs Gamp's henhouse when she refused to give him the duckling he asked for."

"Is this your exhibit, dear Aunt Jessie?"

"Yes, Sophia, dear," Mrs Wirraway explained. "It's my entry for the First Prize for six pots of medicinal herbs. These were hard to come by, I assure you."

"It's quite a masterpiece. Dill, caraway, balsam, fennel, angelica and even mint!"

"That is Patience Boisragon's, next to mine. She has bergamot, lavender, sweet-cicily, costmary, chives, and sandwort. But that is not a herb! It's a kind of minium, I think, so I am pretty certain of getting the award."

"Oh, botheration! Hiram and his mother are descending on us! Let us escape!"

"Too late!" Mrs McCree smiled kindly. "Good afternoon, Mrs Thripp. Good afternoon, Hiram. I see your exhibit is next to mine."

"Yes. Them's Hiram's. Grass-bents stuck in bottles. All he could get, poor lad."

Peering in his half-witted way Hiram held the lanthorn up and scanned each face in turn. He then put the lamp down on the grass—the tent was pitched in Farmer Best's paddock—and, taking all Mrs McCree's herbs in his large fleshy hands he rearranged them in his own bottles.

"Them's mine now," he mumbled, in his thick, blurred utterance. "Them's a lovely prize-winner, shurely."

His queer face with its half-shut eyes and too-red cheeks mapped out with purplish veins showed a furtive satisfaction.

"Tell your son to put back my herbs this instant!"

Mrs McCree spoke crisply.

"Ah, don't bother the poor lad, Ma'am, 'is temper is hawful when it's once aroused. I never thwarts 'im meself, never! It don't do. If you'll please to believe it, Ma'am, 'e's best left to hisself like."

Never had Mrs Thripp better deserved the description "a comfortable body". She was richly soothing in voice and manner.

"But they are my herbs. I grew them."

"Now, now, Ma'am, calm yerself. Don't start a scene. 'Tisn't ladylike. Look at the boy! 'Appy!"

"Start a scene? Me!" Mrs McCree was indignant.

"Come back, dear, and replace your herbs when Hiram has moved away." Mrs Wirraway whispered nervously.

"Ah, well!" Mrs McCree shrugged her thin shoulders; her pelisse was new. "Never mind. Let the afflicted Hiram have them.

The judges have already praised them to me; they should recognize them."

It was easy to suffer themselves to be carried forward by the humming and surging crowd since at that moment the arrival of the Vice-Regal party was announced. The town band played a popular air as Lady Willing-Toper, led by the Lord Mayor, made her way to the dais. She was received by the most loyal demonstrations of goodwill, for during her two years in office she had greatly endeared herself to the populace.

Lady Willing-Toper had brought with her the house-party she had invited to stay at Government House for the event. Both the Admiral, Sir Jason Popham, and the General, Sir David Ochterlony, Commander-in-Chief, Madras, though they were merely passing through the Colony on their way to their respective stations (Sir Jason was Commanding the China Station), wore the full uniform of their rank, and were covered with perfect herbaceous borders of decorations and medals. They looked magnificent and utterly formidable, yet, when seated between them on the platform, which was gay with flags and ferns, "Corporal Cora", true to type, had soon brought them down, as one might say, with a right and left barrel.

To the General she remarked while complacently admiring the bouquet of buttercups and daisies presented to her on behalf of "The Loyal Daughters of Parramatta" by the Lord Mayor's little girl—there was an idea that Lady Willing-Toper had "simple tastes"—"I know you realize as well as I do, Sir David, that the English army nowadays is made up of the rag-tag and bob-tail of the country. And I am sure you'll agree, too, that those poor creatures below us—for instance—the ensigns of the Fighting Fortieth—are weeds, merely weeds! Look at their wretched physique! They are quite incapable, one sees at a glance, of lasting through a long brush with the enemy—let alone a campaign. Look at that white-faced little stripling on your left! *He* couldn't endure hardships! He is weighed down by the weight of all those medals. He could hardly run ten yards burdened by the weight of his own helmet—let alone a pike or a sword. I can't think what the Nation is coming to!"

"The History of the Peninsular War will tell you something of the Fighting Fortieth, Ma'am! We do not ask our soldiers to run."

Sir David's tone was dry.

"But they do run! Look at Corunna! You must get His Excellency to tell you something of the storming of Seringapatam and the Battle of Condore! In his fighting days there were heroes indeed."

Sir David's answer was to rise, bow to his toes, and say, coldly, "I fear I am keeping some of the local worthies from their place of honour beside you. I will call His Worship to take my seat."

This he did, and sat himself down, fuming with rage, at the back of the platform.

"What nice manners Sir David has!" Lady Willing-Toper remarked to Sir Jason, who, covertly amused, was sitting on her right. "And that reminds me! I have a little compliment to pay YOU, Admiral! The Navy, I have found, always knows such *impossible* people, as I am certain you will be the first to admit! I was on this account *more* than pleased, when Sir Jeremiah and I went on board your Flagship, to notice what respectable friends you seem to have! The subjects of the daguerreotypes and chalk drawings that adorn your walls are quite the kind of people one would know oneself. I do honestly congratulate you on the good appearance they make. In the Navy one so seldom meets a gentleman."

Lady Willing-Toper was nowise disconcerted when the Admiral rose and with the stiffest of two fingers saluted her, saying in icy tones, "I am afraid that I monopolize Your Excellency, I will send one of the Aldermen to take my place."

Sir Jason Popham (K.C.B., Order of St Stanislas—with Swords—and so on), white with anger, joined Sir David on the back benches.

"Such a considerate man, Sir Jason," Lady Willing-Toper told the Alderman who took his place, and who was, in fact, Mr Guerdon the Undertaker. "He quite realized that it is more of a treat to a humble person like yourself, to sit next a lady, than it it is to him."

"I usually edges 'em along, feet foremost," Mr Guerdon, remarked, with a hearty laugh, in which "Corporal Cora" joined; she dearly loved a joke.

Here the Mayor rose and twitched his gown, set his cocked hat at a gallant angle, and conscious of his chain and a new ruby ring, launched out into a speech.

He welcomed the Governor's wife in a few well-chosen words and taking the audience completely into his confidence asserted that she was the best customer that the Parramatta tradespeople (except myself—"loud laughter") had ever had. "And, gentlemen, *she pays on the nail.*"

This greatly pleased Lady Willing-Toper, who liked an artless tribute.

He told, next, of his early struggles, of his marriage to Mrs Guerdon, of the birth of his daughter—"the greatest event in my life, and that of my good lady herself"—and he gave anecdotes of her genius; he welcomed the General and the Admiral, and called for three cheers for them, which were heartily given. He extended the hand of brotherhood to the heroes recently returned from the Crimean war.

"No one is more sorry than the Lady Mayoress and me to see so many of you out of work and begging at street corners for a few pence."

Here, to lighten a sad subject, a gleam of wintry humour lightened his Worship's knobby face: "But I deplore the new oaths these young gentlemen have brought back with them. It's *Sacré Bleu* here, and *Sacré Bleu* there!"

The Mayor raised himself on the toes and, hands on hips, demanded, "What's wrong with the good Christian oaths and expletives as we've been used to, and our fathers and mothers before us?" This sally was so well received that he added, "and these French songs as they've brought back—why, I've heard of a popular medico—who shall be nameless—" everyone turned to smile at Dr Phantom and his bride, née Fragrance Thistledew—"who on his return from Scutari was heard singing the *Marcel-looze* as he went his round, when he thought no one could hear!"

Hearty laughter stopped the speech; Mrs Phantom blushed; and the Mayor, suddenly feeling he might have presumed, hurriedly said, "And now I ask Your Excellency to distribute the prizes."

Mr Thripp of the Tool-bar handed up the list to Mr Guerdon.

There was some kind of hitch, and to everyone's surprise it was found that Mr Guerdon could not read. "I read print—but not this high-falutin'-handwriting—" he explained, so Lady Willing-Toper possessed herself of the paper and, standing, a regal figure in heliotrope enriched with bunches of pansies, read out in her high pitched "Englishy" voice.

"First Prize for a Mammoth Watermelon—Mr Hiram Thripp."

An indulgent smile and some patronizing handclapping greeted this first announcement. Hiram, his lamp held high above his head, walked down the alley cleared for the prizewinners and took the shilling.

"First Prize for the best collection of pot and medicinal herbs —Mr Hiram Thripp."

Hiram, wide-eyed and open-mouthed, his lanthorn swinging, made his way to get his prize—another shilling.

Mrs McCree's friends refrained from clapping.

The grower of the mammoth watermelon had by this made his way through the crowd to voice his protest.

"Hush! Don't hinterrupt a lady!" The voice was that of Hiram's father, Mr Thripp of the Toll-bar.

He was on the judging committee.

"First Prize for the best hanging basket of ferns—Mr Hiram Thripp—of the Toll-bar."

Lady Willing-Toper, herself surprised, examined her list. Yes! There was no mistake. It was clearly so. In silence Hiram walked up to her and claimed his shilling.

When, however, the next announcement said, "First Prize for the best six named varieties of Mangel-wurzels" and Hiram again walked up to claim it, loud murmurs arose on every side.

The Alderman begged for a sight of the document.

Lady Willing-Toper handed it over.

A noise only to be described as the growl of an angry animal had gone up from the waiting crowd. There had been foul play. Someone (it was found) had changed all the labels. *Who was responsible*?

The men of Parramatta looked sourly on the men of Hornsby Junction. The stalwarts of Doggett's Patch angrily jostled the men of Dural. Mallow's Marsh and Gander's Pond, a notably bad-tempered lot, began abusing each other in the good Christian oaths approved by the Lord Mayor. The inhabitants of Little Peeping in the Inlet were mostly sailors, and very tough customers at that, for they came, usually, from the Blackbirding Fleet, or from American Whalers; they began a more serious hectoring of the boys from Balmain.

There was a quite noticeable movement for the men of the various communities to get together; they were elbowing their way to collect, as it were, under their rightful banners. In short the seeds of disunion and suspicion had been sown.

Incidents in the past history of the relationship between the dwellers in one place or another were brought openly into conversation.

"Hey, you from Doggett's Patch! What about our beer at the Oddfellows' Picnic last year?"

The beer had vanished; the men of Doggett's Patch had been obviously convivial and a free fight had ended the event.

"Where's your Umpire, Huskies?" Another slogan became dominant.

At the football match between the Dural Huskies and the Mallow's Marsh Wanderers, a wrong decision, as Mallow's Marsh held, had awarded Dural the Victory.

"*Where's our fifty pound?*"

The most flagrant case of chicanery ever known in the history of sport had been the disappearance of the fifty-pound stakes in a cricket match, played between Parramatta and Gander's Pond.

There was certainly going to be trouble.

With great presence of mind the Mayor said: "Tea is now ready in the adjacent tent, and the Lady Mayoress will escort Her Excellency to partake of refreshments there. Will every lady please join them?"

Every lady was only too glad to escape. The rustle of silk, the jangle of crinoline wire, the creak of whalebone, which marked the movements of the Fair Sex, quickly grew to a crescendo and, as they vanished, died down in the distance.

"I'll ask every man who calls himself a man to wait in this here tent—French oath—till the—English expletive—aboriginal spell-word—devil who monkeyed with the prize list is exposed for the —Norwegian whaling phrase—cheat he is. And I hopes all proceedings will be conducted in a gentleman-like manner."

Alas! Not five minutes later His Worship, in a white heat of passion, had cast from him his robes, his cocked hat and chain, and leaping down from the platform had seized the mammoth watermelon and hurled it straight at the head of the Captain of the Dural Huskies.

It was the largest, juiciest and most thickly seeded watermelon that ever left its vine, the consequences of its impact changed the face of local history; the Dural Husky, though blinded by pink juice, riposted by picking up the giant pumpkin, "Pieman's Wonder", weighing seven stone, and planting this very neatly at point-blank range full in the Worshipful stomach. The Mayor crumpled up and was shoved by some kindly soul into comparative safety underneath the platform, where he lay hidden from sight.

Mr Ponting, the Butler from Government House, quickly assumed the leadership of the Parramatta faction, and being a handy man with his fists, and scorning the vegetable missile, quickly engaged the winner of last year's Welterweight contest (held at Little Peeping) in an animated boxing-match. His footwork in keeping his balance in a mixture of vegetable pulp and struggling bodies was admired by all who had time to notice it.

Directly the fun started, Dr Phantom, divesting himself of his top hat and frock coat, leaped nimbly for the Mangel-wurzel stand and, shouting "Doggett's Patch for Ever!" began hurling prize Mangel-wurzels (the "Farmer's Friend", "Dew of Herman", "Nellie Blinkman" chiefly) with an unerring aim at every combatant not claiming allegiance to Doggett's Patch.

(Dr Phantom himself owed no real allegiance to Doggett's Patch except that he visited a ruined stomach there, but he had noticed that the men from that hamlet were outnumbered by fifty to one.)

Within five minutes all available horticultural ammunition was reduced to a foot-deep layer of pulp spread over the grass, and very slippery to the feet, and the champions of Doggett's Patch, Dural, Hornsby Junction, Gander's Pond, Mallow's Marsh and Little Peeping in the Inlet were for the most part engaged in Homeric combat with their fists alone.

Every face was bruised and disorganized, every smock was torn to ribbons, every beard was sopping wet and stained with tomato juice, strawberries and melon flesh.

And the blood! The grunts pumped out by the impact of each mighty fist made an accompaniment to the shouts of derision, the taunts, the challenges bandied from man to man. It was quite impossible to tell friend from foe—but who cared! The fight was the thing!

When the fun was at its height, Donalblain, in his last term at the King's School, looked in, accompanied by the school football team. With shouts of glee they manned the "Hokey-Pokey" Gondola and charged right down the space between "herbs" and "ferns", mowing down all in their path.

Shouts of "King's School for Ever!" rose above the din.

It was at this moment that the goanna eggs hatched.

A spate of lively black morsels, their tails twisted back over their repulsive necks, launched themselves out into a surprising world. To Doggett's Patch, hemmed in between a tent wall and a depleted stand stripped of Mangel-worzels, they were a God-sent form of ammunition, a miracle from on high, too tempting to be resisted. Spreadeagled, they were discharged at point-blank range and with the zip of a *feu de joie* straight into the faces of the men of Gander's Pond, who were winning, and who had formed into a solid phalanx opposite the heroes of Doggett's Patch, their next objective.

"Very nice—*very* nice!"

The men of Doggett's Patch, whose position had seemed so hopeless, raised a loud cheer. Really the goannas made the most perfect projectiles, for they stuck, they ran up and down, evading capture, and the sight of six jet goannas playing catch-as-catch-can round the bald head of the police-sergeant from Gander's Pond was of so compelling a phantasy that several men shut their eyes and were heard taking the pledge all to themselves.

They almost held up the engagement for sheer horror, but not quite. Many contestants could not see them, and leaping up on to the trestles, began cutting down the wire hanging baskets of ferns when a smell of burning assailed every nostril.

Hiram Thripp had at last succeeded in setting fire to the tent. Flames sprang up in several corners.

Hiram, swinging his opened lamp, was visible one moment, yelling with triumph, and then all became a pandemonium past description.

Immediately united, every man, though himself urgent for the safety of the outer air, looked to his stricken neighbour. The rows of men laid out along the tent-flap, dazed or unconscious, were dragged to safety. Trundled out on the "Hokey-Pokey" Gondola, bleeding noses, broken collar-bones, sprained wrists and ankles, and several cases of concussion (for the Mangel-wurzel is a shrewd weapon) were wheeled out to enjoy the comparative safety of the women's care.

The tent burnt rather funnily. The thin, yellow cotton lining flared up first, and lighted up the damp outer covering round which twenty black goannas could be seen to be running in a demonic dance. They finally reached the top of the tent-pole and actually planed down to the safe asylum of the long grass. There must have been some ancient scandal in their family.

Entranced, the crowd watched the fire. Some busied themselves making a firebreak. Some even more busily wondered why the fire brigade did not come? Then someone asked, "Where is the Mayor of Parramatta?"

"Where is His Worship?"

The alarm quickly spread.

"Who saw him last?"

Mr Ponting said he remembered seeing a Dural Husky throw a Pieman's Wonder at him.

The Husky owned to shoving the Mayor under the platform "for safety like".

A shout went up!

"His Lordship is lying senseless under the platform."

"His Worship will be burned to death."

The flames, by this time sky-high, had got a greedy hold of the outer tent. It was Dr Phantom who, as usual, thought most quickly. He rushed forward, and in the midst of an appalling orange glare, was seen to run back into the burning marquee—now on the point of collapsing.

Immediately everyone began shouting, "Where is Mrs Phantom?" "She must be told." "Fetch Mrs Phantom."

As many women as could tear themselves away from the spectacle of so much drama rushed into the refreshment tent and burst in, calling out, "Mrs Phantom! Come at once! Your husband's being burned to death!" "There's nothing can save him!" "The marquee's on the point of collapsing."

While Lady Willing-Toper, always calm in an emergency, burnt the feathers from her bonnet under the fainting Mrs Phantom's nose, these messengers of ill-omen—"*What fun it has been*"—"*She went down like a ninepin*"—"*Expecting, too*!"—rushed back just in time to see a Dr Phantom whom no one could recognize emerging from the tent with the Mayor of Parramatta slung over his shoulder.

Did everyone cheer?

Did everyone then have the gratification of seeing a distracted young wife—the stately Fragrance Thistledew—throw herself into her husband's arms?

Was the Lady Mayoress herself revived with hartshorn?

Did His Worship recover?

Did comparative amity reign for some months between the men of Parramatta and the neighbourhood hamlets? So that, when very man Jack met every other man Jack, they would dig each other in the ribs and exult?

The answer is Yes! Yes! Yes! Yes!